Praise for Nicola Moriarty's *The Fifth Letter*

"Lifelong friendships, secrets, and pages I couldn't turn fast enough. *The Fifth Letter* is one of my favorite books this year, and Nicola Moriarty is now on my short list of favorite women's fiction authors."

—Susan Elizabeth Phillips, #1 *New York Times* bestselling author

"The brilliant unraveling of this sisterhood of secrets will leave you wondering how well you really know the best friends you've known forever. A must-read before your next Girls' Night."

—Mary Hogan, author of *The Woman in the Photo* and *Two Sisters*

"The meandering stories of these women are held together with the powerful question of who wrote the last letter, which reveals just how precarious childhood friendships are. . . . The book . . . adeptly exposes the striking differences among the four friends and the five letters."

—*Publishers Weekly*

"Readers . . . [will] race to the end as a credit to Nicola's fine sense of pacing and suspense. An author to watch."   —*Booklist*

"A delightful, heartwarming exploration of the twists and turns of true friendship, *The Fifth Letter* was simply delicious from the very first page to the last. . . . Relatable characters, a fast-moving plot, and just the right amount of mystery. I was hooked!"

—Rachael Johns, internationally bestselling author

THE FIFTH LETTER

THE
FIFTH
LETTER

NICOLA
MORIARTY

WILLIAM MORROW

An Imprint of HarperCollinsPublishers

P.S.™ is a trademark of HarperCollins Publishers.

THE FIFTH LETTER. Copyright © 2017 by Nicola Moriarty. Excerpt from THOSE OTHER WOMEN © 2018 by Nicola Moriarty. All rights reserved. Printed in the United States of America. No part of this book may be used or reproduced in any manner whatsoever without written permission except in the case of brief quotations embodied in critical articles and reviews. For information address HarperCollins Publishers, 195 Broadway, New York, NY 10007.

HarperCollins books may be purchased for educational, business, or sales promotional use. For information please e-mail the Special Markets Department at SPsales@harpercollins.com.

A hardcover edition of this book was published in 2017 by William Morrow, an imprint of HarperCollins Publishers.

FIRST WILLIAM MORROW PAPERBACK EDITION PUBLISHED 2018.

Designed by Fritz Metsch

Library of Congress Cataloging-in-Publication Data has been applied for.

ISBN 978-0-06-241357-4

18 19 20 21 22   LSC   10 9 8 7 6 5 4 3 2 1

For Liane, Jaci, Kati, and Fiona,
the four very best big sisters in the entire world

The first thing you need to know is that I would never, ever actually follow through on these feelings.

PROLOGUE

J oni's first thought was that she wasn't the right person to find it. It should have been someone else. Maybe Deb. Or Trina. Deb was the straight shooter. She would have just brought it right out into the open. No secrets, no internal monologue trying to decide what to do about it, no panic, no anguish, and definitely no empathy. "What the hell is this all about?" she would have demanded of the group, probably while brandishing the letter out in front of her like a weapon.

And Trina, she came across as quiet . . . restrained. But she had her moments. Catch her on the right day and, like Deb, she knew how to take charge. But her style differed from Deb's. If she'd found the letter, she would have stared each one of them down, brought them to their knees, made them confess.

Eden would have been just as bad as Joni, though. Maybe worse. She crumbled under pressure; she wouldn't have had a clue what to do. Joni supposed Eden would have simply brought the charred fragments of paper straight to her.

She *could* take it to Deb. Make her deal with it. Put it all in her hands.

But here's the problem, thought Joni, *how do I know she wasn't the one who wrote it?*

CHAPTER 1

———

"What's that thing you're supposed to say at the beginning?"

"Ah, what do you mean, love?"

"You know. The thing you're supposed to say first, before you launch into your whole . . . speech?"

"Oh. You mean, 'Forgive me, Father, for I have sinned'?"

"Yes! That's the one. Forgive me, Father, for I have sinned, it's been—oh, I don't know, years and years since my last confession . . . Although, can I just say . . . 'I was expecting you to sound different.'"

"How do you mean?"

"Well, you know, with a name like O'Reilly. I thought you might have a sweet Irish accent. I just didn't think you'd sound so . . . Aussie."

"Ri-i-ight."

Joni readjusted her bottom on the flat wooden seat and leaned forward to press her face up against the mesh window. "Are you sure you're really Father O'Reilly?" she asked, her voice coming out a bit muffled due to her mouth being smooshed against the window. God, imagine if she were just about to spill her guts to some complete random who'd taken up residence in the priest's compartment for a laugh?

"Yes," came the steady reply. "Quite confident."

She leaned back and rested her head against the paneled wall behind her, breathed in the dusty darkness of the small enclosed cubicle. "What happens if a claustrophobic person wants to confess?" she mused quietly.

"Pardon?"

"Nothing. Never mind."

Three bars of sunlight filtered through the gaps in the wall to Joni's left, picking up the flecks of dust in the air. She gazed at the gently floating sparkles and felt her body start to relax.

"I suppose I should really get started," she said.

"If you're ready."

"I wasn't planning on coming here to talk to you, by the way. I haven't been to church since I was twelve. That was the age Mum and Dad let us all make our own decisions about religion. We were allowed to say we didn't want to come to evening mass on the weekends, just as long as we were doing something worthwhile instead—like homework or a load of washing for Mum, or whatever. So as soon as each one of us hit twelve, one by one, we all stopped, until it was just Mum and Dad, driving down the street in the fading light all by themselves.

"Sometimes I felt a bit guilty about that. Like, I wondered if they were lonely. Or if they regretted giving us the choice. I mean, as much as I was starting to doubt the whole 'existence-of-God thing'—no offense—I did sometimes miss getting all dressed up and the whole family piling into the car together at twilight and the church would be warm and glowing and there would be those families that you only sort-of knew, because you only ever saw them once a week and if you ran into them anywhere else, they'd be completely out of context. And sometimes,

Mum and Dad would take us to Pizza Hut for dinner afterward—and the best part of that was the all-you-can-eat dessert bar with the giant vat of chocolate mousse.

"Sorry, I've gone off on a tangent. Anyway, the point is, I was going to talk to a psychologist. Or a psychiatrist. I never know what the difference is. But then I started ringing around, and they were all either booked out for weeks and weeks, or else they wanted me to go to my GP first and get a referral and get put on a mental health plan or whatever. And I couldn't really waste that kind of time. Besides, you don't cost anything, so that's a bonus."

"Um, thank you?"

"You're welcome."

"Not to rush you, love, but did you have something you wanted to confess?"

Joni hesitated, thinking. How was she supposed to do this? Just come right out and start listing off her transgressions like a sinful shopping list?

I almost cheated on my husband.

I've compromised my own morals in my work.

I've betrayed my friends, I've judged my friends, I've pushed my friends to breaking point.

And now I don't even recognize one of my friends anymore.

I don't even know who she is.

And if I'm honest, I guess I've been lying to myself as well.

"Sort of. Well, yes, a few things, actually. It's just hard to know exactly where to start, you know?"

"I understand. Start at the beginning. My mother always said it's a very good place to start."

Joni snorted. "Did you seriously just say that?"

"Yeah, fair call. But come on, work with me here."

"Okay, okay. The beginning. Well, I could start with the girls' holiday. But you sort of need to know the girls first—the dynamic. Otherwise, you won't be able to help me figure it out."

"Figure what out?"

"Figure out who wrote the fifth letter. The point is, Father . . . I'm not the only one who's sinned."

CHAPTER 2

1993

Deborah! . . . Debbie! . . . Deb! . . . Aha!"

Joni took the concrete stairs two at a time to catch up with the tall girl in front of her. When she finally stopped and turned around, Joni grinned up at her. The two of them moved to the side to allow some senior students to push past and join the canteen line at the top of the stairs.

"You like 'Deb' best, then?" Joni asked.

Deb glared back at her. "What do you want?"

"Come and have lunch with me."

"Why?"

"Because, it's like Mrs. Gamble said, we have a connection."

"A connection? Are you high or something? I don't even know you."

"I'm Joni! Joni Camilleri. I'm in your homeroom. Remember, this morning? We found out that we're both Scorpios and we both have surnames starting with C."

"So?"

"So . . . we're supposed to . . ." Joni's voice faltered. She paused and then tilted forward onto her tiptoes so she could lean in closer to Deb. "I don't have anyone to sit with," she said quietly. "I don't know anyone *at all* at this school. No one from my primary school came here. Please, please, just sit with me?"

She pulled back and waited, hid her hand in her pocket, and crossed her fingers. Joni could tell that Deb was the type of person who would easily make friends with the coolest people in the school if she chose to. She was gorgeous in a completely effortless and highly intimidating sort of way. She had a short spiky haircut, sharp, high cheekbones, no makeup, and no jewelry. Somehow, her school uniform seemed to hang off her body in a trendy, uncaring way.

This morning, when Mrs. Gamble had gushed over the fact that four girls in their homeroom all had *C* surnames and were all Scorpios, Joni had known, right there and then, that this was her in. Her chance to form a new circle of friends.

Deborah Camden was the one she had to swing first, though. If she could win Deb over, then she could win anyone.

Deb was still just staring at her, eyes narrowed, jaw set. Then Joni saw it happen. A minute twitch at the edges of Deb's lips. She huffed, noisily, and said, "Oh, okay, fine. But *just* for today."

Joni immediately brightened and all traces of fear and loneliness that had been stamped across her face vanished. "Yay!" she said happily. "Come with me, we'll find the others first."

"The others?" Deb asked as she followed Joni back down the steps and away from the canteen. "Um, excuse me, *the others*?" she repeated when Joni didn't reply.

"Yes! The others," sang Joni.

They found Trina waiting on the side of the basketball court. She had a grim look of concentration on her face as she watched the girls play, her shiny black hair scraped back into a tight ponytail.

"Trina!" said Joni, nudging her with her elbow to get her attention. "Short for Katrina, right?" she asked.

Trina glanced sideways at Joni. "Nope. Just Trina," she said, before turning her attention back to the game, her eyes trained on the ball. "That girl should have passed by now, total ball hog," she muttered under her breath.

"Really?!" continued Joni, ignoring Trina's mutterings. "Just Trina. So like, it says Trina on your birth certificate and everything?"

Trina kept her attention fixed on the play. "Yep. My mum liked it that way."

"That's cool."

"Uh, thanks."

"Anyway, Deb and I want you to come and sit with us."

Trina took her eyes off the court once more. She glanced at Joni and then at Deb. Joni realized that Deb was just kind of glaring back at Trina, so she tried to spread her welcoming smile even wider—although her cheeks were actually starting to hurt.

"Uh . . . why?" asked Trina.

"Wasn't anyone listening this morning in homeroom?" asked Joni. "Your surname, Chan. Is that Chinese, by the way? Or Korean? Never mind, doesn't matter. Anyway, the point is, it starts with a *C*."

"It's Chinese," replied Trina. "But I'm Australian, I was born here in Australia," she added, sounding a little defensive. "But so what, it starts with a *C*, what does that have to do with anything?"

"Your surname starts with a *C* and you're a Scorpio! Same as Deb and me. So we're supposed to be friends. You have to come sit with us."

"Oh, well, but I'm just waiting to get called on," said Trina, waving her hand at the game.

Joni could feel Deb's patience wavering. She thought fast and then said firmly, "They won't, though, I heard two girls in the bathroom earlier. They were making fun of all the people who wait on the sideline hoping to play. They said they were just going to leave them waiting there forever, pretending like eventually they would call you on but never actually do it."

"Seriously?" asked Trina.

"Uh-huh," said Joni.

At that moment the ball bounced toward them and then rolled to a stop at Trina's feet. Joni and Deb watched as Trina reached down to pick it up and stared at it in her hands for a few seconds. "Screw them," she said, and then she hurled the ball toward the hoop before turning away to join Joni and Deb. Joni watched over Trina's shoulder as the ball swished neatly through the net and hoped that Trina would forgive her if she ever found out that she had just lied to her.

It wasn't until the last five minutes of lunch that the three of them finally found Eden, wandering up and down the aisles of the library, examining the books with careful consideration, moving slowly, running her fingers along the spines. She was the shortest of the four of them, and her petite face looked almost comical under the large mess of frizzy blond hair.

Joni was feeling exasperated when she spotted her. As though Eden ought to have known that they'd be looking for her. When Joni suggested that Eden leave the library and come and sit with them—all simply because her surname was Chester and her birthday was in early November— Eden just shrugged and nodded, as though that made perfect sense.

The conversation between the four twelve-year-old girls was a bit stilted, with Joni trying to lead them. Asking questions like she was an interviewer on a chat show. At the end of lunch, she instructed them all to meet back again tomorrow at recess at the same silver benches.

Eden complied happily. Deb offered a terse, "Maybe," and Trina gave a half laugh before agreeing to join them.

Years later, Joni had asked Eden whether or not she would have ever ventured out of that library had they not come and rescued her. "Oh no," Eden had replied. "My plan was to keep myself busy by trying to read every single book in the library by the time I finished high school. I was going to learn new languages, teach myself chemistry, learn how to play the saxophone. Stuff like that."

"I don't know if you can really learn all that stuff from books alone. But you were glad, right? That we did find you?"

"Well. I was a bit disappointed that I never did learn French, but yes. I was glad."

In fact, I don't even know why I have these thoughts.

CHAPTER 3

_____

2016

Four Weeks Before
the Thermomix Party

"What if we get arrested?"

"By who?!"

"The police."

"Why would the police turn up at the door out of the blue?"

"I don't know—because someone could smell it?"

"How unlucky would that be for you? First time you've ever smoked weed and you get a knock at the door from the cops. Stop worrying, Joni, no one's going to dob us in."

Joni stopped pacing and flopped down on the rug in front of the open fireplace. She was relieved that they'd managed to get the fire going. Having the lights dimmed and the room lit by the flickering flames added some ambience and hid the cobwebbed corners, the mildewed walls, and the tattered blinds.

The house wasn't exactly what she'd been expecting based on the photos she'd viewed on happyhappyholidays.com. For one thing, the supposed ocean view was obscured by several overgrown trees that obviously weren't so out of control when the photos were first taken. And the interiors were a far cry from the description in the ad: "A flawless fusion of Hamptons style and exotic décor, this lavishly appointed two-level beachfront haven encapsulates the essence of luxury and tranquility."

Apparently the person who wrote that ad was working with a very loose definition of the words "lavish" and "luxury." It had a very basic layout—the combined living, kitchen, and dining upstairs were about the size of a small studio apartment, while the four shoe-box-sized bedrooms downstairs were dark and musty. The "Hamptons style" seemed to refer to a couple of faded blue-and-white-striped beach chairs and an old wooden oar propped up in the corner, while the exotic décor was presumably represented by the oversized African mask that hung from the ceiling above the kitchen. It kept swaying and spinning because of the gusts of wind that were currently whistling their way through the gaps under the cracked and peeling doors, which meant Joni kept catching the movement out of the corner of her eye and feeling her stomach jolt each time. The remaining furniture looked like it was straight out of a seventies sitcom.

The location wasn't really what you would call beachfront either. The beach was in fact a good twenty-minute walk down a steep, rocky pathway that wound its way through the bush—or you could take the long way around via the road and be at the beach in forty minutes instead.

The four of them had been doing this holiday every year since they'd turned twenty-one. Friends since that first day of high school when Joni had brought them all together, they'd seen each other through breakups, bad perms, and end-of-year-exam panic attacks. They'd written letters to Eden every week for six months when her family moved to Adelaide in Year Ten. They'd hidden Deb from the teachers when she'd turned up to school blind drunk and sobered her up with a sausage roll, a can of Coke, and a Frosty Fruit ice block from the canteen. She'd vomited in the agriculture plot and cried all afternoon. Later they found out her parents were getting divorced.

The first time they took this holiday, it was a joint birthday gift to themselves but they had so much fun that they all promised each other that they would make it an annual event. Joni was always the one who made it happen, though. The one who coordinated and cajoled until they had a date that suited everyone. The one who picked the destination, found and booked the accommodation, paid the deposit, arrived first, and picked up the keys.

It was Eden who had found the marijuana plants in the bush behind the house, just past the perimeter of the backyard. They'd all been exploring their holiday house, oversized glasses of wine already in hand, shielding their faces from the glare of the setting sun. She'd called the others over to take a look. "Is that . . . is that what I think it is?"

"Nup," Trina had said immediately. "It's just one of those plants that looks like pot, what's it called, like a hibiscus or something?"

"That's no hibiscus," Deb had said.

And then they'd all leaned down to smell the leaves and their eyes had widened in mutual surprise.

First they'd argued about whether or not they were actually going to pick some of it, ("What if it belongs to some drug lord who decides to come after us for messing with his crops!"); then they argued over whether or not they wanted to smoke it. And then they argued over whether it was even possible to use it fresh from the plant.

Trina had Googled it ("I'm just curious") and announced that it was possible to dry it out in the oven if you didn't have the four weeks to wait for it to dry out naturally.

Deb was immediately keen; she hadn't had a joint since high school and she thought it would be a hilarious way to start their girls' holiday. She also made the very solid point that they'd all need to get high in order to ignore the fact that Joni had booked them into an absolute dump for five days, to which Joni had defended her choice by bringing up the original real estate photos on her phone and they were all forced to agree that it wasn't her fault.

Trina was on board next. She'd only tried it once during university and it had just given her a bad headache, so she wanted to know what all the fuss was about. Then Eden gave in—"I guess it's legal now in parts of America, right? So it can't be that bad for you. Although I'll need to call Ben first and check in on the kids."

Joni was the only holdout. She'd always liked to think of herself as the rule follower of the four friends. The sensible one. She was the one who always kept her hands at ten and two on the steering wheel, as opposed to Deb, who had started driving with just two fingers resting on the bottom of the wheel the moment she passed her driving exam.

She was the one who never drank coffee after 11 A.M., because she was determined to be in bed by 10 P.M. at the latest, so she could jump up bright and early for the gym before work the next day.

And she was also the one who had been devastated when they hadn't been able to organize a date for their annual holiday the previous year. "It's an *annual* holiday! That means we're supposed to do it every year!"

"Things are different now," her friends had said. "We all have other stuff going on in our lives, it's not so easy to just drop everything and come away for five days." Each one of her three friends had stopped short of saying what Joni knew they'd all been thinking: *You're the only one that doesn't have kids, so you don't understand.*

Joni did understand. She got it. Having kids complicated things, but it didn't mean they had to sacrifice their friendship, did it?

At first it had seemed like they were all following the same path. Each of them settled into their chosen careers by the time they were twenty-five. Deb working in insurance fraud after completing a business and finance degree at university. Trina teaching sports at their old high school. Eden—who had skipped studying in favor of the steady paycheck that waitressing brought her—had been caught by her restaurant manager playing the piano after close one evening. He begged her to perform for the diners and she eventually gave in and that led to her singing and playing piano at various restaurants around Sydney.

It didn't bring in a lot of money, though, so she supplemented it by selling Nutrimetics or Tupperware or Jamberry or whatever the latest craze was, and that suited her perfectly—even though her friends had started to become suspicious every time she invited them around to her place because it usually turned out to be a sales party disguised as a "girls' night."

And Joni, somehow, had fallen into a job as a staff writer for loveliferight.com—a women's lifestyle website—after an internship that she'd applied for on a whim. (A whim that had quite possibly been spurred on by the fact that she had no clue what she wanted to do with her life, but what she did know was that she didn't want to be left behind by her friends, who all seemed so perfectly suited to their jobs.) So she stuck with it, churning out story after story, meeting briefs, pitching ideas, researching new pubs, clubs, fad diets, and skin-care products— any and every topic that was thrown her way. Including the more recent subject matter that she'd been tasked with basing her articles on. She was keeping that to herself for now, though.

So everything was ticking along fine. They had all been on the same track. Earning money, building careers, meeting cute boys when they got together for drinks every Friday night at the wine bar downstairs from Deb's office. (It was always the wine bar near Deb's office, because Deb somehow convinced them all that her job was the most demanding and she couldn't possibly get herself out of the city and over to the pub near Trina's school or even across the bridge to North Sydney to any of the bars near Joni's office. Eden's work had her floating all over Sydney anyway, so she never minded where they met up.)

And then Eden met Ben. A tall, muscly builder who—apart from the matching blond hair—seemed like petite, artistic Eden's complete opposite. Joni loved the story of how they met. He was having dinner at one of the restaurants where Eden played, and after skipping the desserts and sending his date home in a cab, he doubled back to wait until Eden finished her set so he could ask her out. They had a barefoot beach wedding with champagne and carrot cake and Joni had been embarrassingly weak at the knees when she'd seen Ben in his open-neck shirt, his eyes shining as he watched Eden walk up the makeshift aisle on the sand. "Why doesn't this guy have a couple of brothers for us?" she'd groaned to Trina after one too many drinks at the reception. Just six months later, Eden was pregnant.

But that was okay. Nothing needed to change. Deb and Trina were still single like Joni. Plus, Eden was totally relaxed as a first-time mum. She was the epitome of the easygoing earth mother. Leif came with her everywhere in a baby sling and was the poster child for newborns. He would breastfeed and fall asleep against her chest while Eden carried on a conversation as though becoming a mum was the easiest, most natural progression in the world.

Deb was next. She married Connor—a civil engineer who she met when the company he worked for was under investigation for insurance fraud. Deb had flirted with him in order to get him to help out her investigation. After the case was all over, Joni convinced Deb that she should take him out for dinner to apologize for all that fake flirting. But somewhere between the mains and the desserts, Deb realized the flirting hadn't been as fake as she'd imagined. And then she fell pregnant with her daughter, Ruby, around the same time as Eden announced she was having her second.

So Joni and Trina were the last two standing. And Joni was confident Trina wasn't going to be getting married let alone having babies anytime soon because they were all certain that the guy she was dating at the time, a good-looking but arrogant guy named Josh, was going to be cut loose any day now.

That's why it was such a shock when Trina rang around to tell them all she was engaged. Even more so when the wedding was rushed through only four weeks later. Deb was *not* happy about being crammed into a bridesmaid dress at eight months pregnant while Eden was let off the hook because Maisie was only two weeks old. She spent most of the ceremony pacing at the back of the church, trying to get Maisie to stop wailing, while a two-year-old Leif clung to her skirt. That was Joni's first clue that Eden's dream run when Leif was first born was the exception rather than the rule.

At the reception, Deb had bet Joni fifty bucks that Trina's rushed wedding was because she was knocked up.

"No way," Joni had argued. "She would have told us—there'd be no reason for her to keep something like that from us."

"Just wait," Deb had replied serenely.

Seven months later, Trina gave birth to Nate and Joni had to hand fifty bucks over to Deb.

That's when everything started to go wrong for Joni and her "plan to stick together forever" with her best friends. All of a sudden all three of them had families. Families that kept them busy. Babies who wouldn't take the bottle. Husbands who had to work late. Toddlers who went through annoying clingy stages, meaning Joni's best friends would rush off the phone after a terse "No, I can't come and see the new *Hunger Games* movie with you tonight, are you kidding me?! You need to give me *notice!*"

So Joni was left behind, still steadily positioned within the "early

thirties and single" demographic, still heading out to drinks on a Friday
night, but now it was without the company of her three best friends.

And then Joni met Kai. The sweet, redheaded IT guy who she'd seen
at the noisy, German-themed pub on the corner four Fridays in a row
before one of her workmates finally made something happen between
the two of them. The colleague paid for a drink for Joni on the sly, and
told the bartender to pretend it had been sent to her from the redheaded
bloke at the end of the bar. It was enough to get the two of them chatting. And enough for Joni to discover that the low rumble of his laughter
made a warm glow spread through her body. And that the self-conscious
way he would tug at his left ear when he was unsure about something
made her want to take hold of his hand and kiss it gently while she told
him it was *fine* that he didn't know who the premier of New South Wales
was at the moment, because she didn't know either.

So Joni started to catch up. She and Kai had been married now for
two years. And she was happy with him, absolutely she was. But sometimes it felt like these days, they were leading such separate lives. The
two of them so focused on their respective careers—Kai often working
late, Joni up early for the gym. Their marriage just seemed so . . . different from everyone else's. And she knew that shouldn't matter. She knew
she shouldn't be so worried about her friends, knew that she shouldn't
be making these sorts of comparisons. But knowing you shouldn't be
feeling a certain way and *not* feeling that way were two very different
things.

That was why now, as one by one the roughly rolled joint was passed
around the table after dinner (takeaway Thai from the small strip of
shops down by the beach) and several more drinks (Coronas for Deb
and Trina, red wine for Joni and Eden), Joni had given in. Because why
should there be yet another thing that separated her from the others?
Besides, it was just one night. One time. A bit of fun. Not really that dif-

ferent from progressing from wine to a few vodka sodas really. All three of the others had ended up calling their respective husbands before they lit it up, though, Eden making kissing noises into the phone at her two kids, Trina insisting on singing a lullaby down the line to Nate, and Deb offering a terse "Yes, yes, love you too," before hanging up fairly quickly.

Joni hadn't felt the need to call Kai. She'd just seen him that bloody morning.

As the joint had dwindled down to a small, charred stump, the girls had migrated from the dining table across to the rug in front of the fire, leaving the empty containers littering the table but bringing the drinks along with them. That was when Joni's paranoia had set in—hence the pacing and worrying about getting caught by the cops—but Deb's reassurance had helped calm her down. Now, as she sat cross-legged on the floor and looked around at her friends, she asked thoughtfully, "You get the feeling we don't talk like we used to?" It was the music that was causing her to feel nostalgic. Someone had plugged their iPod into the stereo and put on a playlist of nineties grunge and rock music. The song that had just come on, "Good Riddance" by Green Day, had taken her straight back to high school—to the weeks leading up to their final exams in Year Twelve to be exact.

"Yes!" exclaimed Trina. "I was thinking the exact same thing today on the way up here. We don't. We definitely don't." Trina was lying on her stomach, her oversized jumper swamping her slim frame and her chin resting on her hands. Her skinny legs were kicked up behind her and she was absentmindedly chewing on the end of her long, dark ponytail—the way she used to when she was thirteen, back when they used to have sleepovers and giggle and chatter all night until the parents of whoever's house it was would stomp in and shout at them all to go to sleep. The excessive passion in her voice gave away just how stoned she was.

Deb gave a small groan. She was sitting with her back resting against the couch and her knees tucked up in front of her. "Do we have to get into a serious DNM right now? Can't we just sit quietly and enjoy the buzz?"

"No, but she's right, Deb," insisted Trina. "Like, what's *actually* going on in your life right now? I don't even know. I mean, tell me, what did you have for breakfast yesterday?"

Eden giggled. She was lying on her back with her long, white-blond hair spread out around her, making her look like an ethereal angel. "I had crumpets," she said. "Do you feel closer to me now?"

"It depends," interjected Joni. "What was on the crumpets, Vegemite or honey?"

"Jam. Didn't see that coming, did you?" Joni noticed that Eden's voice was sounding slurred and melodious around the edges.

"What do you want to know—I mean, apart from breakfast? Seriously, ask away, I'm an open book," said Deb.

The other three erupted with laughter. "Sure you are, Deb, that's exactly how I'd describe you." Joni giggled.

"What are you talking about—I'm the most honest one here."

"Yes, you're honest—and outspoken—but only on topics that you *want* to be honest and outspoken about," Joni explained firmly.

"What does that even mean?" Deb muttered crossly, shifting her position and picking up her drink to take a long, noisy gulp.

"I'll tell you something," said Trina, rolling over onto her back and holding her hands out in front of her to examine her fingernails. "I watched a Dove promo video the other day that made me cry. They blindfolded kids and got them to pick their mums out of a lineup based on how they felt and smelled."

"Aw," said Eden, "that's so beautiful."

"No!" said Trina. "It fucking wasn't beautiful." She stayed on her back, resolutely avoiding eye contact with the others. "You know why?

'Cause what if you were the mum whose kid didn't recognize you? What if your kid hugged some other mum thinking it was his, and then they take off the blindfold and he realizes he's got the wrong mum and it's all awkward for the mum whose kid couldn't pick her out and the kid probably realizes his mistake is kind of monumental and the other mums are all superior because their kids found them without any trouble, and then for the rest of your life, there's this disconnect between you and your kid, all because Dove wanted to sell some fucking moisturizer."

Joni didn't know what to say. As the only childless one in the group, she had no idea how to react. And both Deb and Eden were remaining awkwardly quiet. *See,* thought Joni—*this is what I mean, we never talk properly anymore. Nobody even knows what the hell to say right now to poor Trina!* But then Eden rolled over and crawled across the rug to Trina, stopping when her face was right above hers. "Trina," she said, "I'm sure that Nate would recognize you in a lineup."

"You really think so?" she said, sounding teary now.

"Yes," said Eden, "I absolutely think so."

They all fell quiet while Trina gave Eden a watery smile and the sound of a low rumble of thunder along with the growing wind from outside filled the room, undercutting the music.

"Oh, hey," said Joni, keen to move the topic of conversation away from children and maybe reconnect with her friends over some old-school common ground. "I have a secret for you three."

"Really? Something good?" asked Eden, moving back away from Trina and facing Joni with eager eyes.

"Yeah," said Trina, sitting up and wiping her nose with the back of her hand. "Is it something super juicy?"

Joni paused for dramatic effect . . . "I had a crush on Luke Berry in high school."

She waited for them to react with amazement, but instead they just laughed at her. "Joni, we all knew that," said Trina.

"You did not!" Joni argued without conviction.

"Uh, yeah we did, it was obvious," Deb agreed. "Although I could never quite understand why," she added. "He and Joseph absolutely tortured us almost every day throughout high school. Remember how they nicknamed us the 'C-word girls'? Mrs. Gamble really regretted pointing out our surnames after they started calling us that, didn't she?"

Trina sighed. "Why do girls do that?" she asked. "Why do we go for the guys who torture us?"

"Excuse me? Not all girls do that. I never had a crush on anyone who was an arsehole to me," said Deb.

"Yeah, but you're an anomaly, Deb. You were always so confident in high school. Right from day one."

"Confident? Or terrifying?" asked Eden.

"Okay," said Joni. "You knew I had a crush on him. But did you know I actually ended up kissing him at a party at the end of Year Twelve?"

"Seriously?" asked Trina. "You kissed that fucker? Why?!"

"I knew," said Eden. "I saw you two making out around the side of . . . whose house was it?"

"It was Kelly Cropley's house," provided Joni.

"Hey! Kelly had a *C* surname, how come she wasn't in our group?" Deb teased.

"Wasn't a Scorpio, though, was she?" Joni replied smoothly.

"Was that the formal after party?" asked Trina.

"No, that was the party after muck-up day. Her parents were in Europe or something. I think her house actually got trashed."

"People got carried away after toilet-papering and egging the school all day," agreed Trina, a wistful look on her face. "So how in the hell did you end up kissing Luke?" she added.

"I don't know. We started talking. He actually apologized for being such a jerk all through school, said he was just going along with Joseph, and then we went outside for a ciggie and next thing he had his hands on my waist and then . . . we were kissing."

They fell quiet again and Joni wondered if the others were all doing the same thing that she was, thinking back to first kisses, first boyfriends, first times.

Trina had been the first one in their circle of friends to lose her virginity. And she'd been so excited that she'd made the others all sneak out to meet her in the park in the middle of the night, just so she could tell them it had happened. They'd taken it in turns pushing one another on the swings while Trina had tried to unsuccessfully convey to the others just how extraordinary the whole experience had been. Deb had been envious; she'd been hoping to be the first one to have sex. Eden had looked slightly frightened by the whole idea of it, but Joni just remembered feeling in awe of Trina's bravery as the four of them breathed puffs of mist into the night as they chatted, the chains of the swings ice cold beneath her fingers.

"Think the rain's started," murmured Eden now.

"Love the sound of the pouring rain on the roof when you're all rugged up inside," said Joni.

"Hey, guess what I did the other day?" said Trina, "I joined a basketball team."

"Don't you already play netball?" Deb asked.

"Yeah, but I've always missed basketball. And I've always regretted not playing it in high school. Remember how those girls on the court were so mean to me when we started Year Seven?"

Joni's eyes connected with Deb's. *Shit!* She mouthed, *I thought she knew!*

"Oy!" said Trina. "What's this?" she asked, waving her hands between Deb and Joni to break their eye contact. "What's happening here?"

"Um," said Joni. "Well . . . it's just that—"

"Trina," interrupted Deb, "surely you knew that Joni made that up. Like, it was obvious, wasn't it?"

"Wait, what?! What do you mean?" Trina looked back at Joni. "You made what up?"

Joni twisted her hands together and gave Trina an imploring look. "I always thought you knew! I just wanted you to come and be our friend. So I made up the story about the players not letting anyone else on the court."

"But . . . but . . . but . . . Oh shit! I stole Kendra Williams's boyfriend in Year Eight just to get back at her over that!"

Eden spat out her mouthful of wine with a huge guffaw of laughter. "*That's* why you went out with Hamish! I always wondered."

"I knew," whispered Joni. "And he had *such* bad skin, didn't he? I'm so sorry, Trina!"

Trina shook her head but she was smiling. "Oh my God, Joni Camilleri. You are *so* manipulative. I believed you completely. I guess it was all worth it, though, because I got to become friends with you three losers."

"Excuse me? Loser? *Moi?*" said Deb, and she reached behind her to grab a cushion off the couch and hurl it across at Trina.

"Hey! Watch the drinks, woman," Joni warned.

"Oh shit," said Deb.

"Nah, it's okay, it didn't spill," Trina reassured them.

"No, no. Not that. I think we might have a problem. I'm pretty sure I just felt a drop of rain on my head."

"What?! How? What do you mean?" asked Joni, tipping her head back to squint confusedly up at the ceiling above them.

"I mean the roof is leaking, you big dork."

"No it's not, you're imagining it."

The three of them all crawled across the rug to where Deb was sitting and held their hands out to feel for the drops themselves. And then, when they had to concede that there was definitely a leak and got to their feet and started dashing about looking for a bucket to position under the steadily increasing drip, drip, dripping, Trina and Eden each discovered two more leaks.

"Okay!" shouted Deb as she leaned down and shoved the heavy, brown couch back far enough so that she could place one of the buckets they'd found in the laundry room in the right spot. "I'm calling it. This place is officially the worst one we've stayed at. Even worse than the one where the air conditioner sounded like a fighter jet."

"What about the one that had a view straight into the apartment next door where that dude was always vacuuming naked," Eden said from the kitchen, where she was climbing up onto the bench so that she could position a large serving bowl above a high cupboard where they'd spotted yet another leak.

"You didn't like that view?!" Joni called from the other side of the room, where she was on her knees pressing a towel against the carpet to soak up some water from one of the worst leaks. "I thought it was especially entertaining when he straddled the vacuum cleaner and pretended he was being bucked off a horse."

Trina appeared at the top of the staircase from downstairs carrying a couple more buckets she'd found. "Oh," she said, "are we talking about the worst places we've stayed? I always thought the country town that had NO liquor store took the cake."

"Yes!" agreed all three girls in unison, and then they started laughing. "Come on," said Joni, abandoning the carpet and grabbing one of the buckets off Trina to position under the last leak. "Let's have another drink while we wait and see if any of our buckets overflow."

Thirty minutes later and the one last drink had somehow turned into several. The joint from earlier had worn off, but instead they were now all completely plastered. Someone had turned the music up and Eden and Trina were dancing together to "Come on Eileen," while Joni was searching through the kitchen in a futile attempt to find chocolate she was hoping might have been left behind by a previous guest. Every time she sprang across the kitchen from one cupboard to the next, she would forget about the hanging mask and bang her forehead against it with a look of complete surprise.

"Even if you did find anything, you'd have no way of knowing how long it's been there," Deb called out from the couch, while simultaneously using her foot to steady one of the buckets that Trina had just knocked as Eden spun her around.

"That kind of negativity will get you nowhere," Joni replied, stopping the search and hoisting herself up onto the bench top to watch the others. Trina and Eden were both always such *fun* drunks. And Deb—well, she just remained cool. No matter how plastered she was, she never got messy—apart from that one time in Year Nine—but that was different, special circumstances. *So what kind of a drunk am I?* Joni wondered. She liked to think of herself as passionate. She was passionate in her search for chocolate. She was passionate in her assertion that they needed to continue this annual holiday regardless of how many children they all had. Or didn't have. When she drank too much, she generally just turned into an even more persistent version of herself. Maybe she really was manipulative, like Trina had said earlier. But only when it was important and for the benefit of others, right? Like when she talked Deb into taking Connor out—she'd said it was because Deb ought to apologize, but truthfully, she'd been able to tell from the way Deb spoke about Connor that she had a huge crush on the guy. Joni wondered if she used to sound just as enraptured about Kai back when she'd first met him.

Joni slowly became aware of the fact that the music had switched to

"Linger" by the Cranberries and that Trina and Eden were now slow-dancing romantically around the lounge. It was nice to see them both relaxing a bit. So far tonight, each time there had been a lull in the conversation, Joni had worried that it was a sign the four of them were drifting apart—that they didn't have as many common topics to chat about anymore. But now it was starting to feel more like the old days— more like the holidays they took *before* husbands and kids—back when minimal planning was required and no one needed to check in on home and the conversation flowed, much like the wine.

She lay down on the kitchen counter, her head resting on the sink's draining board, and wondered if she was in danger of passing out. She couldn't remember the last time she'd been this far gone. And it had definitely been a while since the four of them had all been this drunk together. The last time they'd even seen one another had been at a barbecue at Eden's place almost two months back and everyone had stuck to a respectable one or two drinks. An entire gathering of responsible designated drivers. Boring. No one had been able to have a proper conversation either because each and every sentence was punctuated by "Ruby! Share!" or "Leif! Gentle!" Kai had bugged her that day as well—she could tell that he was keen to get back home and keep coding a website he'd been working on.

Kai was always bringing his work home lately. Laptop on his knees in front of the television most evenings. Up late into the night, so by the time he came to bed, Joni was fast asleep. She wouldn't mind climbing into bed with Kai right about now actually. That joint had left her feeling turned on. She had an unexpected flashback to being in the back of his black Holden Commodore when they'd first started sleeping together, the windows all fogged up with their hot breath. Sweaty skin and awkward thrusting and fingers fumbling with the condom wrapper. So ridiculous, two grown adults having sex in a car because they couldn't agree on whose apartment they should head back to after the movie.

Although then again, being this drunk, if he *was* here right now, she'd take *forever* to come.

Not that he'd be up for it anyway. He was never up for it lately. Even on the odd occasion that she *was* still awake when he came to bed. She reached into her pocket and pulled out her iPhone. Was it weird that she was the only one not to call her significant other earlier this evening? She checked her Facebook notifications and her text messages—but there was nothing there from Kai. Obviously he wasn't worried about the fact that he hadn't heard from her. She considered sending him a dirty text as a bit of a joke. But then what if he ignored it? The same way he'd ignored her suggestive hints the last time he'd walked into the bathroom to brush his teeth while she was having a shower. She always felt at her sexiest when she was in the shower. The room all filled with steam. Her brown, curly hair slicked back. Hot, wet skin. It was humiliating when he'd just shoved the toothbrush in his mouth without bothering to respond to her purred request for him to join her. What kind of man turns down a wet, naked woman in the shower?

The music changed again and Joni heard Trina whoop and Eden laugh; from the corner of her eye she could tell that Trina had started spinning Eden around the room. "What's this song?" Joni murmured to herself. "So familiar . . ."

Suddenly she sat bolt upright and leaped off the counter to run over to the others. "This song!" she shouted triumphantly, bouncing up and down on her toes in front of Trina and Eden. "Listen, Eden! It's your song!"

Eden stared back at Joni, swaying dangerously on the spot. She paused, then said, "'What's Up?' by 4 Non Blondes. Okay . . . how is that my song?"

"Because! It's the song you were singing when we first all found out about your voice!"

"Ohhh," said Eden, a look of realization crossing her face. "It is, too."

Joni could remember that day in Year Eleven so clearly. Eden had been singing to herself in one of the music rooms when Joni had overheard her and rushed off to find the others. Five minutes later, the three of them had burst through the door and demanded to know why Eden had never told them she could sing.

Joni always liked to call it Eden's "aha moment" because she'd been so genuinely surprised. She'd argued with them that there was nothing all that special about her voice, but then next thing Joni had dragged the music teacher in to listen to her as well and he was begging her to take up music classes the following year, and finally, the "aha" crossed Eden's face.

Aha, that's what I can do.

Aha, that's who I'm meant to be.

"Hey," said Trina, "do you still sing at Pete's restaurant these days?"

Eden's face flushed. "Yes," she said, sitting down on the couch next to Deb. "Fortnightly."

"Who's Pete?" asked Deb.

"The head chef at Bellacinos," Joni supplied immediately, "Don't you remember? He was Eden's first serious boyfriend." Joni shoved Eden aside so she could squeeze onto the couch between her and Deb. "Was Pete the first guy you slept with?" she added, looking sideways at Eden with interest.

Eden's hands flew up to her mouth and her cheeks bulged. "Oh shit!" said Deb, and she reached down to grab a bucket and pass it over to Eden.

They all waited, watching Eden with a mix of fascination and revulsion. A second later, she took her hand away from her mouth.

"Sorry," she said. "I think I've had too much to drink."

"You gonna chuck?" Trina asked.

Eden shook her head. "I'm fine," she said. "I swallowed it back down."

"Eww!" chorused Trina, Deb, and Joni all at once, and then they laughed. Despite the hilarity, though, Joni was feeling suspicious. The way Eden had reacted to that question. Was she feeling guilty? Did she still have feelings for Pete?

"Oh," said Trina, "I just remembered! I brought something with me. You guys will love this." She darted from the room and disappeared down the stairs, reemerging just a minute later, holding a thick envelope in her hand. "Old photos!" she announced. "I found them in a shoe box when I was sorting through some junk the other day. Thought you guys might like to see them."

She sat herself down on the floor by the couch and rested her head against Joni's legs, before opening the envelope and handing a stack of photos up to Deb. "Pass 'em round," she instructed.

"Oh my God," said Joni, immediately snatching the first shot out of Deb's hands. "Deb! Look at how short your skirt was! I can't believe that was even allowed as part of the school uniform."

Eden leaned in to see. "I look like a nun next to her," she huffed.

"That's nothing compared to those paisley headbands I always wore," offered Trina.

"Oh yeah," said Deb. "And Joni's knee-high socks, look!"

They spent a good ten minutes passing the pictures around, laughing at their silly poses, trying to remember the names of random students or teachers caught in the background and *all* swooning when they spotted Steve Highbury, a gorgeous guy who'd been two years above them at school.

"Hey, remember this?" said Trina, twisting around and holding out a photo of the four of them sitting side by side against a low brick wall at the edge of the main quadrangle.

"What?" said Deb, "What are we looking at here?"

"That," said Trina, jabbing the photo. "See, on my lap. It's that purple notebook we used to share."

"The one we were supposed to use to write letters to one another?" asked Eden

"I vaguely remember it," said Deb, squinting at the photo. "I don't think it lasted very long, did it?"

"No," said Joni. "Because pretty much the very first day we started writing in it, Eden told us her family was moving to Adelaide for six months. I think it just sort of petered out after that."

"Don't blame me!" Eden exclaimed.

"I liked it," said Trina, pulling the photo back to stare at it in her hands. "Even though it didn't last long. I never kept a diary of my own when I was younger, but I remember how nice it was to write down my thoughts instead of trying to find a way to talk about what was going on. I wish we'd kept going with it for longer."

"You want to start it up again or something, Trin?" asked Deb.

"Ha. No. How weird would that be? Four grown women sharing a diary."

"Not *that* weird," said Joni. She was thinking fast. This could actually be a good idea—*if* she played her cards right and made sure everyone else could see what a great opportunity it was. Earlier tonight, Trina had agreed with her when she'd suggested that they didn't talk like they used to. This could be the answer! The catalyst she'd been looking for to *really* restore their friendship.

Joni could feel a bubble of anticipation growing inside her chest.

But then Deb shot her straight down. "Um, yes, Joni, it *would* be strange. We're not in high school anymore." The bubble popped.

"Although," said Eden, tapping the tips of her fingers together, "what about a one-off? We each write down just one thing we want to share. One secret?"

Deb screwed up her face in distaste. "I don't think I like the idea of writing some sort of secret confession and then you all reading it and knowing it's mine."

"Well, we could make it anonymous?" Joni suggested carefully, trying hard not to give away how much she wanted to do this. "Each write one secret but not sign our name to it?"

"And so then what?" asked Deb. "What would be the point?"

"And then . . . well, we mix them all around and each pick one out to read out loud to everyone else? Then we don't have to tell our own secrets. Someone else can tell them for us."

"But what about handwriting?" Deb argued. "We went to school together, I could pick out every one of your handwriting styles in an instant. Eden's writing is always all flowing, like she's doing calligraphy, yours is big fat letters, and Trina's is small and neat."

"And yours is an indecipherable scrawl," Joni shot back, irritated that Deb kept finding a way to shut her down.

"I saw an old desktop computer downstairs in one of the bedrooms," said Eden. "It's a dinosaur but it has a printer. We can type them up. We could go into the room one at a time to write our letters."

"Well, Deb would have to make a conscious effort not to swear every two words, otherwise we'll know straightaway which letter is hers," said Trina.

"Yes, writing style, we'll have to disguise our 'writing voices' as well," said Eden.

"So, then . . . we can do this, right?" exclaimed Joni—and the bubble of excitement re-expanded. "I mean, there's no reason not to! It would probably be good for us. Such a great chance to get some things off our chests?" She was unable to hide how thrilled she was now.

"Yep," said Eden. "I think we should."

Trina shrugged. "Why not?"

Deb gave a massive sigh as the others all stared at her expectantly. Eventually she shook her head with a half smile. "Oh, okay, fine," she said, "I'm in."

Sometimes, an idea just pops into my head and afterwards, I think, fuck! What the hell was that? Where did that thought even come from?

———————

"Everything started out so well. It was beginning to feel like old times, you know? Instead of spending the entire time talking about whose kid has taken their first steps or what food Leif now hates or how Ruby's stopped sleeping through the night or whatever, we were reminiscing about the old days.

"Oh, and you should have seen Eden's face when Trina mentioned Pete. I'm sorry, she might be happily married with two kids and all, but there is no denying the fact that she still has some kind of feelings for Pete. He was her first serious boyfriend out of high school and I'm pretty sure they did sleep together. That kind of a thing creates a connection between two people, don't you think?"

"Ah, I wouldn't really know about that."

"Oh! Sorry, I kind of forgot about the whole celibacy thing you guys have going on. But anyway, the point is, when Trina pointed out the old notebook in that photo and we came up with the plan to write the letters, I honestly thought it was going to be a brilliant idea. Ha. I'm such an idiot."

CHAPTER 4

———

The first woman entered the room and closed the door firmly behind her. She walked over to the computer and pressed the start button and then checked to see that there was paper in the printer while it powered up. The room was dimly lit by just a desk lamp, and as she waited for the computer, she started to feel strangely nervous. This was silly! There was no need to feel nervous, these were her friends. And she didn't have to own up to the letter being hers if she didn't want to anyway.

Finally, the screen lit up, ready and waiting for her fingers to hit the keyboard. She opened up a new Word document, took in a sharp breath, and then started to type.

The second woman was feeling uncertain. The alcohol was starting to wear off and, like her friend before her, she was doubting this idea.

There was definitely something that she'd love to tell her friends. A secret that she'd kept to herself for such a long, long time. But could she do it? Could she finally reveal it?

Or should she hold it close for a little longer?

Should she tell a lie instead—make something up?

Truth or lie?

Truth or lie?

Someone banged on the door. "Hurry up in there! There's still two more of us who need to write our letters, you know!"

She closed her eyes and willed herself to make a decision.

Truth or lie?

Truth or lie?

The third woman sat in front of the computer for a good five minutes, just staring at the blank screen. She didn't know where to start. Upstairs it seemed like a good idea. They'd all gotten worked up about it, carried away. In the flickering light of the fire, it had seemed like this warm, beautiful moment among friends—a revolutionary idea!

Now, downstairs in this cold, dark room with just the harsh light of the computer screen, it didn't feel as good anymore. The idea of each one of them creeping in here alone and typing up their deepest darkest secrets suddenly felt sort of sinister.

Although, then again, she supposed it didn't have to be something dark, did it? This was just about revealing something about yourself to the others, something that they didn't know. Something you were going through in your life right now. Probably something that you really did want to talk about but just didn't know how. She lifted her hands up to the keyboard and began to type.

The fourth woman found it easy at first. She knew exactly what she wanted to say—it was obvious really. This was the perfect medium for her to reveal this secret that had been biting away at the back of her mind for some time now, chewing on her brain, sending her a little crazy, making it so hard to think of little else.

Her fingers danced across the keyboard as she let go of wave after wave of freshly turned feelings. It wasn't until she reached the end and reread what she had written that she started to doubt.

I can't tell them this. Even if it is anonymous, they might not understand. They might judge. They might make a big deal of this, a bigger deal than it really is.

The mouse hovered between the print button and the delete button. But she had to go through with this. She had to hear their opinions, she had to know if she was being crazy or not. She had to know if anyone else ever felt this way too.

She hit the print button.

It was just after 2 A.M. when one of the four friends crept back into the bedroom. The sleeping figure in the bed under the window shifted slightly and then rolled over, facing her way. An arm fell out from the covers and hung over the side of the bed.

She held still, waiting to see if she would wake. Wondering what her explanation for being in here would be if she was caught.

But her friend slept on, and so she sat down at the computer, ever so slowly and carefully tapped at the keyboard to wake up the computer from sleep mode. She was mostly worried about the glow from the screen—would the light wake the sleeping figure to her left?

It didn't, though.

When she had a new blank document opened up, she typed as quickly and quietly as she could. A new letter, a replacement confession for the one she had written earlier. Fear had made her change her mind. She had gone to bed with her first letter tucked safely under her pillow—

their plan was to put all the neatly folded letters in a common spot in the morning, ready for them to pick out the first one at dinner that night. As she had lain there in bed, feeling the paper under her pillow, she had begun to worry. She'd played out scenarios, possible reactions from her friends to the secret she had shared. Eventually she'd pulled the letter back out from under her pillow for one more look.

She'd reread it three times, trying hard to see it from their perspective. One final skim over the last few paragraphs cemented her decision. She just couldn't share this with anyone after all. She would have to destroy it, write something new. Come up with another secret to share. There was plenty more material from her life—other things going on that would suit the situation just as well.

Now, as she finished off her new letter, she hesitated before hitting print. Surely the sound of the printer would be too loud? But if she didn't do it now . . . she didn't want the others to know that she was changing her letter. They would wonder why. They would be desperate to find out what was in the first one—she knew that *she* would want to know if the situation was reversed. She was just going to have to do it and hope and pray that it didn't wake the other woman in the room. She hit print, closed her eyes, and crossed her fingers.

The printer was even louder than she'd first expected, but she supposed that was because of the silence of the night. Everything was louder in the vacuum of darkness.

Hurry up, hurry up, hurry up.

The woman next to her stirred again. Rolled back the other way, snuggled farther into her pillow.

Hurry up, hurry up, hurry up.

Finally, the printer finished. She snatched up the paper and was about to shut down the computer when she remembered her first letter. Quickly, she found the original document, which had been saved to the desktop, right-clicked on the icon, and hit delete. Okay. It was gone. She would get rid of the hard copy of the first letter as well. Maybe burn it when they lit the fire again tomorrow night, just to be sure it was completely destroyed. For now, she could keep it hidden under her pillow or in among the clothes in her suitcase.

She turned off the computer and scurried from the room, feeling an extraordinary sense of relief that she'd gotten away with this. No one knew she'd changed her letter. No one would ever find out the original secret she'd first typed. She would deal with that on her own.

She had no idea as she carefully pulled the door closed behind her that the woman in the bed was actually lying wide-awake now. That she'd woken as she'd rolled back to face the window again, having heard the sound of the printer whirring to life. That she'd lain still, wondering why one of her friends was sneaking around in the middle of the night. Wondering if she should just turn over and ask her what was going on but then thinking that perhaps she should let them get away with it, because perhaps she needed that moment of privacy. She wasn't entirely sure who it was, she couldn't risk turning back the other way to take a look, but she did have an idea of who it might be. Something about the way she moved, the way she breathed, something about the shape of the figure in her peripheral vision told her who it was. Although she couldn't really be certain . . . She wondered if she should ask her about it in the morning—or if she was better off just letting it go.

I suppose you could even call it jealousy, really.

———————

"As soon as I went into the room to write my letter, I started to doubt the whole idea. I mean, I know I was the one who really pushed for it in the first place, but to be honest, I don't know what I was thinking. Why didn't I just suggest that we chat it out like every other normal group of friends? Why didn't I come right out and tell them what was going on with Kai? Or about the problems I was having at work? Or ask Eden about Pete? Or explain to the three of them that I was feeling like the outsider. That I was feeling like we were falling apart?

"I guess it was because we were high. Uh, I mean, drunk. Wait, does confession get covered by that same confidentiality thing that doctors and patients have? Do priests have their own version of the Hippo-whatsit oath?"

"The Hippocratic oath? In a sense. Look, it's fine, you're safe to share here."

"But do you have some sort of moral duty to report serious crimes? Like, what would happen if someone came in here and confessed to murder?"

"Have you murdered someone?"

"No. It's not as bad as that. Not quite anyway."

"Then we're all good. Please, continue."

CHAPTER 5

—————

"I swear to God I'm going to kill her."

"Come on, Deb, you know what she's like. She can't help herself."

"You guys know I can hear you back there, right?" Joni made the mistake of glancing behind her to give Deb and Trina an admonishing look, and when she turned back again, a branch that Eden had pushed aside immediately whipped back and slapped Joni in the face.

"Shit, sorry," said Eden, who was looking distinctly comical in a thick woolen beanie with a pom-pom on top. "I didn't mean to let that go. You should be the one leading, anyway."

They were supposedly following a walking track that led through the bush and down to a hidden beach that couldn't be reached by the road—although Joni was harboring a secret fear that this wasn't actually a real track and was hoping she wasn't leading her friends to their certain deaths over a cliff edge or something. She hadn't admitted to them that she was lost yet, though. They were already all cross enough with her after she'd announced her big surprise that morning. She'd signed the four of them all up for "The Dirty Thirty Challenge" for the second-to-last day of their holiday. It was one of those mud-run obstacle courses, but it was specifically designed for people over the age of thirty, which Deb had found particularly insulting. On top of that, Deb, Trina, and Eden had all proclaimed that they had zero interest in putting their bodies through some grueling obstacle course or crawling through mud when they had intended spending their holiday drinking, relaxing, and drinking some more.

Joni supposed she'd known that it was going to be a hard sell, but she just really wanted to do something fun—something different. They never seemed to do crazy stuff anymore. Ever since those women had had children, they'd completely lost their spontaneity and Joni was determined to bring it back. Trina was right—she couldn't help herself. Plus, there was the fact that Joni had never been particularly athletic at school, but now that she spent so much time at the gym, she kind of wanted to show off to her friends about just how fit she'd become. And why shouldn't she take that chance to show off? She'd worked hard and she was proud of it!

So Joni tried to cheer them up by taking them on a bush walk to find a beach with a hidden waterfall that was supposed to be absolutely magical. She'd thought it would be easier to find than this, though. Although, if it were so easy, it wouldn't be secret, would it? "Ha ha," she muttered crossly to herself.

To her left, Eden stopped short and Deb almost crashed straight into her.

"Shit, Eden, what's up?!"

"Shhh!"

"What?!" Trina hissed back.

"Snake, just over there . . . look." Eden pointed through the trees and down a slope to their left. They all followed Eden's gaze and one by one they focused in on the long, smooth, black body.

"Fuuuuuck!" said Trina, reaching out to grab hold of Joni's arm and digging her fingernails hard into the skin. "A fucking snake! A mother-fucking big black snake. Fuck, fuck fuck!"

"Calm down, Trina," said Eden. "It's not interested in us. If we don't bother it, it won't bother us. Now, if it was a brown one, then you could get worried. Come on, it's moving off in the opposite direction. Let's keep going."

Trina was jumpy for the rest of the walk, slapping at her legs any-time a branch brushed against her and leaping into the air if she thought anything moved near her feet. They were all relieved when the bush sud-denly gave way to sand and sea—Joni most of all, who had no idea how they'd finally happened upon the beach.

"Told you guys it would be worth it," she said happily as they all trooped onto the beach, injecting a note of confidence into her voice so they wouldn't realize she was just as surprised as everyone else that the beach actually existed. "See, we're the only ones here."

"Has it occurred to you that we're the only ones here because it's the middle of winter?" asked Deb.

"Speaking of which," said Trina as she pulled off her backpack and yanked a picnic blanket out of it, "why wasn't that bloody snake hiber-nating?" She spread the blanket out on the sand and sat down.

"Because this is 'straylia mate," said Eden helpfully, putting on an ex-aggerated Aussie accent as she flopped down on one side of Trina while Deb sat down on the other.

Joni stood in front of them, bouncing up and down. "We just got here! Aren't we going to explore a bit?"

"Nope," said Deb, lying back and covering her face with her arms. "I'm going to take a nap."

"I'm going to get a winter tan," said Trina, lying down next to her and tugging on her leggings to roll them up and expose her legs to the sun.

"No one's going to walk with me?" Joni asked.

"We just walked all the way through the bush with you," Deb said, her voice muffled from under her arms. Eden tilted her head to the side, looked longingly at the two stretched-out figures beside her and then up at Joni. Joni batted her eyelids back at her friend.

"Oh, okay, fine," said Eden, putting her hands out for Joni to pull her up.

"Thank you!" said Joni. "You're the best."

They both pulled off their sneakers and socks and headed down the sand toward the water.

"So what'd you write in your letter last night?" Joni asked as they stood at the water's edge and let the freezing-cold water wash over their toes. The air was crisp but the sunshine was warm on their backs.

"I'm not telling you!" Eden exclaimed. "They're anonymous, remember?"

"Yes, but I can't wait until tonight," Joni whined. "We should have just read them all straightaway this morning."

Eden laughed. "You *do* remember that it was you who told us all we should read them one at a time over the next few days?"

That morning, Joni had presented the others with a Mexican-style ceramic bowl that she'd found in the kitchen during her frenzied search for chocolate the previous evening. "We're all going to fold up our letters and place them in this bowl, then no one is to touch it until we pick one out to take with us to dinner tonight," she had instructed them in a very formal voice. They'd all agreed—probably because they knew that sometimes it was easiest to just go along with Joni. The process had been very ceremonial then, with Joni tapping out an ominous rhythm with the palms of her hands on the bench top while each of them deposited their letters in the colorful bowl.

"Yeah, okay, okay. Hey, do you think those two are heaps mad with me for booking the mud run?" Joni asked, jerking her head back toward the two figures farther up the beach.

Joni watched Eden's face carefully. She knew Eden couldn't lie. If Deb or Trina were angry with her, Eden would have to confess. When they were nineteen and Joni had borrowed Deb's favorite leather jacket without asking and then left it at a nightclub, Eden had sold Joni out— not because she wanted to, but because she simply couldn't help it. And right now Eden's face was contorting as though she was trying to get a fly off her nose without using her hands.

"I don't think they're *mad* as such," she said eventually. And she reached out to gently tug on one of Joni's curls, pulling it until it was completely straight before letting it go, so it sprang back up into a ringlet again. "Maybe more just . . . a teeny bit annoyed."

"But why?" Joni asked, batting Eden's hand away as she reached out for another curl. "Stop that! You don't mind doing the race, do you?"

"Nooo."

Joni felt a horrible sinking sensation. She was an idiot; she shouldn't have tried to make them do something when deep down she knew they wouldn't want to. Once again it felt like it was her against the other three.

"No, no, I don't mind, Joni. I don't. I think it will be fun. It's just that . . . we've got a limited amount time away from our kids and mostly we just want to relax. But this will probably be good for us, get us out doing something different . . . oh, stop looking so sad!"

Joni hadn't meant to let her face give away so much. She forced herself to grin back at Eden. "I'm not sad! You're so right," she said, keeping her voice bright. "I totally didn't even think of it that way. Do you think I should cancel the tickets?"

"No way, you won't get your money back. It's okay, Deb and Trina will do it. Hey, let's go find that waterfall you said is supposed to be around here somewhere. Which way you reckon, left or right?"

They found the waterfall eventually, hidden within a cave at the head of the beach. Joni was pleasantly surprised by how impressive it actually was; she'd been terrified that it was going to turn out to be a trickle coming out of a storm water drain with a nasty sewerage smell or something like that. Instead, it was a steady gush that fell over the rock face into a sparkling pool and the whole cave smelled of fresh rain.

"Oh, hey," said Eden, having to raise her voice so Joni could hear her over the constant roar of the waterfall, "I've picked my next venture. You're looking at the newest Thermomix sales rep."

"Will you be offended if I say I have no idea what that means?"

"You haven't heard of the Thermomix? Excellent. That means I'll be able to give you the whole pitch when you come to my first Thermomix dinner party."

"Yay," said Joni, but her tone was contradictory.

"Shut up!"

"Kidding. You really like doing all that pyramid salesy stuff?"

"I don't mind it. And it's not pyramid sales anyway. I guess sometimes I wonder about having a more . . . grown-up sort of a job, like you guys all do, but . . ."

"You think we've got more grown-up jobs? Trust me, I don't feel like a grown-up," said Joni as she hopped from one damp, mossy rock to another, continuing to explore the dank cave.

"Me neither. And I have two kids and I *still* don't feel like a proper adult. Sometimes when I'm at home by myself with Leif and Maisie, I feel like I'm waiting for someone to walk through the door and say, 'Right, thanks for babysitting these two, but I'll take it from here now.'"

"That's a bit disturbing."

"Is it?"

Joni stopped exploring and perched herself on a rock shelf, patting the spot next to her for Eden to come and sit down too. "You think about a stranger walking into your home and taking your children away. Yes, it's disturbing."

"Oh no, it's not really like that." Eden sat down beside Joni. She pulled the beanie off her head and ran her hands through her hair to fluff it out. "I don't mean I'd like some psychopath to kidnap them or something like that. I just mean someone more . . . capable. Like Mary Poppins maybe."

Joni realized that Eden was looking worried that she'd said something wrong and she quickly changed the tone of her voice. "Oh, well, sure, if it's Mary Poppins then that's completely different. Mary Poppins is the bomb. But in terms of work, I don't think my job is going anywhere more than yours. At least you're using your amazing musical talents."

"You use your talents too, though—writing is a talent."

"But I just sort of fell into it and I don't know if it's what I actually *want* to do. Plus . . . well . . ." Joni hesitated, wondering if she should share her latest work news with Eden or not. But she'd started now, so she decided to just spit it out. "I sort of changed roles recently."

"You did? I didn't know that!"

"No one does. I haven't told anyone yet."

"Why?"

"Well, the thing is my new job is a bit . . . ah, morally compromising."

"What does that mean?!"

"So, Live Life Right have partnered up with another site . . . a parenting site. And anyway, I wrote this article—this satire 'mummy blogger' piece—and sent it around to a few of the other writers as a joke when the merger happened. Somehow it landed in my boss's in-box. She called me into her office and I thought she was going to grill me for not taking the new partner site seriously, but instead she told me she loved it and they wanted me to switch sites."

"Okay, so what's wrong with that? How is writing satire mummy blog articles morally questionable or whatever?"

"Because they don't present them as satire. They publish them under a pseudonym as genuine opinion pieces written by a parent. And they're controversial stories that are intended to get the readership really riled up."

"Oh. Which site is it?"

"Parentingdoneright.com."

"Oh no. Deb and Trina both read that site. They're always commenting on the articles on Facebook."

"Eden, you can*not* tell them," said Joni, immediately regretting having shared this news.

"What's your pseudonym?" Eden asked.

"I don't want to say."

"Why not?"

"Because I don't want you to read what I've been writing. You might not like the stuff I've been saying."

"Is it really that bad?"

Joni shrugged. "I don't know. At first I didn't think they would really bother people that much, but some readers do get pretty worked up in the comments section. My boss loves it—apparently my articles get the best click-through rates and the highest amount of direct interaction. I even got a pay rise."

"And so you're not going to tell the others about it?"

"I really don't think I should."

"Come on, I doubt we'd be offended—especially if we knew that it wasn't your true opinion."

"Yeah, I guess," said Joni. "But please, Eden—I know it isn't easy for you, but do me a favor and don't mention it just yet, okay?"

"Okay," said Eden, holding her hands up in defeat. "Come on," she added, standing up. "We should probably head back. The others might start worrying that we're lost at sea or something."

As Joni followed Eden back out of the cave she wondered if Eden would be able to figure out her pseudonym. Celine Fletcher. She'd used that old porn-star-name formula to come up with it: Celine Avenue, the name of the street she grew up on and Fletch, their family dog who passed away when Joni was in Year Seven. She just hoped Eden wouldn't start looking into it.

When they arrived back at the picnic rug, Joni immediately got the sense that Deb and Trina had been talking about them, and for a second she panicked, thinking that they somehow knew what she and Eden had just been discussing. The way Trina was snickering and exchanging sideways looks with Deb, it reminded her of Eden's wedding day when she'd made them all have hideous beehive hairstyles and they'd all tried their best not to let on how much they hated it. Joni wondered what it was that was going on between them now. Eden, on the other hand, seemed completely oblivious—just as she had been on her wedding day.

"Okay. What's going on with you two?" Joni asked.

"Don't look at me," said Deb. "Ask this one," she added, elbowing Trina. "I had nothing to do with it."

"Nothing to do with what?" asked Joni.

Trina reached under the picnic blanket and pulled out a folded-up piece of paper. She waved it around in front of her with a wicked smile on her face.

"What?" asked Joni. "What's that?"

"One of the letters from last night," she replied.

"Trina!" Eden gasped. "You dared to touch the sacred vessel?"

Trina laughed. "Seems like I did."

"Hey!" said Joni. "We agreed we'd wait until dinner tonight to read it as a group!"

"So? I couldn't wait, I was too curious."

"Joni," said Eden, "didn't you say you were wishing you could—"

"Shush! Irrelevant," Joni interrupted her. "So you've already read it, then?" she added, turning her attention back to Trina.

"I'm sorry, I couldn't help it. Stop giving me that 'I'm disappointed with you' look, it's a pretty good first letter. I thought everyone would just write stupid stuff, like . . . I don't know, 'I secretly love Justin Bieber' or something like that. But someone shared an actual proper secret in here."

"Did you read it too, Deb?" Joni asked.

"I may have glanced over Trina's shoulder," Deb said casually. "I concur. It's a decent letter."

"All right. Hand it over. I'll read it out loud for me and Eden, then."

It was this vibe you gave off, as though you've always thought you were better than the rest of us . . . Better than me.

———————

"I'm always pushing them—that's the problem. I'm always pushing them to do things that, deep down, I know they don't actually want to do—like the time I bought us all tickets to the Silverchair concert when we were seventeen without asking any of them first. It turned out that Deb didn't even like Silverchair anymore, so she didn't want to go. And Trina's mum wouldn't let her go—she was a single mum, so she was super protective of Trin back then—and Eden had this really bad relationship with her parents at the time—I think it was because she was so angry with them for moving her to Adelaide the previous year—so they wouldn't let her go either. In fact, I'm not sure that Eden's relationship with her parents—especially her mum—has ever been the same again. Anyway, I kept begging and begging them to come with me. Eventually Deb gave in, but I know she resented being there, and Trina agreed to sneak out and join us.

"I got so dressed up for that concert too. With my tartan skirt and my fishnet stockings and my crimped hair. I thought that for once my outfit was going to live up to Deb's usual level of cool. But then there was Deb, looking about ten years older than me, sitting on the back-seat of the bus in her genuine leather jacket and ripped Levi's. She's absolutely stunning, you know? Could have been a model if she wanted. And she still has the exact same haircut that she had the day I met her in high school. Short back and sides, like a twelve-year-old boy. Anyway, I digress. Once I saw Deb, I can tell you I really regretted the heavy eyeliner and the hot-pink crop top layered under black lace and finished with several strings of beads. I looked like a ten-year-old play-ing dress-up next to Deb! But anyway, Trina ended up getting busted by her mum and she was so upset about disappointing her. I felt ter-

rible. And yet here I was again—pushing them to do something they don't want."

"And why do you think that is?"

"I don't know."

"I bet you do."

"Hey, are you a priest or a psychologist?"

"Funny story, I actually studied psychology first, before I switched to theology and eventually joined the Church."

"Oh. That's handy."

"Yes, well, technically, I am supposed to just sit quietly and listen and then issue you your Hail Marys at the end, but I like to read the room, you know what I mean?"

"You know, I think that's another one of my issues? Not knowing how to read the room. Not knowing when to pull back, when to ease up. Can I make a confession?"

"I thought that's what you were already doing."

"The truth is; I hadn't already signed them up for the mud run. I just told them that I had so they'd think they had no choice. But I didn't want to risk wasting four hundred bucks if they refused outright to go through with it. I entered us online once I'd got the final yes."

CHAPTER 6

Hey, guys,

Here's my secret:

I've joined a support group for divorced women.

And obviously, I'm not divorced. I know, I know, it's weird and it's wrong and it's probably even a little bit creepy. But you have to understand how good it is. Let me explain: First of all, there's all the crazy stories you get to hear. I swear to God, it's better than television. You hear about custody battles and fights over divorce settlements and prenups that get thrown out in court because someone breached it by cheating. It's like a real-life soapie!

And then there's the best part: you get to vent about your husband with absolutely NO judgment. You wouldn't believe how freeing it is to sit there and just complain about him to this group of women who really don't know me at all, who don't know a single thing about me or my life. Who are all on my side—

regardless of how petty or unfair I'm being! All I do is alter the stories slightly, make out like it's stuff that happened before we "got divorced" even though it could be something that actually just happened that morning or whatever.

You see, everyone is always telling me how lucky I am to have my husband. How great he is, how easygoing he is. How amazing it is that we hardly ever fight. So it's like I'm never allowed to complain about him because it means I'm being ungrateful or whatever. So this is the only place where I can whinge about him without people wanting me to get over it because other people's relationships are apparently so much worse than mine.

Anyway, I've been a part of this group for a couple of months now, and still not one of the women knows that I'm "happily married."

Look, I'll admit sometimes I do feel bad about it, like I'm this naughty, voyeuristic person prying into the private lives of these other women. But on the other hand, I feel absolutely awesome, like I'm getting exactly what I need from these meetings. It's like I get to learn from their mistakes at the same time as getting this opportunity to air all my own dirty laundry.

The other day I even found myself wishing that something *could* go wrong with X—just so I could have some more material to talk about with them. Like, some sort of big blowup fight between us. Even though I know that I don't actually want to get divorced, I want to be a genuine member of the group so that I don't have to feel guilty anymore about taking advantage of the other women. I kind of feel like they're somehow above me, somehow better than me—because they've been through something so profound that I don't understand. I feel like I want to reach this magical plane of existence that they're a part of. Which I know is ridiculous. There's nothing magical about divorce. I know it's an absolutely horrible thing to think and I don't mean to feel that way. I just feel like now I've developed this strange connection with these women and I want it to be somehow validated.

All right, judge away—you know you want to.

"What if she gets caught?" asked Joni, looking back over her shoulder at the others. They'd been discussing the first letter nonstop since Joni had read it aloud on the beach and they were now on their way back through the bush again, having put their faith in Joni's ability to retrace their steps back to civilization.

"You know, what if one of the women from the support group runs into her at the shops and she's with her husband?" Joni continued.

"Yeah, I was wondering that too," called Deb from the back of the group. "But maybe she could get away with pretending he's her new boyfriend or something?"

"Okay, that works until the other person starts asking about her ex," said Trina.

"Would they, though?" interjected Eden. "Surely they leave all that sort of talk for within the meeting?"

"Maybe," agreed Deb. "You sure you know the way back, Joni? I don't recognize any of this."

"That's because this stupid bush all looks the same," said Trina.

"All good," called Joni. "I'm pretty sure we're nearly through to the road. Tiny bit further."

"It's pretty bad, though, isn't it?" said Deb. "How she's taking advantage of the support group?"

"I guess it does sort of undermine the concept of the group," said Joni.

"I don't know, it's not that bad, is it? All she's doing is chatting with them. It's not like she infiltrated the group to scam money out of them while they're vulnerable or something like that," said Trina.

Joni wondered if everyone else had noticed the same thing that she had—the fact that somehow not one of them had brought up the issue of whose letter it was. It was as though they all knew they should tread carefully now that the first secret was out in the open. But the fact was, one of them was clearly lying—or at least . . . omitting the truth, anyway. One of them was pretending to casually join in on the discussion about the letter as though they were just hearing about it for the first time like everyone else. And Joni felt like this knowledge was now hanging uneasily in the air between the four of them.

"You guys think there must be something really serious going on in her marriage for her to feel like she needs that kind of support?" asked Eden. "Even though she says everything's fine and she's just getting stuff off her chest, maybe she really was heading toward divorce and there was a part of her that joined the group to stop it from happening."

"So she's getting the help that she needs before something serious actually goes wrong? Like, she's trying to save her marriage before it's too late? I guess that's smart," said Joni, briefly wondering if her own marriage could do with a bit of a tune-up via some sort of similar means. "I think I can see the road up ahead, by the way. Told you we weren't lost."

"Trying to save it? Pfft," said Deb. "Sounds to me like she wants it to fail. She actually said she's wishing more shit would go wrong just so she can justify going to her special little meetings."

"Deb!" said Trina. "Tone it down, you're talking about someone who's right here in front of you, remember."

"And when has that ever stopped me before?" Deb retorted.

They all stopped as they stepped out of the bush and onto the road. The four of them all looked around at one another nervously. Joni exchanged a brief look with Trina. Was the discussion around the first letter about to turn nasty? She saw a flicker of worry cross Trina's face, and when she spoke again, she sounded like she was trying to be more careful. "True," said Trina slowly, "but don't you think you're coming down on this person a little hard?" She hesitated before adding, "And maybe the reason you're being a bit harsh about it is because you're looking at this from the point of view of someone who's been through all of this before."

"What are you on about? I've never been divorced. None of us have," snapped Deb.

"No—but you've been through a divorce, just in a different way. Your parents."

Deb tossed her head and laughed. "Ohhh!" she said. "No, that's completely different. Besides, it was a long time ago. Sorry," she added, "I didn't mean to get bitchy about the letter."

"Your parents' divorce was pretty hard on you, though," said Eden. "I mean . . . considering what happened at school."

Joni widened her eyes at Trina yet again: What the hell was Eden doing?! They all knew that there was an unspoken rule that no one was ever supposed to talk about the "incident" at school that had happened after Deb's parents told her and her brother they were divorcing. The one and only time that any of them had seen cracks in Deb's tough-girl demeanor.

But Deb just laughed again. "It wasn't that bad," she said. "Come on. Let's keep walking. I want to take a shower before dinner."

They followed the road up the hill toward their holiday house. "Anyway," said Joni, hoping to defuse the leftover tension, "either way, I think the person who wrote this letter needs to stop going to the meetings, and maybe just talk to her *friends* about her husband instead of these strange women she barely even knows. And we'll all just promise not to take his side or anything like that. Otherwise, if she keeps going, maybe she'll end up doing something to sabotage her marriage, just so that she can justify attending."

"Or how about she just talks directly to her husband?" said Eden.

"Well, I don't think she should stop going," disagreed Trina. "If she's getting something that she needs from it, then why not keep taking advantage? Who does it really hurt?"

"I can't offer any more advice as long as we're walking up this hill," said Deb between her heavy breathing. "Not if you want me to actually make it to the top."

A beat-up old car suddenly flew around a bend up ahead and hurtled toward them, honking its horn and making all four of them scatter off the road. They heard a snatch of loud rock music as it passed them and then disappeared around the next corner and they all stayed where they were as two more cars followed almost instantly—all going at the same breakneck speed, all playing loud music. As the last car passed them a blond-haired head stuck itself out of the window and hollered something unintelligible at them.

"Slow down, you little shits," Deb shouted after them, but they were already long gone.

"What the hell was with that?" asked Trina. "This is supposed to be a sleepy little beach town. And it's the middle of winter. I thought we were pretty much the only tourists up here."

"Oh, crap," said Joni, scrunching up her face before looking guiltily around at the others.

"What?" asked Eden.

"The surfing competition. I completely forgot. When we were trying to sort out a date that would suit everyone, I originally had this week blocked out as a bad idea because I read there was going to be this big competition on up here. But then we were having so much trouble getting a date picked out between the four of us that I ended up coming back to these dates and couldn't figure out why I'd eliminated them in the first place."

Yet another two cars full of young guys flew past them. "How many teenage surfers do you think this place is about to get overrun with?" asked Trina.

"Um, I think . . . a lot," said Joni.

"Joni," said Deb, "can we talk?"

Joni looked up from the coloring-in book she'd been working on. Trina and Eden were both downstairs getting ready to go out to dinner and Deb had spread herself out across the couch to read a psychological crime novel, while Joni had set herself up at the coffee table with a packet of colored pencils and her "mindfulness" coloring book. She got the sense that it had taken all of Deb's self-control not to make fun of her for her chosen pastime. Apparently the novel wasn't holding Deb's interest, though.

"Yeah, what's up?"

"I'm worried about Trina."

"Why?" Joni continued to color absentmindedly as she listened to Deb.

"Well, you know what Josh is like—I mean, we *all* know what Josh is like—and we tolerate him because he's Trina's husband and, from what I've seen, he's never really crossed a line, like he's not actually abusive toward her or anything. But, we all think he's a bit of an asshole, right? It's just . . . have you noticed how skinny Trina is at the moment?"

Joni swapped her green pencil for a pale pink then tapped the end of the pencil thoughtfully against her lips. "Yeah," she said, "but that's just Trina, isn't it? She's always been pretty fit and sporty."

Deb was still lying on the couch, her eyes on the ceiling above her.

Joni followed her gaze. The water stains on the roof looked like dirty clouds.

"She doesn't look fit to me," continued Deb. "She looks underweight. She looks unhealthy. Haven't you ever looked at her wrists and wondered how on earth they don't just snap?"

Joni was taken aback. It wasn't like Deb to sound so worried or to voice her concerns behind someone else's back; usually, if she had something to say, she would just come right out and say it directly to the person.

"Maybe," said Joni.

Deb sat up and then slid down to the floor and made her way across to Joni on her knees. She picked up an orange pencil and indicated the book. "You mind?" Joni shook her head and Deb began to color as she continued. "And I think the reason she's lost so much weight is because of Josh. I think he's pushed her to do it. Plus, when we were on our own on the beach today—before we read the letter—Trina told me that Josh didn't want her to come away on this holiday, that he even made her feel guilty for going away and leaving Nate for a few days, but then she just laughed it off. I don't know, it's like, when it comes to Josh, sometimes she seems like a different person. With us, she's assertive and she speaks her mind. She's not like that with him. It worries me."

Joni tipped her head sideways, watching Deb as she colored. "Okay, I can tell that you're really serious now because you're coloring in. And I know that you were desperate to make some sort of derisive comment about adult coloring-in books when I first got it out." She paused and then they both turned to look over at the kitchen bench as a loud ding sounded.

"That your phone?" she asked.

"Nope," said Deb. She hesitated. "Actually, that's Trina's, isn't it?"

"Deb," Joni warned, "don't do what I think you're about to do."

"What?" said Deb as she stood up and crossed to the phone. "All I'm doing is making sure there's not an urgent message for her or something."

Deb picked up the phone and frowned down at the screen. Then she brought it over to Joni and held it out in front of her. Joni read the text that was showing up on the home screen. It was from Josh and all it said was, TAKE YOUR TABLET.

"That's weird, right?" said Deb.

"Why?" asked Joni. "He's just trying to help her remember to take her tablet. No big deal."

"Yeah, but what tablet? And why is it so . . . so commanding? Like he doesn't even say, 'Hey, babe, just a quick reminder,' or anything like that."

"Maybe he was typing it in a rush. And could be she's just on a course of antibiotics for something."

"I still don't like the way it sounds." Deb put the phone back where she'd found it and then sat down on the floor again to pick up one of Joni's pencils and continue coloring. Though now her pressure on the page looked a little harder than before.

"Look," said Joni, "do you think the first letter was Trina's? That she's the one going along to the divorced women's support group meetings? Because if she is, then maybe that means she knows herself that her marriage isn't great. Maybe she's preparing to divorce Josh."

"I suppose," said Deb. But she still looked worried as she continued to shade the Celtic pattern on the page in front of her.

The woman reached her hand into the pocket of her jeans, caressed the edges of the paper under her fingers. The fifth letter, folded up tight, waiting to be destroyed. She couldn't just simply throw it in the bin. Too risky. What if someone saw it in there, picked it out from among the soggy scrapings of someone's breakfast cereal and the orange peels? What if they were curious, if they opened it up and read it? They wouldn't understand.

She wanted to throw it in the fire, but they hadn't lit it since last night. And now they were heading out for dinner. Would they light it when they came back afterward? Or should she get rid of it while they were out? She was so deep in thought that when she felt the touch of fingers on her upper arm, she spun around on the spot, more aggravated than perhaps she should have been.

"Sorry! I didn't mean to startle you, are you ready to go? We're about to lock up."

She tried to smile. Tried to pretend it was just because she was lost—daydreaming in another world. But her friend continued to scrutinize her face.

"You okay?" she asked.

Am I okay? she wondered. *Good question. Great question. But you know what? You're the last person in the world I'd want to talk to about it.*

And sometimes it gets more . . . involved,
this . . . obsession, this hatred of you.

———————

"The first letter was pretty strange. And I'm sure we all had an idea of who wrote it. I was just wishing she would own up to it, I mean it was so awkward. All of us talking about it in this weird, careful way— avoiding accidentally saying her or her husband's name. And then there she was—talking about herself in the third person! Did she really think we didn't know it was her?!"

"Which one was it? The one you said had the divorced parents? What was her name—Debbie?"

"No way, not Deb! Trina! Trina's the one with the marriage problems. I mean, it's crazy that she thinks we all love her husband and would be on her husband's side if she complained about him to us. But I guess that's just because we're all good actresses. We actually can't stand the guy. None of us has ever thought he was good enough for her. And there she was, pretending to be all shocked by the first letter, joking about how it was a juicy secret first up. Besides, I had that conversation with Deb where I suggested the letter might have been Trina's and she agreed with me. Plus, there's no way Deb would go along to meetings and betray the trust of those women just because she found their stories interesting. Not after the way she acted out when her mum and dad split. She went through her parents' liquor cabinet and mixed herself up a bottleful of rocket fuel from every different type of spirit they had. I don't think I've ever seen anyone that drunk—not before or since. In fact, I think she was this close to needing to be hospitalized so she could have her stomach pumped.

"Whereas Trina still tries to pretend that she and Josh got engaged right before she found out she'd fallen pregnant, when everyone knows it happened the other way around. I mean, it's not like it matters, does *it? No one would care! I do have a theory, though. I think it's because her mum raised her as a single parent after a one-night stand. And maybe she thought if people knew she fell pregnant by accident before she got married, they'd judge her the same way people used to judge her mum. I mean, Trina has always claimed that it didn't bother her, growing up just her and her mum—and I have to admit, her mum is pretty great—she had that way of looking out for us all and striking that perfect balance between being our friend but also being strict with us when she needed to be. She was really cool—that's probably why Trina felt so bad when she got caught sneaking out to come to the Silverchair concert with me. But anyway, I once saw Trina standing in front of a mirror with a photo of her mum in her hand. And I think she was playing a game of spot the difference—you know, trying to figure out which of her features might have come from her dad. She doesn't even know his heritage. She has no idea if he's Chinese like her mother or Australian or from somewhere else altogether. So as much as she says she has no interest in knowing who her dad is, I think she does care. And so that's why it was important to her to marry Josh even though he was never the right guy for her. She wanted to make sure Nate knew his dad."*

"Really? But she could have made sure of that without marrying the guy. That's a big step to take just to make sure people don't judge you."

"Yes, but Trina has always been the type to worry about what people think of her."

"Still, from what you told me, I don't think she sounds like the type to join a group for divorced women when she's not divorced yet."

"Seriously, Father? You hear about my friends for half an hour—"

"Ahem, ahem."

"Okay, okay, for an hour and a half, then, and you think you know them better than me?"

CHAPTER 7

T here," said Eden. "In the corner, an empty booth. Someone grab it."

Joni scanned the area, unable to see what Eden was talking about, but then Trina broke away from them and strode through the groups of drinking patrons to reach the table first. She stowed her umbrella in a corner and peeled off her wet coat. The others caught up with her and started delayering their damp clothes as well. They'd plucked a second letter out of the Mexican bowl that afternoon and brought it with them to read over dinner. Trina now placed this in the center of the table, where it taunted the four of them with its potential.

It was raining yet again, pouring in fact. Dark clouds had rolled in from across the sea that afternoon. Thanks to the surfing competition, the pub was absolutely packed, though. The floor was gritty with sand and several people looked suspiciously underage.

"Nicely spotted," said Joni.

The four of them slid into the semicircular booth seat and then pro-

ceeded to follow the rule they'd set out many years ago for group din-
ners: no one was allowed to start making conversation until every one
had looked at the menu and chosen their meals. Otherwise—as what
used to happen—they'd sometimes still be sitting there two hours later,
too busy chatting to notice just how hungry they all were.

Joni could remember how much it had killed Eden having to wait
when she'd found out she was pregnant and was ready to give them
the good news. Deb had guessed she had something big she wanted to
share and had purposely scrutinized every item on the menu, sending Eden almost insane with the anticipation. Eventually, in a move
quite unlike the usually calm and sweet-natured Eden, she had reached
across the table and wrenched the menu out of Deb's hands, shouting,
"You're having the schnitzel, you always have the bloody schnitzel—I'm
pregnant!"

They'd all clapped and laughed and hugged her and Deb had leaned
sideways to whisper to Joni, "As if that news wasn't half-obvious."

Tonight they all made their choices quickly. They were wet and
hungry and all four of them were curious about what was going to be in
the second letter.

Sixty minutes later, their empty plates cleared away and the next
round of drinks in front of them, Joni leaned back and said contentedly,
"Hashtag perfection," before she picked up her glass and clinked it with
Eden's.

Deb choked on her drink. "Joni," she said, "did you just say '*hashtag*'
out loud?"

"Yes, well, Trina confiscated our phones, so we'd all be 'present' at
dinner, which means I can't tweet it, can I?"

"Oh my God, it's possible that you're actually more of a dork than
Eden."

"Hey!" said Eden.

"Oh, you know I mean it in a fondish sort of a way."

"What's wrong with saying 'hashtag' anyway? Internet speak is becoming the norm. Soon people won't actually laugh when someone says something funny, they'll just say 'LOL.'"

"How depressing is that?" said Trina.

"Not depressing. Just the future. Very now. Much current. So trend."

Eden looked around at the others, perplexed. "Why is she talking in those weird sort of haikus? Is she having some sort of a seizure?"

"Just ignore it and it'll stop," suggested Deb.

"No," sighed Trina. "It's another Internet thing. I don't know where these weird trends come from, but it's like this whole new way of writing on social media. Maybe a symptom of character-count restrictions or something."

"I can't help it if I'm all up with the latest lingo," said Joni, oblivious to how old she was making herself sound by saying "latest lingo." "I've already posted eighteen photos, four different updates, and several tweets about our holiday, all with the hashtag 'girlsgetaway,' so we can easily look up everything from this week again later."

"Joni, I think you may have a slight problem," said Deb.

"Intervention?" asked Trina.

"Absolutely," said Eden

"Shut up," said Joni, amicably enough. "How's all the kids?" she asked the group at large, because she was feeling generous and knew that they would all want to talk about their babies eventually anyway. In fact, it was remarkable that they hadn't already spent hour upon hour stuck on the topic of parenting thus far.

"Ruby's good," said Deb. "She's taken to the terrible twos with excellent gusto. I'm very proud."

"Yeah, Maisie's been getting to that stage as well," said Eden. "I keep trying to remind myself that it wasn't so bad with Leif, you know, that you get through it, but I think she might be a bit more stubborn than he was. The other day she decided that bananas were like, I don't know—poison or something—even though she'd eaten one perfectly happily the day before, and when I tried to give her some cut-up pieces, she actually smooshed them into my face."

"Ewww!" said Joni.

"Good to know that's what I have to look forward to next year with Nate," said Trina, looking worried.

"You'll be all right," said Eden. "Nate's so cute, you won't even be able to get mad at him."

Trina laughed. "I hope you're right," she said. She gave Joni a funny look and then reached out for the letter that was still waiting in the middle of the table. "I guess we should get on with this now, shouldn't we?" she asked.

What was that look for? Joni wondered. Was Trina changing the subject on her behalf? Was it really that obvious that Joni *actually* didn't want to hear every little detail about their kids?

"Go for it, Trin," said Deb.

Trina unfolded the paper and began to read.

Hello ladies!

Okay, I have several confessions to share with you all:

1. I've taken up smoking in secret. This probably seems a bit
   silly. I'm a grown woman, why would I need to smoke in
   secret? But with all the bloody information out there about
   how bad it is for your health, it seems sort of stupid to actually
   choose to smoke at this stage in your life—when you're old

enough to know better. I have to keep it hidden from my husband because he would be LIVID if he knew.

2. Sometimes I like to tell LIES on Facebook! I make up stuff to make my life seem more interesting. Once I downloaded a picture of a recipe and pretended that I'd cooked it for my dinner that night.

3. Every now and then when I go through the self-serve checkout at the supermarket, I steal one item. I "forget" to scan it.

4. I like watching porn.

5. I accidentally killed my pet budgie when I was nine. My parents think he died of natural causes, but I was trying to clean out his birdcage and it was taking forever to wipe it out . . . so I got the vacuum cleaner thinking it would be a quick way to suck up all the birdseed. I don't even know how it happened—one second he was sitting on his perch, next second there was this phlerp noise and he'd vanished down into the vacuum pipe. I felt TERRIBLE. By the time I got the vacuum open and found him inside the bag, he was already dead. I still have nightmares about it.

6. I have a teeny tiny crush on the husband of someone else in this group. Don't freak out, though. I promise I would never, ever, EVER try and act on it. And it's not like I'm in love with him or anything like that. I promise I love my husband. It's a minuscule crush, purely physical.

Okay, those are my "deepest, darkest" secrets!! Don't judge me! And pleeeease don't figure out who I am. I'll be mortified if you do.

Lots of love

From

Mrs. XYZ

Trina had been shouting a bit as she read the letter out, in order to be heard above the noises of the pub, and Joni had been spending the entire time as she listened trying her best to keep her face composed. But it was bloody hard—hearing her own words yelled out in the middle of a pub—it took all of her self-control not to reach across the table and snatch the letter out of Trina's hands, to yell, "Stop! Stop shouting my secrets out to the world!" Now that Trina was finally finished, Joni chanced a look around at the others, half expecting to find them all staring straight at her, waiting for her to own up to it. But instead, both Eden and Trina were staring at Deb, who had one hand across her mouth and looked like her face was turning red.

"What?" said Trina. "What's wrong? Are you choking or something?"

"No." Deb's voice came out as a tiny squeak then she slapped a second hand across her mouth and starting rocking in her seat.

"Oh my God," said Eden. "She's laughing. She's laughing at that terrible budgie story."

Deb shook her head quickly but then she glanced over at Trina, who looked like she was trying hard to hide the edges of a smirk on her face, and all of a sudden it was clear Deb couldn't hold on to it anymore. The laughter burst out and she said between wheezes, "I can't . . . believe . . . she killed . . . her bird . . . with a vacuum . . . cleaner."

"Stop!" cried Trina as she attempted to hold herself together and not fall apart along with Deb. "You can't, you can't laugh at something so horrific."

Joni watched the two of them in horror. She couldn't believe that she'd held that awful story about her pet budgie inside for so long, always harboring this horrendous guilt, and there were her friends, just laughing at her. At least Eden looked suitably horrified. Besides, she'd just confessed to having a crush on someone else's husband! How was that not the first thing they all jumped on?

"You two are pure evil," said Eden. "One hundred percent, pure evil."

Finally, Deb started to calm down. "Sorry," she said. "Sorry to whoever's letter it was—it was just such a strange image . . . anyway, forget it, I didn't mean to laugh."

Trina coughed uncomfortably and nodded. "Yes, sorry, sorry. It's dreadful, not funny at all. Besides, let's focus on the important part of this letter. Who the hell has a crush on my husband?"

"Why do you assume it's your husband that she has a crush on?" asked Deb.

"Because Josh is the hottest," she replied.

Joni hoped Trina wouldn't catch the look of distaste on her face. She could honestly say that she'd never found Josh to be attractive. Okay—so in the *traditional* sense he was handsome. But that personality, God, it turned you off and completely transformed his features the moment he spoke. And it was unlikely that any of the others would ever covet Trina's husband either.

"Bullshit. Connor is way hotter," said Deb.

"Disagree," said Joni, thinking she should join in and pretend like she was just as interested in who it was that had this secret crush. "Kai is clearly the best-looking one."

"He's a redhead," said Deb dismissively.

"So?"

"He has a *beard*!"

"*So?!*"

"Joni," said Deb. "Look. We all know it—so I'm just going to come right out and say it. Your husband is a hipster."

"He is not!"

"Yes, yes, he is."

"Doesn't it come down to personal preference?" Eden interrupted. "Surely we're all attracted to different things? And besides, Ben has the sexy Latino vibe, so he's obviously the hottest."

"Ben's Latino?" Trina asked. "That's news to me. Is Benjamin a particularly Latino name? You do realize he's blond and fairly pale, right?"

"It's on his mother's side," said Eden defensively. "Do you think that means there's trouble in whoever's marriage it is?" she added.

"Nah, it's just a crush—perfectly normal," said Deb. "I don't think she needs to worry that there's any deeper meaning there. I used to have a bit of a thing for the guy who sold me my fresh juice and bagels every morning on the way to work in North Sydney, but that didn't mean I wanted anything to actually happen with him."

"So, we're not worried?" Joni asked. "No one is freaking out about this?"

"Yeah actually, I agree with Deb," said Trina. "It's not that big of a deal, is it? I mean it says in the letter that she would never act on it. As long as that's true—then it's fine."

Eden reached across the table for the paper. "Okay, what else was in this essay of a letter," she said as she scanned the contents. "Right. The first thing she's got is the smoking. Hmm, I would have thought we'd have noticed if one of us was smoking. Surely we'd smell it on them."

"Check Deb's handbag!" shouted Joni, partly in an effort to cover herself and partly because she really did want to know if Deb was hiding something in her bag. "When we ordered the first round of drinks to-night," she continued, "I went to get her purse out of it and she snatched it back off me like I was mugging her!"

"It's not *my* letter!" shouted Deb, grabbing her handbag and pulling it close.

"So why were you secretive about your bag, then, Deb?" Joni asked.

"I wasn't! I just didn't want you taking my money, thank you very much—it was supposed to be your shout."

"Yeah, but you practically launched yourself at me! You were totally trying to stop me from seeing something in there . . . Tell us the truth!"

There was a brief pause and then Deb said crossly, "Okay. There might be something in my bag—but it's not cigarettes. I'll *think* about telling you. Let's focus on this letter right now, though."

"Should we search everyone else's bags for cigarettes?" Trina asked thoughtfully.

"No!" shouted Eden.

"Ooh, she sounds guilty."

"I do not! It's just that we seem to have gotten off topic. We're sup-posed to be helping, not doing an investigation."

"Oh yeah, I forgot," said Trina, looking disappointed.

"All right," said Joni, "The first thing we need to figure out is why she's started smoking."

"Does it matter?" asked Eden. "Surely we should just convince her to quit."

"Well, maybe we need to know why she started to help get to the root of the problem. Maybe she can't quit without first dealing with what it was that caused her to start up?"

Yes, come on, thought Joni, *tell me what's wrong with me. Tell me why I'm doing this.*

"Who cares?" said Deb. "We're adults, if someone wants to smoke, it's fine by me. I just don't see any reason to sneak around doing it. Besides, you're all big enough and ugly enough to know the risks. I'll visit you when you're in hospital with lung cancer and I'll make fun of you when you have to speak through one of those voice thingamies 'cos your voice box is shot, and I'll hug your kids when they're devastated because their mum died before she got to watch them get married or meet her first grandchild."

"Holy shit, Deb, way to manipulate with the reverse psychology," said Trina.

"And way to bring the mood down," added Joni.

"Okay, Deb, you've made your point. It's bad for her, she should quit. Let's move on to the next issue in the letter," Trina said, double-checking the paper. "She lies on Facebook," she read out.

"Who doesn't?" said Deb. "Next."

"Hang on," said Eden. "I'm seeing a pattern. She's lying about smoking. Now she's making stuff up on Facie. Underlying issue here? She's not happy with her life?" She took a sip of her vodka lemon lime and scrutinized the others from over the top of her glass. "Who's feeling unhappy?" she whispered.

"Well, how are we supposed to deal with that without knowing more information?" asked Joni. "Why is she unhappy?" And for a moment she'd almost forgotten that she was analyzing her own actions rather than an anonymous friend.

Yes, why am I unhappy? she thought.

Ha. As if I don't already know the answer to that.

"Because she has financial problems?" asked Deb.

"Why do you think that?" asked Joni, probably a little too quickly.

"Further down in the letter," said Deb. "She says she steals stuff sometimes from the supermarket."

"I don't think that's got anything to do with money," said Eden. "It sounds more like rebelling. Same as the smoking."

I'm rebelling, am I? Huh. Interesting, thought Joni.

"This would go a lot easier if we just knew whose letter it was," said Trina.

"Well, we don't know, so quit trying to make someone admit to it," snapped Deb. "And by the way, on the fourth point, the fact that she likes porn. Honey, whichever one of you it is, that's no biggie. This is the twenty-first century. You don't have to keep that a secret just because you're a woman. I like watching it with Connor."

"You do?!" Eden sounded slightly scandalized.

"Oh, screw it," said Deb, and she reached under the table for her handbag. "I may as well show you what's in here as well." She searched around through the contents inside and pulled something out and slammed it onto the table.

"Is that . . . is that a vibrator?" asked Trina.

The girls all squealed with laughter. "Please tell me it's clean right now!" shouted Joni, delighted to have the distraction from her letter, and Trina spat out her drink with a fresh wave of laughter.

"Why is it in your handbag?" asked Eden.

"I like to keep it close at hand," Deb replied. "In case I need a bit of stress relief."

"So . . . what? You just duck away into the bathroom or something?" exclaimed Joni.

"What about the noise it makes?" asked Eden.

"It's discreet," she replied. "Very quiet, barely purrs." That was too much for Trina, who laughed so hard that she almost fell out of the end of the booth.

"I so wouldn't have picked you as the 'sexual deviant' of the group, Deb," said Joni.

"It doesn't make me a sexual deviant. It just means that I know what I want, what I need—and how to get it."

"Do you think we're being helpful enough with this letter?" asked Eden.

"Probably not," said Deb. "Have we at least covered everything in it?"

"Let's see," said Trina, snatching the letter away from Eden. "There's the bird thing. Very sad and all, but it was just an accident. I think she should forgive herself and move on."

Joni chewed on her bottom lip. If it were that easy to just simply forgive herself, she would have done it already!

"So does that mean we've solved this person's problems, then?" Deb asked. "Because if so, I'm going up to the bar to order another round of drinks."

Joni dipped her head while she tried to hide her disappointment. Her issues were far from dealt with. For God's sake, she had a crush on another man. Why didn't they all think this was a major problem? And lately, her relationship with her husband was more like roommate and roommate than husband and wife. But she couldn't argue with Deb without giving herself away. "I'll have the same as Eden this time, please," she said.

Deb extricated herself from the booth and then Trina jumped up to follow her, saying with a resolute sigh, "Ah, I *suppose* someone should come and give you a hand."

For instance, when we were eating the Thai takeaway—you made this comment that, to be honest, was thoughtless and totally egotistical. I was right in the middle of cutting up my spring roll and I just about threw my knife at you!

CHAPTER 8

J oni was wishing that the glass in front of her was full. She'd been left on her own at the table with Eden while the others had gone to order the fresh round of drinks. She tried to swallow but the top of her mouth felt like it had been encrusted with the barnacles she'd seen on the wall of the cave that morning.

Eden slid over a little closer in the booth and lowered her voice. "How long have you been smoking, Joni?" she asked.

Joni's neck made a horrible creaking noise as her head snapped up to look at Eden. "How did you—" she began. But then she stopped.

Ben.

That's how Eden knew.

Eden's husband, Ben, had sold Joni out. She thought back to that day outside the gym, when she'd been caught smoking.

She'd always taken such pleasure in lighting up her cigarette right underneath the sign outside her gym: WE DON'T SMOKE BUTTS; WE TONE THEM, said the witty Virgin Active sign. All of their signage was like that. Quirky jokes—usually some sort of a play on words. Inside, several of the staff members matched their signage. Bright, bubbly people, full of helpful advice, with quirky hairstyles and accents, bulging muscles and taut skin stretched over rock-hard abs.

She knew it was a contradiction to spend ninety minutes working out, to follow it up with a healthy shake and a coconut and cacao protein ball, and then step outside and fill her lungs with nicotine. But she couldn't help it. It was her secret defiance. Her secret defiance against who? Against what? The current society that had become so obsessed with health?

"Look at you, you rebel." The voice had come from her left and Joni had turned, expecting to see one of the male gym junkie staff members making fun of her. She'd been startled when she realized it was Eden's husband, Ben, walking toward her from the car park.

"Ben! You don't come to this gym."

She'd instantly dropped the cigarette to the ground and stomped on it.

"Don't feel like you need to do that on my account." Ben had laughed. "I was just joking around because of the sign."

"No, no, I was done with it anyway," she'd said, even though she'd barely had one drag.

"I joined the other week," Ben had continued. "Eden said you always rave about this place and I've been meaning to find somewhere to start working out again. Funny I ran into you so soon."

"Ha," Joni had said, as though she didn't find it funny at all. She'd felt uncomfortable asking but she'd said it anyway: "Um, Ben. Listen, no one actually knows that I smoke. In fact, I don't really smoke properly anyway. It's just a once-in-a-while sort of a thing. So, I'd appreciate it if maybe you wouldn't . . ."

"It's all good," Ben had said. "Promise I won't say a word."

"Even to Eden?"

"Cross my heart," he'd replied, crisscrossing a finger across a broad chest under a tight-fitting T-shirt.

Now Joni stared at Eden, feeling a strange mix of annoyance and guilt. "I can't believe he told you!"

"What?"

"Ben! Ben told you that I've been smoking."

"Uh, no. I just knew it was your letter. From the way it was written—it just sounded to me like your voice. I doubt the others will guess, though—you're the least likely one of us to be a smoker, especially considering how you were with that joint the other night. And I assume you're just having the occasional cigarette, it's not like a pack a day, right? Anyway, what do you mean *Ben* told me, how would he know?"

"Oh, sorry. I just thought . . . he goes to my gym. A little while back he saw me having a cigarette out the front and I asked him to keep it a secret."

"I promise, he never mentioned it. I mean, he said that he'd seen you at the gym, that you'd worked out together once or twice, but that's all. So . . . Do you want to talk about it a bit, about your letter, before Deb and Trina come back? Like . . . why are you doing all these self-destructive things? Smoking and stealing and lying and stuff?"

Joni tipped forward and put her head on the table. She spoke in a muffled voice against the smooth, cool surface so that Eden had to lean in even closer to hear what she was saying.

"I don't know!" she said miserably.

"Yes you do," said Eden firmly.

"Yes, okay, I do. But I don't know if I want to talk about it yet."

"All right, all right," said Eden, patting Joni on the back. "Just tell me when you're ready to talk about it, okay?"

Joni kept her face hidden. Ben was the husband that she had the "teeny tiny" crush on. And since that day when they'd first run into one another, they'd worked out together at the gym more than "once or twice." Not that a single thing had happened between them. There was absolutely nothing to indicate to Joni that Ben reciprocated her silly crush. And that was all it was really, just a silly crush. A result of the fact that she and Kai were having some troubles at the moment. Plus, it didn't help that she kept seeing Ben in tight-fitting T-shirts with his muscles all rippling and stuff.

Although, as she sat there, continuing to refuse to lift her head, something occurred to her. Ben had kept her secret. From his wife. Did that mean anything? The moment the thought crossed her mind, Joni felt terrible. Of course it didn't mean anything!

She pushed the thought away and figured she really should lift her head back up and make conversation with Eden. She wasn't being particularly nice sitting here ignoring her. And what did it matter if she had a minuscule crush on Ben? Eden didn't know that it was Ben she was referring to, and as she'd said in her letter, there was no way she would ever follow through on her (almost nonexistent and completely irrelevant) feelings, so it didn't matter one bit.

"Actually," she said, "I just have to go to the bathroom. Be right back." Joni slid out of the booth and walked away briskly, feeling bad for leaving Eden on her own. Squeezing her way through the throngs of people—the place seemed to have gotten even busier since they'd arrived—she got close to the bar and realized she was right behind Deb and Trina, who were still waiting to be served.

They didn't notice Joni and she caught a snatch of their conversation.

"Whose letter do you reckon it was?" Trina was asking Deb.

"Joni's. Hundred percent," Deb replied.

Joni rolled her eyes. Great, so everyone knew. Apparently everyone could pick her "voice"—her "style." Although considering how closely she *usually* abided by the law, she was surprised that they would peg her as the rule-breaker so quickly. Maybe it was a case of the three of them making the assumption that just because they all had children, Joni, as the childless one, would be the most likely to be doing all these stupid, crazy things—smoking, stealing, pining after someone else's husband.

Not pining. Just a silly crush.

She stayed still, continuing to listen in on Trina and Deb's conversation.

"So did you really mean what you said?" she heard Trina ask. "About it being fine because it's just a crush?"

"Truth? I was just trying to make her feel better because I could tell she looked worried. But in my opinion, if you've got a crush on another man, then there's something seriously up in your own marriage."

Joni felt her skin turn cold. She wanted to move away, wanted to stop listening, but her feet felt rooted to the spot.

"Really? Joni and Kai? But they've always been such a cute couple. The king and queen of public displays of affection!"

"Not anymore. Haven't you noticed that there's something a bit *off* between them lately? They were definitely acting weird when Eden had that barbecue a while back. Remember how they had that hushed argument over in the corner of the garden? They thought that no one noticed, but I mean, come on, we could *all* tell they were fighting."

"Ooh, you reckon we need to lock up our husbands, then?"

"Ha! I think you need to slow down on your drinks, you sound sloshed. You nearly fell off your chair before."

"Excuse me! That was your fault—you with your bloody purring vibrator."

Trina was speaking quite loudly and two guys next to them at the bar both turned and looked pointedly at them, instantly taking an interest in their conversation. One of them caught Joni's eye and he grinned widely at her, wanting her to join in on the joke. But this was enough to make Joni realize she needed to get away, before the girls followed his line of sight and discovered her listening in on them.

As she blended back into the crowd and headed again for the bathrooms, she overheard Deb say to Trina, "Don't worry, though, I'm fairly sure it's Connor she has the crush on—I've always known she had a bit of a thing for him."

In the bathroom, Joni leaned against the basin and stared at her reflection in the mirror. She felt sick, deep within her gut, sick and dirty and angry. How could they chat so flippantly about her and Kai behind her back like that? Her reflection stared back at her. The rain had made her hair frizz up and her mascara smear and the bright red lipstick she'd put on before they'd headed out tonight now looked ridiculous. She resembled a sad, drunk clown.

She twisted the tap on and cupped her hands under the running water, then scrubbed roughly at her lips and her eyes, wiping the makeup away. This wasn't supposed to be how her letter turned out. No one was meant to know who had written it. And even if they did, they were supposed to reassure her, make her feel better, not make her feel worse.

I am a terrible human being, she thought as she continued to splash water on her face. *But so are my so-called friends. And apparently my friends seem to think they know me better than I know myself.* The question was, if they all knew that the letter was hers, did that mean they were all going to figure out that it was Ben she had a crush on?

She wished Trina hadn't confiscated their phones earlier and hidden them in the bottom of her handbag. Because suddenly she wanted to call Kai. She wanted to hear his voice. She wanted to be reminded of why it was that she had fallen in love with him in the first place. But maybe it was lucky she didn't have her phone. Because maybe speaking with Kai would have the opposite effect. Maybe he would tell her he was too busy to chat. Maybe he wouldn't even answer her call.

After a few more minutes, she realized she couldn't hide in the bathroom forever. So what was she going to do when she got back out there? Admit to them that she'd overheard their conversation at the bar? Get angry? Deny that the letter was hers? Or pretend she hadn't heard a single word?

Deb and Trina were on their way back from the bar when Joni finally left the bathroom, and she joined them seamlessly, taking one of the drinks off Trina without a word.

When they reached the table, though, she was distracted from any thoughts of herself and how upset she was with her friends. Three guys were sitting in their booth—surrounding a visibly uncomfortable Eden.

"You're in our seats," Deb said bluntly.

"Yeah, well, we saw your friend sitting all alone and we just thought— that's not right," one of the guys replied, smiling up at them and making no attempt at moving.

"There's room," another bloke added, and he slid in farther to create space to his left while simultaneously pushing himself up against Eden. He patted the seat. "Sit down," he said.

"How about you get up?" said Deb.

Joni could see the look on Eden's face as she signaled each one of her friends with her eyes, the message quite clear: *Get these guys away from me.* Joni was just considering going to find a security guard to help them get rid of the persistent guys when the one who'd pressed himself up against Eden leaned in and whispered something in her ear. Joni had no idea what he said, but she saw Eden's face change right in front of her. Next thing, Eden snatched up one of the half empty glasses from the table and threw the contents right in his face. Then she stood up and started clambering across the table to get out from in between them. As she reached the other side of the table, and Trina quickly took her hands to help her down, the man who'd just received a faceful of vodka and cranberry reached out and grabbed hold of her ankle.

"Fucking bitch!" he began, pulling her back. Joni and Deb both lurched forward, ready to tear his hands off of Eden, but they didn't need to. Eden kicked her leg out, catching him on the chin and making him drop her foot as his hands flew up to his face.

Eden scrambled down from the table and the four of them gathered up their bags, coats, and umbrellas and made for the exit without looking back.

When they burst through the door and were out on the damp street, the cold night air hit Joni like a sharp slap across the face.

"Oh my God!" shouted Deb. "Eden, you were awesome in there! What the hell did that guy say to you to make you dump that drink in his face?"

"Walk and talk," suggested Trina. "I think we should head back to the house in case they try to follow us out here." But her face was shining with excitement. Joni could see that all three of them were pumped about what had just happened, but she was glad Trina had suggested getting out of there. "Good idea," she said quickly.

The four of them started walking briskly up the hill. The air was still fizzing among them as they pushed against the steep incline. *Adrenaline*, thought Joni, *we're all running on adrenaline. But isn't anyone else worried that Eden just completely overreacted in there? For God's sake, she just kicked that guy in the face—that was assault! What if they go to the police! We could get arrested! God, I wish I could have a cigarette right now.*

She didn't say any of this, though. For a start, she didn't feel in the chatting mood. But even if she was, it was clear her concerns on the matter would put her in the minority. Deb and Trina were both in awe of Eden. It wouldn't have been this way when they were younger. In high school, it would have been Eden panicking if one of them had done something like that. Whereas Joni would have been the one reassuring her that everything was going to be okay. And Deb would have been the one doing the assault. In fact, Joni wouldn't have thought that Eden could have had a violent bone in her body.

So, when did we all change so much?

And why didn't anyone let me know that we were swapping roles?

They were about halfway home when they heard the sound of a car approaching from behind. This time they were already off to the side, walking in single file on the graveled edge of the road, right next to the bush. As the car flew past them, two things happened at once: something hit the ground right in front of Trina in an explosion of glass and an angry voice yelled out of the car: "Fucking sluts!"

Trina stopped short, her hands flying up in front of her face to protect her from the airborne shards of glass.

"What was that?" gasped Deb, throwing out a protective arm across her friends even though the car had already continued on past.

"A beer bottle," said Trina, standing still, visibly shaken. "It was a bloody beer bottle. God, if it had hit one of us in the head . . ."

"Oh shit," said Eden. "It's my fault. I bet it was those guys getting back at me. I'm so sorry."

Trina spun around to look at Eden. "Stop," she said. "This is not your fault. It's their fault. They're the ones who were invading your personal space and they're the ones who threw that bottle, not you. Do not blame yourself."

"Shit, Trina," said Deb. "Is that blood on your knee?"

"Shush," said Trina. "Don't undermine my feministic speech here."

"Okay, but still, can we just take a look and make sure it's not a deep cut or anything?"

"All right, fine," Trina agreed, "but, Eden, believe me, this isn't your fault."

Joni tried hard to keep her face neutral as she gave Eden an encouraging nod. But inside she couldn't help but feel just a tiny bit of irritation with her. Eden hadn't told them what it was that the guy had said to make her so angry, but could it have really been that bad? What could he have possibly said to make her react in that way? And, truthfully, had she just stayed calm, they would have got her out of there and away from those guys and none of this would have needed to happen.

When the beer bottle had exploded in front of them, her immediate instinct had been to thrust one hand deep into her pocket and hold tight to the secret letter. She didn't know why that was. A strange reaction to have. She'd meant to get rid of it at the pub, but somehow the opportunity hadn't presented itself.

Or maybe that wasn't true. Maybe it was a case of her not being able to let it go just yet. Did she still want the others to discover the truth? Was she still thinking about sharing this letter?

But that was madness. Besides, she'd already made the decision that she couldn't let them know what she was hiding deep inside. And she'd written that replacement letter. No. She needed to stick with the plan. She needed to destroy it. She needed to find a way to make these feelings go away.

Don't stress, okay? Because I'm not actually violent!!! Even with all these exclamation marks, I promise I'm not crazy.

———————

"My letter was next. And that's when things started to get complicated. You see, somehow Eden knew straightaway that it was mine."

"A perceptive friend."

"Maybe. Or maybe Ben actually did tell her he caught me smoking. But either way, it was uncomfortable. And anyway, as it turned out, apparently Deb knew as well. I overheard her tell Trina that it must mean there's major problems in my marriage. Pretty upsetting to hear—I do love my husband, I really, really do. But lately, things have been . . . difficult. There have been some issues. Still hurt to hear my friends just chatting about it so casually, though. I didn't think we looked that bad from the outside. And look, maybe that's what I should have shared in my letter, instead of just listing off all these insignificant things. I should have just come right out and told them the truth about Kai and me."

"You think you were deflecting?"

"I guess. Anyway, at least I told them about the crush . . . but I suppose I wasn't entirely honest about that either. Ben and me, we'd already spent quite a lot of time together at the gym at that point. And we'd flirted. But I thought it was all just harmless. It felt like Kai never even looked at me in that way anymore, whereas Ben, he made me feel attractive. I'm a horrible, horrible person, aren't I?"

"No."

"Why did your voice just go all high?"

"It didn't."

"Yes it did."

CHAPTER 9

Joni drummed her fingertips on the bench top as she waited while Trina tightened her laces. She'd been up since 5 A.M., unable to sleep, still feeling uneasy about what had happened at the pub the previous evening. Both about the conversation she'd eavesdropped in on and the incident with Eden and that random guy. Trina had been the next one to wake, and as soon as she'd emerged from her bedroom, Joni had pounced on her. "Come for a run with me! I need to get *out*." She'd decided to place the blame for that horrible conversation she'd overheard solely on Deb—after all, she was the one who had stood there and said outright that there was definitely a problem in Joni's marriage. Trina wasn't to blame; she'd just been going along with it because she was drunk. Besides, Joni really needed someone to come for the run with her.

Trina had shrugged and agreed and Joni had immediately dressed in her fluoro striped leggings and Nike singlet, while Trina changed into a much more casual outfit of tracksuit pants and an old T-shirt.

"One sec," said Trina as she stood up from doing her laces and then headed around to the kitchen to grab a glass of water and wash down a tablet before she and Joni headed off out the front door and down the steps to the driveway.

"Hey, what was that you just took?" Joni asked as they reached the end of the driveway and paused to consider which way they should turn. The rain from the previous evening had cleared and the newly risen sun was shining weak winter light across the landscape in front of them.

"Huh?" said Trina.

"What was that tablet you took?"

"Oh, just a multivitamin."

"I always wonder if I should be taking multivitamins; are they any good?"

Trina shrugged. "Yeah, I guess. Do you need to walk a bit to warm up?" she added as they made their decision and started down the hill.

"Do you?" Joni replied.

"Not really."

"Let's go, then."

They both put their earphones in. Joni's iPod was filled with her favorite eighties and nineties dance hits that spurred her on whenever she was starting to lose her motivation while she ran. They both then broke into a light jog, pacing themselves against the steep slope as they headed down the hill.

Beach? Trina mouthed at Joni when they finally reached the bottom of the hill.

Joni nodded and they turned right and jogged down the road, beginning to pick up speed now. On one side, the street was lined with colorful shops and cafés, while to their left, a grassy slope led down toward the beach, where the morning waves were crashing lazily against the shore.

They took a walkway from the main road through to the beach and then jogged evenly down toward the water's edge so they could run where the sand was more compacted. Joni was trying to lose herself within the music, but she was having trouble concentrating. It was because she knew full well that Trina had lied to her just now when she'd asked about the tablet. The only reason she'd even asked was because Deb had put the idea in her head that the text they'd seen from Josh to Trina was somehow sinister. And to be honest, there *was* something shifty about the way Trina had popped it into her mouth before they'd left. She'd pulled the foil packet out of her handbag, taken the pill, and then immediately stashed the pack again while glancing across at Joni to see if she was paying her any attention. It didn't look like any multivitamin Joni had seen before and there was definitely a funny sound to her voice when she'd answered Joni's question.

Her first guess was antidepressants.

Although Joni hadn't really noticed any specific signs that Trina was depressed. Then again, as far as Joni was concerned, being married to Josh would make anyone feel depressed. Deb had always said he suffered from short-man syndrome. Josh was stocky but definitely vertically challenged and he often felt the need to throw his weight around with the other husbands when they all got together.

Maybe she was wrong. Maybe it was nothing at all and she was just imagining things. She tried to put it from her mind and focus on the feel of the sand beneath her shoes. The steady rhythm of her heart. She lifted her chin and pulled her shoulders back. She often had to remind herself as she was running to check her form, to make sure she wasn't letting herself get all hunched up or tense as she concentrated on pushing through the pain barriers and keeping her breathing even.

Trina was fast! And she didn't even look like she was breaking a sweat yet as she ran elegantly alongside her. She had that casual loping sort of running style that you normally saw women in sportswear ads employ. So much for Joni showing off about her improved fitness.

Joni realized that Trina had increased her pace another notch and she pushed herself to match it. She hoped Trina wasn't going to keep increasing her speed; she wasn't sure she'd manage it if she did. Thank God it wasn't hot at least; it was much easier to keep her body moving fast with the cold wind whipping the salty sea spray onto their faces. And it was equally nice that Trina was just as happy to listen to music and shut out the rest of the world while they ran. She hated it when people wanted to go running with her and then spent the whole time trying to make stilted, out-of-breath conversation.

Twenty minutes later they both slowed down to a walk and Trina pulled her earphones out and elbowed Joni to get her to do the same.

"What's up?" Joni asked.

"Can I make a confession?" Trina said.

Joni fiddled with the earphones in her hands. Either Trina was going to admit that she'd lied about that tablet, or she was going to tell Joni about the fact that she and Deb had discussed her behind her back last night.

"Trina," began Joni, ready to tell her that it was fine, that she could tell her anything, but Trina interrupted her.

"I'm really annoyed at Deb about something."

Joni stopped walking and Trina stopped next to her. "Oh," said Joni, "are you? Why?"

"Well, first of all, she keeps telling me she thinks I'm too skinny, and considering how hard I've worked to get back into shape since having Nate I find it really offensive! But the other thing is, I tried to make a joke with her yesterday about how Josh was a bit . . . difficult about letting me come away with you guys and she totally turned it into a contest between Connor and Josh. Like as if Connor is so much better than Josh just because he was all 'Oh, honey, go, you need this holiday, I'll be *fine* with Ruby.' I mean, where does she get off? Comparing them like that and acting like Connor is the perfect husband!"

Joni was trying to make sure she chose her words carefully, but she was stuck on the fact that Trina had just used the exact phrasing "*letting her come away.*" What the hell did she mean "he *let* her"?

Joni realized that Trina was still waiting for her to respond, so she said quickly, "Oh my God, I know exactly what you mean. Deb's done that to me before. Acted like Connor was somehow above Kai because his job is apparently more 'demanding.' But don't let it bother you, it's just what she does. You know Deb, she's always thought she was somehow above the rest of us—so much cooler. But I don't think she means anything by it."

Trina nodded and Joni noticed that she looked a little less anxious than she had when she'd first brought it up. Had Joni done the wrong thing, though?

The four women all peered over the edge of the cliff face, then Eden took several quick steps backward and Joni turned to see that her face had a noticeably green hue about it.

"I don't think I can do this," she said.

"Hey, don't look at me," said Joni. For once, she hadn't been the one to push them all into signing up for some crazy, bonding activity; Trina had been the instigator. She'd seen a poster in a shop window after their morning jog and had convinced them all to spend the afternoon climbing up a rock face and then rappelling down—all because it supposedly had amazing views of the sea.

"The views are incredible, Trina, really they are, but I don't know if they're actually worth it."

"Come on," said Trina, "don't be daft! It's completely safe!"

Brett, their rock-climbing guide, put a hand on Eden's shoulder. "I'm going to guess you'd like to take first turn holding the fort down at the base of the cliff, then?"

Deb immediately raised her hand. "I'll join her," she said.

Trina and Joni were on their way back down again after an agonizingly long climb up to the top when Joni looked sideways at her friend and gave her a tight smile. "Okay," she said, "the outlook is sensational, I'll give you that, but it's harder than I thought it would be. My arms are seriously killing me."

Trina laughed and then used her feet to push off and bounce against the rock face a couple of times. "Are you kidding me?" she asked. "It's easy! You just have to relax into it."

"Yeah, well, at this point I'm starting to get why Eden and Deb both decided to stay on the ground and man the ropes for us," said Joni. "Because right now I'd much rather be down there—and I don't think they're going to be swapping over with us to take their turn when we're done."

"Look, see if you can sit back into the harness a bit more, your body is so tense, it's like you're trying to support all your weight with your arms. You need to trust in the equipment."

Joni concentrated hard on loosening her shoulders, tried to lean back a tiny bit further, the way Brett had showed them when he was getting them all geared up.

"That's good!" Trina called. "I can already see a difference in your form."

Joni had to admit that Trina had a point, it was only now that she was paying more attention to her body that she noticed just how tense her muscles had been.

"So since when are you such an expert anyway?" she asked, "I didn't know you were into rock climbing."

Trina put on an overly exaggerated tone of superiority, "Oh darling, I *must* be a natural!" Then she laughed at herself. "No, I don't know what it is, heights have just never bothered me for some reason. Have another look out at the ocean, see if you can distract yourself a little more."

Joni twisted around slightly so she could see the view better. It was postcard perfect, an uninterrupted panorama of the water, sparkling in the afternoon sunshine. Her body relaxed further as she emptied her mind and drank in the sight. There was a cargo ship off in the distance, edging its way lazily across the horizon, she loosened her grip some more, settled back even further.

Trina was right, this did get easier the more you relaxed. She gave Trina a much wider grin. "All right," she said, "I guess it's not *that* hard."

"Right? Told you! Now try this!" Trina kicked off from the wall yet again to swing out in a wide arc and that's when it happened.

Joni was laughing, about to tell Trina she was a long way off from trying that, but she didn't get the chance to reply, because Trina was gone.

One second she was right beside Joni and the next, she was flying towards the ground, screaming at the top of her lungs.

"TRINA!" Joni shouted, clutching tight to her own rope and twisting around to watch as her friend plummeted; powerless to help. It felt like the fall went on for minutes, but within seconds Trina had stopped short with a nasty jolt and was hanging like a rag doll, about fifteen meters from the ground. She spun around as she tried to right herself and Joni saw her bang her head painfully against the rock. Then her feet found the rock and she gained control. She looked up at Joni and gave a shaky thumbs-up.

It took Joni a good hour to complete what should have been a twenty-minute rappel to the ground. She was so frightened after what happened to Trina that she moved at the rate of a lethargic snail. When she finally touched the bottom, she was surprised to find a perfectly calm Trina who was laughing about the incident.

"Honestly, Joni, I was still safe," Trina insisted. "There was a tiny mix-up when Brett was helping the girls with the ropes and my rope slipped through their hands for, like, a second. You shouldn't let this put you off abseiling, I didn't even get hurt."

Joni thought the bruise on Trina's forehead told a different story, and regardless of Trina's assurances, Deb and Eden were happy to call it a day without tackling the rock face. They unclipped themselves from all the equipment and trekked back through the bush to Trina's car.

It was Deb's idea to play a couple of rounds of truth or dare that evening after they arrived back at the house. They ordered in takeaway pizza for an early dinner and all agreed that they should have an alcohol-free night after having felt a bit too seedy the past two mornings, not to mention the fact that Deb was certain Trina shouldn't have any alcohol after her bump on the head. Their dinner had just arrived when they decided to spice things up a bit with a game of truth or dare.

It started out with little things. Eden announced that she knew they'd all hated the way they'd had to wear their hair for her wedding. "Eden! You're supposed to wait till we actually ask you a question!" Then Deb was dared to eat three slices of pizza in under fifteen seconds and Joni had to tell them the weirdest place she'd ever had sex (the answer was a graveyard, which they'd all ascertained was weird and creepy and obscenely morbid).

But then Deb dared them all to try sneaking into the spa of the hotel by the beach. The surfing comp had been on that day, so she suggested that it would be easy because most of the guests were still on the beach or out celebrating.

Now they were all creeping their way through the lobby of the hotel—despite the fact that the reception desk was abandoned and there was a sign on the desk that said, GONE TO WATCH SURFING COMP. HELP YOUR-SELF IF YOU NEED EXTRA TOWELS.

Eden flattened herself up against the wall and started making weird hand signals at Joni. She touched the side of her hand to her forehead and then cut it through the air before tugging on her ear and tapping on her nose.

"What?!" Joni hissed, "I don't know what any of that *means*!"

Trina stifled a giggle. "I can't tell if she's doing baseball signals or special-ops hand gestures. Is this some sort of combat mission?"

"Guys!" whispered Eden. "I'm trying to tell you we're all clear over here. Deb! You go in first, I'll cover you!"

Joni and Trina started laughing again, and Deb just shook her head at the lot of them and then strolled out from her hiding spot while Eden stayed pressed against the wall. "Amateurs," she said, "you're supposed to act like you belong. Like you own the place!"

They found the pool area, which Deb was right about—it was completely empty—and they all stripped down to their swimmers and climbed into the hot, bubbling Jacuzzi.

"Why on earth didn't we stay here in the first place?" groaned Deb as she immersed her shoulders in the water.

"'Cause I thought the house was going to be beautiful," said Joni. "Now, let's get on with the game. Whose turn is it?"

"Trina's," said Eden, who, far from looking like she was relaxing into the spa, was instead casting furtive glances around as she checked for any hotel staff who might catch them out.

"Truth or dare?" Deb asked.

"Double-dare, torture, kiss, or promise," Joni chanted automatically.

"Oh, I forgot about the rest of that rhyme," exclaimed Trina. "I'll take kiss!"

"There's no guys around for us to dare you to kiss," said Joni.

"So? I'll just have to kiss one of you, then."

"Are we playing spin the bottle or truth or dare?" Eden asked.

"Ha," said Trina.

"Spin the bottle sounds interesting," said a voice from behind them. And they all turned to see two guys walking over to the spa.

"Oh, crap," whispered Eden. "They'll get us kicked out."

"Um, I highly doubt that's what's on their minds," Joni muttered back, but then she saw that Deb had an uncharacteristically worried look on her face.

"Actually," Deb said, "we were just about to go."

"What?" said Trina. "No, we weren't."

"Yes," said Deb firmly. "We were. Remember? We were going to go and have that bonfire on the beach." And she gave them all a significantly pointed look.

Joni joined in then because she'd just realized what Deb had already picked up on. Those guys were actually familiar. "Of course," she said. "The bonfire! Yep, let's get moving." It was the guys who had taken their seats at the pub last night. The one that Eden had kicked in the face wasn't with them, but there was every chance that he might be about to join them and Joni knew that Deb was trying to get the four of them out of there before the guys recognized them.

"Hang on," said one of the blokes as he got closer to the Jacuzzi. "Aren't you four . . ."

Too late.

They all started scrambling out of the spa and grabbing their towels and clothes. "Nope, we're not," said Deb as she and Joni each took hold of Eden's hands to pull her along, because she still hadn't realized who they were, while Trina gathered up loose bits of their clothing. Then they rushed out of the pool area and back through the lobby. The guys weren't following them, though; they were too busy laughing to themselves about the fact that they'd managed to scare them away and had sent them out into the cold in their swimmers.

Back outside, they started walking toward the beach, wrapping their towels around them and shivering against the cold as they went. "Shit," said Eden. "I just clicked who they were. Sorry, guys, we'd only just got comfortable."

"Forget about it, Eden," said Trina. "It's all good. Besides, I'm liking Deb's idea of a bonfire on the beach, let's do that instead."

"Are you sure that's allowed, though?" asked Eden. "What if we get into trouble?"

"From who?" asked Deb.

"A fireman?"

"Hmm," said Joni. "How sexy will this fireman be and how physical will he get . . . Perhaps forcibly remove us from the beach?"

"Ha ha," said Eden as they all turned down the walkway to head onto the beach. "Aren't there rules, though? Against lighting a bonfire in a public place or something?" She dropped one of her shoes and then, while bending down to pick it up, dropped the other one.

"Here," said Joni, taking her clothes off her while Eden gathered her shoes up again. "I don't think there are any rules. Our family always used to have bonfires on the beach when we were younger." They reached the sand and looked down the beach, where they immediately saw at least three bonfires dotted along the sand at various intervals, each one casting a flickering glow on the groups of people who were gathered around them in the darkness.

"I guess that answers our question," said Deb.

"Wait," said Trina. "How are we going to get it set up? Do we even have anything to light it?"

"I've got it covered," said Deb. "Wait here," and she strode away from them toward one of the groups.

Fifteen minutes later, Joni stood at the water's edge and then reached out to grab Eden's hand. "This. Is. A. Stupid. Idea," she said.

"Come on, you two," shouted a voice from behind them. "Are you going to go through with this or not?"

They turned around and peered through the darkness to see Deb and Trina watching them from farther up on the sand, both looking comfy and warm in their thick jumpers, jeans, and boots, now that they'd re-dressed. Joni and Eden hadn't actually made it back into their clothes yet.

"Why are we doing this again?" asked Eden.

"Because we were dared."

"And?"

"And I've never in my life turned down a proper dare during a game of truth or dare."

"Well, I have," said Eden.

While they'd been waiting for Deb to come back, Trina had decided to continue their game and had issued the challenge of Joni and Eden taking a quick dip in the ocean. "Come on," she'd cajoled. "We're going to light a fire as soon as Deb gets back anyway, so you'll warm up again."

Joni considered for a moment that she really didn't have to do this—that she should just head back up the beach with Eden and laugh the whole thing off. But there had always been something about the idea of being given a dare that made Joni determined to follow through, as stupid as it was.

So they'd both dropped their towels. When Deb had joined them again, carrying with her an armful of kindling, a lighter, and even a bag of marshmallows, she'd suggested that the dare would be more interesting if they skinny-dipped, but Eden had point-blank refused. "Are you kidding me?" she'd said. "There are other people on this beach! And besides, this is bad enough, thank you very much."

Joni wasn't really sure that it would have mattered, though. It was pitch-black and the other groups of people on the beach were all too busy having their own fun. They had no interest in what a couple of midthirties women were doing a bit farther down the beach. Actually, it would probably be easier to dry off if they were naked, but she hadn't wanted to go nude all on her own, so she'd kept her swimmers on like Eden.

"On the count of three," said Joni. "One . . . two . . ."

"Ye-e-e-s?" said Eden when Joni still hadn't got to three.

"Okay . . . Three!" she shouted. And they both sprang forward and sprinted into the water, leaping over the waves until they were deep enough to dive under. Beneath the water, Joni opened her eyes, trying to orient herself in the darkness. The shock of the cold water had made her lose her breath completely and she struggled for a second to get back up to the surface. But then her body's instincts took over and her head popped back out into the frigid night air. Eden appeared next to her and they both stared at one another for a moment, mouths gaping and eyes bulging. Finally, Joni got her breath back enough to speak. "Holy shit, it's fre-fre-freezing!" she said, her teeth chattering.

Eden just nodded vigorously.

"Hey, listen, E-E-Eden," stuttered Joni. "There's some-something I need to s-say."

"Now?" exclaimed Eden.

"Yes! Just qui-quickly. About those guys we saw just now, y-you were okay with seeing them, were you? I mean 'cause, you d-did sort of freak out the other n-night? And so I was wo-wondering. What exactly did that one that you kicked—what did he s-say to you?"

"I'm fine," said Eden. "I promise, it was nothing really. I probably overreacted, to tell you the truth . . . Now let's get the hell ou-ou-out of he-here," she added, starting to stutter herself and jerking her head back toward the beach.

Joni nodded and started swimming back to the sand, starkly aware of the fact that Eden had still managed to avoid answering her question.

Once they were out of the water, Trina ran down to meet them with two towels. "Okay," she said as she handed over the towels, "that was impressive. I did not expect you two to follow through."

"You're the one who dared us," said Joni indignantly.

"Yeah, but still, I assumed you'd just tell me to get fucked. Come on. Deb and I have started putting the fire together. We would have got it lit faster if I'd known you were really going to do it."

Joni and Eden followed Trina back up the beach to where Deb was crouched, piling the dry sticks and leaves up on the sand. "Solid effort, girls," she said without even looking up. "But did you wonder what creatures were under the water there that you couldn't even see?"

Joni and Eden exchanged looks and then Joni kicked sand at Deb, possibly a little harder than she might otherwise have if it weren't for the fact that she was still feeling mad with her about the overheard conversation from the previous night. She'd managed to keep it out of her mind for most of today, until she'd started talking to Eden about last night and it had popped back into her head again. "Thanks for that," she said.

"What? At least I didn't say it before you went in, did I?"

Eden rubbed her body down with the towel and looked at Joni. "Hey, did you think to bring underwear so you could change out of your swimmers?"

Joni had at least stopped shivering now and was holding the towel around her with one hand while carefully extracting herself from her damp swimming costume with the other. "Yeah, I shoved some undies in the pocket of my jeans, didn't you?"

"Nope," said Eden. "I thought we were just going in the Jacuzzi, remember? And that we'd be able to dry off completely at the hotel before walking back up to the house. Guess I'll just put my jeans on over noth-ing." She followed Joni's lead and started pulling off her sixties-style polka-dot bikini underneath her towel.

"Come on, Deb, hurry up and light it," Joni said as she watched Deb put the finishing touches to the fire. "Eden and I are going to bloody freeze to death here."

"Bit dramatic," suggested Trina, "but a fair point all the same. Plus, I want to get the fire going so we can start roasting these marshmallows. I can't believe you convinced those teenagers to give you a bag of their marshmallows as well as the kindling and the lighter! You know, I do often wonder what's even the point of marshmallows without a fire?"

"Hot chocolate," mused Deb as she pushed the lighter into the center of the sticks. "That's their other use."

"Hey, Eden," said Trina, "I have a spare pair of undies, by the way, in the bottom of my handbag, if you want to wear them?"

"Why do you carry spare undies around?" asked Joni, with a note of amusement in her voice.

Trina glared at her. "You'll understand when you have kids. My blad-der control isn't what it used to be."

"Oh my God, I'm so glad to hear you say that," said Eden. "I thought it was just me!"

"Of course it's not just you," said Deb, pulling her hand back from the fire as the flames started to take hold. "I'm in that club too. Granted it's not the most fun club to be a member of, but still, at least we're in it together."

"Gee, pregnancy sounds like an absolute blast," said Joni sarcasti-cally. But she was covering the fact that there was yet something else for the three of them to all share those annoying knowing looks with one another over.

Joni and Eden were both done getting dressed and the four of them all sat down around the fire, rubbing their arms and shivering as they waited for it to heat them up.

Trina had pulled a piece of paper out of her handbag and waved it in the air. "Guess what I have with me?" she asked.

"You grabbed one of the letters again!" said Joni. "Nice idea." *Especially considering I don't have to worry about it being mine,* she thought with relief.

"Whose turn is it to read it out?" Trina asked.

"I'll do it," said Deb, reaching out to take it from Trina. "Unless someone would like me to just throw it straight into the fire and forget all about it?" she added, holding it out over the top of the flames.

"No!" shouted Joni. "There's someone's heart and soul poured into that letter. Go on, read it," she said.

"Oh, okay, fine. Are we all ready?" she asked. And she began to read.

Although there's one more thing that went through my head tonight. And I guess it did worry me a little bit.

"Too many secrets. That was the issue. The letters were supposed to get everything out in the open, but instead the opposite thing was happening. There was Eden and that guy at the pub. Look, fair enough, he and his mates were being assholes, refusing to get up out of our seats, but I still think there was something weird happening. The look on her face! Like something came over her—there was something else going on there, a reason why she snapped. And why wouldn't she tell us what he whispered to her?

"And then Trina, with the tablets, she lied to my face, I know she did. Plus, she still hadn't owned up to the first letter."

"And you hadn't told them the truth about you and Kai, had you? About why the two of you had been having problems. Or about your new job. Or your feelings for Ben?"

"Hey! I didn't have feelings for Ben, it was just . . . I don't know . . . a bit of chemistry? A bit of lust? An unconscious reaction to his flattery? But no, I hadn't told them about my job or my issues with Kai."

"Do you want to tell me?"

"Sort of."

"Then go ahead."

"Okay. Fine. Deep breath, here we go . . ."

"Come on, just blurt it out."

" . . . "

"Trust me."

"We were trying to get pregnant. For almost a year, we had been trying to have a baby and we couldn't. We just couldn't make it happen."

CHAPTER 10

Hi, girls,

Well. This is a bit weird, isn't it? I wonder how everyone else is starting their letters. Like, are you all just jumping straight into the nitty-gritty of it? Or are you making small talk first? Because I've decided I'm going to jump straight in—you ready for this? Oh, and FYI, you're going to work out who wrote it pretty fast, so I'm prepared for the fact that this isn't going to be so anonymous after all. But I'm still not going to sign my name to it! I may as well let you guys do the detective work, hey?

So here it is. My big secret . . .

When I was sixteen, I got pregnant and I gave the baby up for adoption.

Okay. Let's talk.

xx

Deb looked up from the paper in her hands. There was silence apart from the crackling of the flames. She stared at the others. "What the hell?" she asked.

Joni stared back. She could feel tears prickling at the back of her eyes. Why was this making her want to cry?! It was the shock of it, she supposed. The shock of hearing the impossible. "Nope," she said, shaking her head vigorously. "That's not right. We've all known each other since Year Seven. I *know* you guys. I know everything about you all. I think I would have noticed if one of you got pregnant and had a baby."

Maybe this was all a joke, Joni thought hopefully. A stupid, ridiculous, and completely unfunny joke—but *still*—a joke.

But then Trina spoke. "Eden," she said quietly, and they all turned to look her. "Eden was in Adelaide for most of Year Ten. That's the only time any of us were apart for long enough."

"Shit," said Joni. "You're right. How did I not think of that?" She looked at Eden, tried her best to keep the accusatory tone out of her voice. Eden just stared back at her with an apologetic sort of a look on her face. But inside, Joni's mind was racing. How could she possibly not have known this?

"You had a baby in high school?" said Deb. "And none of us even knew? Fucking hell. Why did we have to pick tonight as the alcohol-free night? In fact, why did we have to have an alcohol-free night at all?"

"Because we've all gotten far too pissed the last couple of nights," Trina hissed. "And besides, don't think we didn't see you hiding your head in the fridge and sneaking a swig of wine before dinner. Now shut up and let Eden talk."

"If you only saw me do it once, then I did pretty well," Deb muttered to herself.

Eden shrugged. "What do you want me to say?" she asked.

"Um, I don't know, start from the beginning," suggested Joni, and this time she couldn't stop the tone of her voice from giving away how upset she was, the telltale note of hysteria. Secrets! Too many damned secrets. She saw Trina give her a pointed look, but she ignored it, continuing to stare at Eden, waiting for her to explain.

"Okay, well, Dad didn't *get* transferred," began Eden. "He requested a temporary switch to the Adelaide office. Mum and Dad both thought it would be easier that way. If no one knew about it. I was already almost four months along when we moved, but you couldn't tell, I wasn't really showing yet."

"Far out, Eden," said Trina. "Why on earth have you been holding on to this for so long?" She shifted her way around the fire to put one arm around her friend. "Are you okay?" she whispered.

"Yeah," said Eden, "I'm fine. It was a long time ago, right?"

"Who was the father?" asked Trina.

Eden looked uncomfortable and Deb cut in. "It must have been Jared, right? That guy you dated in high school . . . that was right before Adelaide, wasn't it? But I didn't think you actually slept with him! You know this means you were actually the first one of us to lose your virginity. And we all thought that Trina held that crown."

"Deb!" exclaimed Joni. "Have some tact." It wasn't really her concern for Eden making her say that. It was because she needed them to get back on track. She needed to know more. Like why hadn't Eden ever told them about this? Her three best friends—how could she keep something like this from them for so, so long?

"What?" said Deb. "It just occurred to me, that's all."

"Yes but it's a bit *off point,*" Trina scolded.

"It's okay," said Eden. "It doesn't matter." But her voice sounded a bit croaky and Joni realized that both Trina and Deb were instinctively moving in toward Eden to give her a comforting hug. Joni quickly followed suit and made a mental note to snap out of it. This wasn't about her. This wasn't about the fact that Eden had hidden something from them—it was about the fact that she had been through something so very profound when she was so young, and as her friend, Joni would have liked to have been there for her.

And it also has nothing, absolutely nothing to do with my own problems with conceiving right now. That's irrelevant, Joni. Completely and utterly irrelevant.

So why do I feel like Eden just punched me in the gut?

When they finally pulled apart and took their places around the fire again, Joni pushed herself to speak first. *Pull yourself together! It's not about you!* "Was it a boy or a girl, Eden?" she asked, her voice cracking with nerves.

"Boy," said Eden.

"Did you get to name him?" asked Deb.

"No. I didn't want to."

"Did you get to hold him?" asked Trina.

"Just briefly," she said, and Joni was surprised to realize that Eden's voice was hollow, devoid of any emotion.

"Do you have any idea . . . where he ended up?" Trina continued.

"Um, I'm not really that certain," said Eden. "Mum kind of dealt with all of that."

"Did you want to keep him?" The words had tumbled out of Joni's mouth before she could stop herself. She shouldn't have asked that. It was insensitive. But Eden answered without hesitation. "No," she said, "I don't think that I did, really. Either way, though, there wasn't any opportunity to stop and wonder about what I wanted. Mum and Dad were pretty set in stone that that was what had to happen. And I went along with it, I was just so relieved that they didn't get angry and kick me out or anything like that."

"Hang on," said Trina. "Does Jared even know?"

Eden looked panicked. "No!" she said. "He has no idea."

"It's okay, Eden," said Trina. "I wasn't planning on plastering the news all over Facebook or something."

"Sorry," Eden said. "It's just a bit strange having this finally all out in the open."

"Wow," said Deb. "Can't wait to see what's gonna be in the last letter." They all laughed and Deb passed the bottle of lemonade around that they'd brought down with them. "Here," she said. "It's a pretty lame substitute for wine and I forgot to bring the plastic cups, but . . ."

They took turns taking unceremonious swigs from the bottle while Eden answered more questions: What it was like giving birth so young, and was it weird knowing that Leif and Maisie had a half brother out there somewhere? Eden kept her answers short enough that eventually they stopped asking.

They stayed on the beach talking about other things for a little longer, but as the fire died down, they agreed it had got too cold to stay out any later and kicked sand onto the last of the flames and gathered their things to leave.

On the walk back to the house, Joni and Eden fell back behind Deb and Trina. "Can I ask one more question?" said Joni.

"Sure."

"Does Ben know?" Joni didn't know why it was important, why it was relevant—but there was something about the idea of her having spent all that time working out alongside Ben at the gym, with him knowing this huge secret about one of her best friends while she had no idea. Of course, he was her husband, so why shouldn't he know more about Eden than Joni? But still, she couldn't explain it, it just felt odd.

"No. No one does. Just Mum and Dad and now you three."

Joni felt some of the tension drop from her shoulders. He didn't know.

"Do you think you'll tell him now?"

"I don't really know. Maybe. But then again, he might wonder why I didn't just tell him sooner, right?"

"Why didn't you tell him sooner?"

Eden shrugged. "Don't know. Same reason I kept it from you three, I guess. Because my mum always made me feel like it should never be spoken about again. You think I should tell him?"

Joni thrust her hands into the pockets of her jeans, puffed up her cheeks, and then breathed out slowly, letting the air whistle through her teeth. She shouldn't have brought this up. She wasn't the right person to answer this question. For goodness' sake, Eden should probably be talking to a professional about this, not asking the advice of her idiotic friend who was selfishly wondering how Ben might react if he knew this secret from his wife's past. God, this stupid crush! She needed to get over it. It wasn't real. These feelings weren't authentic. They were just a by-product of her own issues and insecurities.

Finally, she forced herself to give Eden a comforting smile. "Oh gosh, I don't know, hon. That's got to be your decision."

Eden stopped and turned around to look back toward the black ocean as they reached the top of the steep road. "I don't know," said Eden. "Maybe I really should tell him the truth."

I took a pillow and I crept up to you and I put it over your smug sleeping face and I held it down and smothered you.

It was just a fantasy, though.

––––––––––

"How's that for irony? There I am, trying and trying, month after month, to fall pregnant. And I'm thinking, I know that there's something wrong with me. It's like I just have this instinct about it. Over and over again I think to myself: 'It's not Kai, it's not Kai, it's not Kai . . .' You want to know why it's not Kai? Because it's me. I'm the problem. I'm the one who's broken inside. I'm the one that can't do this one simple, everyday, all-natural, womanly task. I'm the one who can't get pregnant. And meanwhile there's Eden telling us all how she can do it so damn easily that she does it by accident. She has a baby and she gives it away like it's a doll she got for Christmas that she doesn't want anymore, and then she waits a few years till the time is right and she does it all over again—and again, until she has the perfect little family. A pigeon pair of kids. A husband who adores her. And meanwhile she's still spending time with Pete at Bellacinos, a guy who she totally has feelings for. Fuck. I'm not being fair, am I? I know. I know I shouldn't feel this way, I know it and I don't mean to, but I just can't help it."

"Can I tell you something, love? There is nothing simple or everyday about conception. Every single time it happens, it's a miracle."

"Okay. So then where's my miracle?"

CHAPTER 11

————

When they arrived back from the beach, the woman seized her opportunity. They were all still shivering from being out in the cold, so they lit the fire. They sat around chatting for a while. All she had to do was wait them out. Wait them out, and one by one, they would all disappear downstairs to their beds, and then she could get rid of this damned letter. The thing that was burning a hole in her pocket—metaphorically speaking anyway. It wasn't actually in her pocket anymore. She'd stuffed it inside one of her shoes earlier today.

When the last of her friends finally went off to bed, she grabbed the letter from its hiding place and then hurried over to the fireplace. The fire was almost out. They hadn't wanted to leave it roaring in case the place burned down while they slept—but they also hadn't put it out completely. She rolled up the letter and shoved it in among the dying embers. She waited for a moment and then saw flames start to shoot up as the last of the fire hungrily took hold of the paper.

Good, *she thought*. What's done is done.

As she tiptoed down the stairs to bed, a part of her wondered if by burning the letter, she might be able to somehow also destroy the inner thoughts that had plagued her for so long.

Back upstairs, the letter slipped sideways in the grate. The flames died back down. It was burned, but it wasn't destroyed—not completely.

It was around three in the morning when Joni slipped out of bed and crept upstairs. She couldn't sleep. Her mind was a lasagna of thoughts. Layer upon layer of feelings. Peel back the top layer and there was another.

Eden's confession. A teenage pregnancy. A baby adopted in secret. A huge life event that had been kept from them all for so long.

Peel that one back and find something else.

Joni's jealousy. Why her? Why Eden? Why was it so, so easy for her to conceive?

And underneath that, there was Kai. A mixture of guilt and resentment: Kai turning her down when she wanted to have sex. Kai making her feel unsexy. Kai making her feel unloved. Kai making her feel like a failure.

And beneath that, there was Ben. Ben's extremely muscly arms pumping as he ran on the treadmill in front of her. Ben's smile as he turned back to look at her. Ben's kind words when he encouraged her to run faster, to push harder, to lift more.

And under that layer, she was right back to indignation. Why hadn't Eden told them sooner? Didn't the four of them always tell one another everything? Weren't they closer than that?

The hypocrisy of this wasn't lost on Joni.

And around and around in circles she went.

Stop it, Joni. Stop it, stop it, stop it.

She slipped outside with a cigarette and lit it up, shivering against the bitter night air. The taste of the nicotine didn't comfort her anymore, though. She knew why she'd been smoking. Eden was right when she'd suggested it was a sign of rebelling. She was rebelling against her stupid failure of a body. Two more drags of the cigarette and she looked down at it between her fingers and thought, *What's the point? I'm not even enjoying this.* She crouched down and stubbed it out against the ground.

Back inside, she poured herself a glass of water and then sat down on the couch to wait for sunrise. It felt like only five minutes later that Joni was jolted awake by the feel of the cool liquid on her lap. She jumped to her feet, disoriented—then she realized what had happened. She put the glass down on the coffee table and plucked at her wet pajama top. She was about to go into the kitchen and find a tea towel to try to dry herself off when she saw it. A small, broken-off piece of charcoaled wood had rolled out of the still-smoldering fireplace and was burning a hole into the rug. A wisp of smoke was curling its way up from the dark, dimly glowing shape.

"Shit," she hissed, looking around for something to pick it up with. Dammit, there was nothing. She ran around to the kitchen, wrenched open the top drawer, and snatched up a set of tongs, then dashed back to the fire and carefully pinched the crumbling chunk of wood off the rug and dropped it back into the grate.

Now that the risk of burning the place down had been avoided, she sat back with relief and then leaned forward to examine the damage to the rug. This might make it difficult to get their security deposit back— great. She looked back up at the grate to make sure nothing else looked likely to come tumbling out. It was as she was examining the fireplace that she noticed the curled remains of a piece of paper with typed words on it, sitting to the side of the ashes. It was mostly burned—and it would be impossible to read more than the odd word—but her curiosity was piqued. She picked the tongs back up and reached in with them to carefully extract the last crumbling bit of the paper. Once she had hold of it, she stood up and carried it carefully to the kitchen table and placed it down on the surface, hoping it wouldn't disintegrate before she had the chance to make out some of the words.

She grabbed her phone so that she could use the light from the screen to take a closer look at it without making the room too bright and risk waking up the others downstairs.

Most of the paper was blackened and unreadable but there were a few small brown-tinged sections where she could make out two or three words here or there.

"Would never, ever" were the words she read first. *Would never what?* she wondered with interest. She squinted at the paper and found some more words:

"what the hell was that
the thoughts are actually
thought this might be a good chance"

And then farther down the page:

"problem with one of yo
. . . stems back to this one . . . incident"
"then you'll know who it is
. . . ough the telephone and strangle you!"

Joni felt her stomach flip. Was she reading that right? Something about wanting to strangle someone? She found one more readable part:

"kick me out of the grou . . ."

She pored over the rest of the paper to make sure but they were the only parts of the letter that she could read. What the hell was this all about? Something that had been left in the fireplace from a previous guest? But no, she was sure the grate had been empty when they'd arrived. They'd filled it with those fire-starter cubes, some kindling, and a few twisted-up pages of newspaper to get the first fire going before adding a couple of logs from the supply held in the large wire basket next to the fireplace. So this piece of paper had been put in the fire by one of her friends. Who? Why? What did it mean?

Then realization dawned.

It was a fifth letter.

Someone had written an extra letter.

Someone had written an extra letter and then changed their mind and burned it.

She reread the words again—and then again. Trying each time to fill in the blanks. But there really wasn't enough to go on. Some of the words were definitely worrying, though. Someone was "irritated" with someone else in the group. Irritated enough to joke about strangling them. Because it must have been a joke, right? And they talked about being "kicked out of the group" as well. Whoever this person was, they didn't want anyone else to know their feelings.

She needed to know more. But there was no way she was finding out anything else from the burned paper in front of her on the table.

The computer.

Would the person who had written this letter have been careless enough to leave the document on the computer downstairs? Presumably not if they had gone to the trouble of burning the printout. But it would be worth checking. And she was too anxious to wait until the morning.

Joni made her way down the stairs, keeping her steps as light as possible. The bedroom door with the computer was ajar. She pushed it softly and the door swung inward. Joni crept into the room and tiptoed across to the computer. She tapped the keyboard and waited for the computer to come to life.

The home screen of the computer finally appeared and Joni scanned the desktop, looking for any documents. There were two left on the desktop. One was her own, titled "Diary Letter"—she hadn't really thought to delete it when she'd typed it up back on the first night. The other was untitled. She double-clicked it and it opened up. But a quick scan of the first few lines and she recognized it as the one that had been read out first. The divorced-women-support-group letter. Obviously Trina hadn't seen a need to delete her document either.

Joni wasn't finished yet, though. She opened up the document folder and started searching through the various folders: My Documents, downloads etc. There was the odd file here and there left behind either by the owners of the house or perhaps previous guests. One titled "Chicken Recipes," another called "Xmas Party Invite," and one called "SongsThatAprilLikes." She briefly considered opening that one up—momentarily curious about this "April" person and what her music taste was—and then she realized she was wasting time.

Her eyes flicked to the bottom of the screen and she spotted the re-cycle bin icon. Would the person who wrote the letter have been stupid enough to delete it but not empty the trash? Worth a try. She clicked on the small icon of a bin and the folder expanded. *Jackpot.*

She opened up the document and began to read. This was definitely the one. As she read, her stomach tightened.

She went through it three times. Tried to swallow and found that the back of her throat had dried out.

Finally, she closed the document and shut down the computer.

She crept from the room and back upstairs to sit on the couch. There was no way she was going to get any more sleep tonight.

Hey, all,

The secret I want to share is going to sound bad. But try not to freak out, because it's not actually as bad as it sounds and the first thing you need to know is that I would never, ever actually follow through on these feelings. In fact, I don't even know why I have these thoughts. Well, okay, I do know—sort of, where they come from, like I know why they first actually started, but still, sometimes, an idea just pops into my head and afterward, I think, *Fuck! What the hell was that? Where did that thought even come from? That was taking it a bit too far!*

But I guess the fact that the thoughts are actually there does sort of worry me. And I suppose that's why I thought this might be a good chance to tell you all and hopefully you guys can give me some advice? I don't know, maybe some of you have had these kinds of thoughts before and you'll just say, "What?! No way, you're not crazy, forget about it, it's completely normal, we all feel that way sometimes!!"

I guess I better stop going on about this and actually tell you what the thoughts are.

Firstly, though, you need to know that I do love you all—you guys have been my best friends for so, so long and you've all been there for me through so much. But the thing is, over the years, I've had a bit of a problem with one of you, I suppose you could even call it jealousy, really. And it's sort of grown . . . bigger and bigger over time. And please know that I DON'T WANT to feel this way.

It stems back to this one . . . incident. Although actually, it was more than just one incident, I guess you could call it a prolonged incident. It's hard to explain without going into too much detail and I'm not ready to share all of that just yet. But, the thing is, you did something; something that really, really upset me.

Anyway, from there it slowly got worse. Other things about you, things that I used to like, started to really irritate me.

Sometimes it would just be the way you spoke or the joke you made or the clothes you wore. It was this vibe you gave off, as though you've always thought you were better than the rest of us. Better than me.

For instance, when we were eating the Thai takeaway—you made this comment that, to be honest, was thoughtless and totally egotistical. I was right in the middle of cutting up my spring roll and I just about threw my knife at you!!

And sometimes it gets more . . . involved, this . . . obsession, this hatred of you.

I thought I'd just get over it. But for some reason I haven't been able to shake this horrible feeling. It's like you've left this bad taste in my mouth. And the thing is, because of this bad taste, every small thing you do these days seems to just ANNOY me!

A couple of weeks ago we were chatting on the phone and you said something—and it was something so silly, just small and trivial—I can't say what it was because then you'll know who it is that's writing this, and I swear to God, I wanted to reach through the telephone and strangle you!

I mean, not really of course. It's just a figure of speech, right?! But okay, I'll admit the feeling was pretty strong. Don't stress, okay? Because I'm not actually violent!!! Even with all these exclamation marks, I promise I'm not crazy.

Although there's one more thing that went through my head tonight. And I guess it did worry me a little bit. So we were all lying on the floor in front of the fire after we'd sorted out the leaks. And you had this look on your face. I will admit you looked very beautiful, though!! All glamorous with the flickering firelight and your petite features and your gorgeous eyes—but anyway, the look on your face. It was sort of a combination between smug and superior and it was like you were judging the rest of us.

It was in between the conversation about which schools we'd all want to send our kids to one day and then the argument about dark chocolate vs. milk chocolate. You really were sitting there thinking that you were better than the rest of us, weren't you? Specifically better than me. Well, that's how it felt anyway, but I'm pretty sure I'm right about that. And so I had this little fantasy where I waited until everyone was asleep, and then I took a pillow and I crept up to you and I put it over your smug sleeping face and I held it down and smothered you.

I know! I know, crazy, right? It was just a fantasy, though. And I'm sharing this 'cause I'm hoping you'll all say, "Oh, don't worry about it, we all have thoughts like that sometimes."

But then I am a bit concerned that you might not say that. I suppose there's a chance that you guys don't have these kinds of thoughts. Or that you do but you won't be willing to admit it out loud! And then if you figure out who I am . . . will you kick me out of the group? Will you be afraid to be around me anymore? I hope not, but I suppose that is a possibility. Especially if you think I'd actually hurt one of you! Which I wouldn't! They're just thoughts, okay?!

Okay, I'm just rereading this letter and now I'm starting to worry. It kind of sounds worse now that I'm reading my own words back. I'm trying to picture it from your perspective, like, how would I feel if one of you wrote this? I suppose it would make me a bit afraid!

I don't know, maybe I should just deal with these issues myself? Keep on acting the part, pretending I still like you? You have to admit I've been a pretty good actor over the years, by the way? I bet you have no idea I even feel this way, do you? And maybe the bad taste will fade over time anyway and in a few years I'll forget that I ever even felt this way. But then again maybe not.

Oh, man. I don't even know what to do now. I guess I should just hit print. I should just go for it, shouldn't I?

XX

As Joni sat on the couch again, wide-awake, eyes burning as the hazy light of dawn started to filter through the blinds, going over and over the words that she'd just read, her first thought was that she wasn't the right person to find it. It should have been someone else. Maybe Deb. Or Trina. Deb was the straight shooter. She would have just brought it straight out into the open. No secrets, no internal monologue trying to decide what to do about it, no panic, no anguish, and definitely no empathy. "What the hell is this all about?" she would have demanded of the group, probably while brandishing the letter out in front of her like a weapon.

And Trina, she came across as quiet . . . restrained. But she had her moments. Catch her on the right day and, like Deb, she knew how to take charge. But her style differed from Deb's. If she'd found the letter, she would have stared each one of them down, brought them to their knees, made them confess.

Eden would have been just as bad as Joni, though. Maybe worse. She crumbled under pressure; she wouldn't have had a clue what to do. Joni supposed Eden would have simply brought the charred fragments of paper straight to her.

She *could* take it to Deb. Make her deal with it. Put it all in her hands.

But here's the problem, thought Joni, *how do I know she wasn't the one who wrote it?*

———————

"It's chilling, isn't it? The idea that within a close group of four women, one of them could hate another one so much that she thinks about hurting them."

"Well, yes, I suppose 'chilling' is one word for it. I'd go with 'disturbing,' though. You realize this is your life, right? Not a piece of fiction. Not a crime thriller."

"Stop judging me! I'm just saying, it was horrifying, but it does make for a good story, doesn't it? I mean, you've stopped asking me when I'm ever going to get around to my actual confession, so obviously you're invested now. It's lucky no one else is waiting to confess, though, isn't it?"

"I think there was actually someone, but he gave up and left. Hopefully, he hasn't decided to go to the Protestant church across the road."

"Or the Buddhist temple around the corner. Hey, what do you think of Buddhism anyway? I've been thinking about taking it up. I've always held off, though, because I hear they don't allow alcohol. That's one thing about the good old Catholics; at least they like a glass of wine, am I right?"

"You're procrastinating. I can tell. And you can't ask my opinion about you swapping your faith. That's like walking into an Apple store and asking them if you should swap from your Mac to a PC. Now, back to the story, what happened next?"

CHAPTER 12

G uess what?" said Joni.

Deb pulled the covers up over her face. "What?! Why are you in here, what's going on? Why is it so bright?" She shifted the blanket back down far enough to open one eye and squint at the room, and then made a hissing noise and disappeared back under the covers.

Joni grinned at Trina and Eden. She was forcing herself to be cheerful, but inside she felt nauseated about today. Last night had been too much. First Eden's secret and then the anonymous extra letter she'd found. Right now all she wanted to do was get away from her friends, just be by herself for a while, think all of this through properly. But how could she do that when she now knew that one of her friends had some sort of weird obsession with someone else in their circle? What if they did something to hurt the object of their obsession? And what if this marked the beginning of the end for their twenty-plus-year friendship? They couldn't fall apart, not now. Not ever. Joni needed to stick close.

She needed to keep an eye on everyone. She needed to figure out who it was who'd written that damned letter and she needed to fix it.

They all stared down at the Deb-shaped lump under the quilt.

"Why is everyone in my room?!" Deb demanded from under the covers.

"Take one guess," said Trina.

"Oh shit," said Deb. "The fucking mud run."

"Yes," said Joni firmly. "And we're in your room because you're the last one to wake up, and if you don't get up now, we're going to be late."

"Fine," said Deb. "Just give me a minute to wake up properly, okay."

"You snuck some more wine last night, didn't you? When we got back from the beach," said Trina suspiciously. "You totally look hungover."

"No, I didn't," argued Deb. "And I do not look hungover." She re-emerged from under the blankets to reveal a tired-looking face with eyeliner smeared across her cheekbones, dark circles under her eyes, and her short hair sticking up at the back of her head.

"Of course not, sweetie," said Eden, giving Deb's leg a comforting pat. "You look gorgeous."

"Come on," Joni said briskly, backing away from the bed, "up and at 'em. We have to leave in fifteen, okay?" Then she ducked out into the hallway just as Deb hurled her pillow across the room at her.

"That's the spirit," she called out. "See you at the car."

In all honesty, the "Dirty Thirty Challenge" started out so much better than Joni could have imagined—and this was despite everything that had come to light since Joni had signed them all up for it. Funnily enough, had she known what she knew now when she'd booked these tickets, she never would have considered putting the four of them into this sort of a situation. And yet the camaraderie of it all—the way it was forcing the four of them to work together and to forget about all of the secrets that had been coming out over these last few days was probably exactly what they needed.

Plus, it was a chance for Joni to watch her three friends closely. To scrutinize their actions. Was that intentional when Deb kicked mud in Eden's face? Was it a sign when Trina slid back down the rope she was trying to climb and Eden laughed? But no, it didn't seem like anyone was being intentionally vicious. In fact, it was the exact opposite. The combined focus among the four of them was on moving forward. Helping one another up and over the wall. Encouraging one another through the ice-cold water. Grabbing one another's hands to stop from slipping in the mud.

And there was no time to chat—no air in your chest to allow you to talk even if you did have the time—and that was for the best. Too much talking lately. Too much sharing.

Adding to the positive vibe in the air was the fact that it was the same with everyone else around them. At each obstacle, there would be groups of people helping each other out. A guy offering his mate a hand to help hoist him up out of a mud pit. A stranger guiding someone as they eased their way back down from the rope swing. No one seemed to be interested in competing with anyone else. It was all just people having fun, all of them wanting to see everyone else make it to the finish line along with them. Everyone laughing at the absurdity of hundreds of grown men and women having paid good money just to get caked in mud.

At least that was how it began.

It was about the halfway mark where things started to go wrong. There was a decent stretch of straight-out running between obstacles. Along the track, different groups of people were taking it at different paces—some walking, some jogging, some running. The four women started off from the previous obstacle—a commando crawl underneath heavy rope nets—at a light jog.

But somehow, they split into pairs. Eden and Joni out in front, Deb and Trina behind them. And that's when Joni found herself falling into step beside Eden, just as she and Trina had when they'd run on the beach the previous day. And the more they picked up on one another's rhythm, the faster they ran. Until, almost without realizing it, they'd shot out in front, unexpectedly leaving Deb and the usually much faster Trina behind. Trina must have been taking it slow on purpose so that Deb wouldn't be left on her own.

At the next obstacle, a short swim across a muddy dam, they stopped at the edge and looked back behind them, finally noticing that they were alone. Joni had a moment where she felt guilty. She was supposed to be sticking close to *all* three of her friends, in order to keep an eye on them and pick up on any kind of homicidal vibes.

She wiped the back of her arm across her forehead, tried to clear away some of the mud that was dripping into her eyes, and then she became aware of a rancid smell that was emanating from the dam. She briefly wondered if they ought to skip this obstacle and she was almost going to make that suggestion to Eden, but then she glanced sideways at her—and that's when she saw it. The look of determination on Eden's face. Her crazy blond hair had been wrestled back into two long plaits and the way it pulled against her head seemed to somehow make her features sharper, her skin stretched tight, her eyes more intense. She didn't want to just muck around and have fun anymore. She wanted to compete. She wanted to win. And it was Joni that she had decided to pit herself against. In that moment, Joni seemed to just forget everything else that was going on. It was as though something primal woke up inside her in response.

During high school, Trina had always been the sportiest one in their circle. The natural athlete who picked up all the ribbons at the cross-country or the swimming carnival. Deb always preferred to find somewhere to hide out and have a cigarette, while Eden was more likely to be seated at the volunteers table, recording people's times, handing out medals. Joni, on the other hand, always wanted to join in on all the different activities; she was just never particularly good at any of them.

Now, though, after all the time Joni had been spending at the gym, not to mention working out with Ben, who always pushed her to work harder and harder, for the first time in her life, Joni felt like she was in with a chance to beat someone. And apparently Eden had become a better athlete as well.

Joni knew that she should suggest they wait for Deb and Trina to catch them up. Knew that turning this into a race was against the spirit of the day. This wasn't what it was supposed to be about. And they'd been having so much fun up until this point. But she convinced herself that Deb and Trina wouldn't really mind. That they would continue to enjoy themselves without her and Eden. That this was just as much Eden's fault as it was her own.

And without needing to say a word, Joni and Eden both dove into the dam. The heart-stopping icy water pressed in on her and she took a moment to adjust her body to the temperature before she struck out in an inelegant freestyle through the thick sludge. When they reached the bank on the other side of the dam, they both scrambled up out of the water without offering a hand and then they took off without so much as a glance at one another.

The track was heading into the bush when Joni heard a faint shout from behind her. She slowed down and looked back to see Deb and Trina, on the other side of the dam, calling out to them and waving their arms. But then Joni realized that Eden hadn't slowed and she turned back and kept running, pretending not to have seen her friends calling after them.

At the wooden balance beams, they both had to wait while the group in front of them took their turns, and Joni found herself tapping her foot impatiently as two giggling girls tried to guide their friend across. When the beams were finally free, Joni and Eden took one each, and against her better judgment, Joni put one foot in front of the other at top speed while the volunteers who were keeping an eye on the competitors called out, "Easy there, those beams are pretty slippery from all the mud." But Joni ignored them. Right at the end, her foot slipped and she waved her arms wildly, steadying herself. Out of the corner of her eye, she saw Eden reach the end of her beam and jump down to the ground. She looked back at Joni—a note of alarm crossed her face—but then Joni righted herself, took the last two steps, and jumped down to the ground as well. Eden's face went blank again. They took off again.

At the next obstacle, they were supposed to pair up and help one another carry a massive, heavy log out around a tree, through a muddy trench, and then back to the starting point. Joni was just about to ask Eden if she wanted to take the front or the back when she saw her approaching a tall stocky guy who'd just arrived at the obstacle. "Need a partner?" Eden asked him.

"Sure!" the guy replied. Joni was stunned as she watched Eden crouch down and hoist one end of the log up and onto her shoulder without even looking at Joni, and a flash of anger on behalf of Ben flared up inside of her: What would he think if he knew his wife was flirting with some guy in order to get him to help her beat Joni? Another guy appeared beside Joni and she spun around and grabbed his arm. "Help me beat them," she demanded.

The guy laughed. "Yeah, all right," he said. They each lifted up one end of the next log and then they took off after Eden and her partner at a fast walk.

Eden was ahead right up until they entered the mud trench—when her partner got his shoe stuck in the mud and Joni was able to overtake. She gave Eden a big grin as they passed her. "This is fun, right?"

she asked, making her voice sound overly sugary and friendly on purpose.

Eden matched her tone. "Yep, so much fun!"

Eden caught up with her on the next stretch between obstacles. "Getting tired?" she asked as she ran alongside Joni.

"Nope," Joni replied.

"You sure? You sound pretty puffed!" And then Eden started sprinting and Joni had to summon every ounce of strength from within in order to coerce her legs into speeding up so she could keep up with her.

At the fire pits, they were neck and neck as they leaped across the smoking mounds. Crawling under the barbed wire, Joni gained a little ground and came out ahead. But then at the next wall climb, Eden got lucky, picking the best handholds, and she took the lead back off Joni.

The last obstacle was monkey bars over the top of a man-made trench of water that was being constantly topped up with buckets of fresh ice. Beyond that it would be a fifty-meter sprint to the finish line.

"Fuck," Joni heard Eden mutter. "I haven't done monkey bars since primary school."

Joni smiled to herself; she'd practiced monkey bars at the gym just last week with Ben's encouragement. She had this one in the bag.

Joni started out strong. She was halfway across before Eden had even made it through the first couple of bars. But then Eden hit her stride and she started taking the bars steadily, one after another. Joni made the mistake of looking back to see how close she was getting and misjudged the next bar. Her hand grasped empty air. For a second, she dangled by one arm—and then her muddied fingers slipped and she fell.

The chilled water made her splutter and splash for a few seconds, and when she looked up she saw Eden looking down at her with a wide smile on her face. In that moment, Joni knew. She knew that Eden knew about her crush on Ben. And that those feelings *were* real, no matter

how much she tried to convince herself that they weren't. And she understood that this entire competition was about Eden showing her that
while Ben might have flirted with Joni, Eden was the one who had him.
Eden was the one who was married to him, who had two children with
him, and who would be sleeping in the same bed as him tomorrow night
when they all returned home. And then Eden looked ahead again and
continued on, swinging from one bar to the next with the form of a practiced gymnast.

"Shit," said Joni, and she pushed herself to wade through the ice to
the end of the trench.

"Joni! Eden!"

Joni was just reaching the edge when she heard their names being
called out. Eden had already landed from the monkey bars and was a
good ten meters up ahead, but she stopped to look back.

Joni looked around to see where the voices were coming from. Suddenly hands were grabbing hold of her arms and helping to pull her up
over the slippery edge.

Her eyes met Deb's first and then Trina's, and immediately she knew
they weren't happy. "Where did you guys come from?" she asked confusedly. "How'd you catch up with us?"

"We took a shortcut," Deb said tersely. "What the hell is up with you
and Eden?"

"Eden! Where is she?" Joni looked around; had she taken advantage
of Joni being distracted and gone off ahead? But then she saw that Eden
was walking back to the three of them.

"Hey!" Eden said casually, as though a moment before she hadn't
been gloating up above Joni. "Where did you two come from?"

"Oh well, Deb found this track and we—" Trina began, but Deb cut
her off.

"Forget that. I want to know what's going on with the both of you?"

Eden looked up at the sky as though she'd just spotted an interesting cloud and Joni folded her arms. "What do you mean?" she asked, trying to sound innocent.

"You know what we mean."

Eden finally lowered her gaze and looked at Joni. Joni stared back at her. A couple jogged past them, the woman glanced across at them, probably curious as to why they'd all stopped so close to the end of the course. Then she turned back, took hold of her partner's hand, and grinned at him as they continued on to the finish line.

There was a moment then. A moment where if just one of them had given in—had admitted that Deb was completely right, that they were being silly and immature about this—then the other one would have agreed. And they probably would have stopped it all then and there. Joni and Eden would have pretended that the truth about Joni's crush hadn't crossed between them. The four of them might have looped arms and crossed the finish line together—as a team. But instead, as they continued to stare at one another, a silent message passed between them. *Let's find out who's going to win this thing.*

"Can we talk about this after?" Joni asked.

"Yeah, it's almost done, we'll chat once we're across the finish line," said Eden.

And then the two of them took off running again. Leaving Deb and Trina standing still, staring after them. Eden was in front and that was no surprise; she wasn't worn out from having to fight her way through that iced water just now. But Joni was being fueled by desperation.

My body has already failed me once.

It's failed me as a woman.

And it's about time I came out on top for once.

Eden doesn't need this.

She doesn't need to win.

She got pregnant. She's had her win.

Pregnant to the perfect guy. The perfect husband. Twice.

A guy who I know *was checking out my bum on the treadmill just the other day. While my husband . . . my husband doesn't even want to fuck me anymore.*

And you know why that is? It's because he's given up on me. It's because he knows it's pointless. I'm a dud bang. I'm useless.

So I'm the one who needs this.

Joni broke through the pain barriers and propelled herself forward.

She was neck and neck with Eden.

She was in front.

She was in front by just one foot—but she had taken the lead.

They were about to cross the finish line—she was going to win. She was going to do it! For once she was going to come out ahead! And then the front of her shoe caught on a rock.

It was during the second or third obstacle of the day that the woman felt herself snap. Before the four of them split off into pairs. When they were all still having fun, acting like they used to when they were teenagers, back before she'd ever started feeling this way about her friend. And at first, it really was like the old days. She was actually enjoying herself. She was managing to keep the snipy thoughts at bay. And she was thinking: Maybe I can get past this. Maybe I can stop these feelings from coming. And she felt relief knowing that the letter was finally gone. That it had been safely destroyed. There was no longer any evidence of her feelings. So all she had to do was make those feelings go away.

But then her friend said something. Something stupid and wrong and there it was. That flash of irritation. That familiar flicker of rage. And all the feelings came rushing straight back, and when she was sup-

posed to be helping her up out of one of the mud pits, a strange sensation came over her and she imagined herself reaching out and placing her hands on top of her friend's head. Saw her hands pushing her down under the mud. Felt the top of her friend's head pushing back against her and imagined herself holding her down. Keeping her down until she stopped.

She gave her entire body a shake. No! That was an awful thing to think. A horrible, horrendous, terrifying thought. And she didn't mean it. She absolutely did NOT mean it.

She briefly closed her eyes, mentally pulling herself back together.

What is wrong with me?

———

"Maybe I should have just asked them all about it straightaway. But I didn't want to show my hand—you know? Because if whoever it was denied it then, what was I going to do? And once she knew I knew, then she could be careful around me. Cover her tracks, right? Whereas this way, I could keep watching them, try and catch her out. It was harder to tell than I thought it would be, though. And the mud run . . . well, I guess it sort of blinded me a bit. I had this stupid desire to win, for God knows . . . oops, sorry, I mean, for who knows what reason, and when I should have been playing detective, I was too busy racing Eden."

"You really don't know why you wanted to win? I would have thought it would have been obvious to you."

"Okay, fine. I knew why I wanted to win—I just don't know why I got so . . . weird about it."

"So—did you get your win?"

"No. But I would have, if I hadn't tripped at the end there. I was definitely in the lead."

"Tell me. Why did it matter? I know we both know the answer, but I think it might help to say it out loud: What was so important to you about winning?"

"Would you stop psychoanalyzing me, Father?"

CHAPTER 13

Joni winced as the antiseptic was dabbed against her chin.

"Come on," said the paramedic with a laugh. "Haven't you just been leaping over hot coals and crawling under barbed wire?"

"So," said Joni, screwing up her face, "that stuff stings."

"Well, then it's lucky that we're done with it now. Just a couple of Steri-Strips and you'll be good to go."

Eden hovered behind him, biting her fingernails as she watched Joni get patched up.

"You really want to chew on those?" Joni asked. "Considering how much mud is under them?"

Eden looked down at her hands and gave a small laugh. "Good point," she murmured. Eden had rushed to help Joni up as soon as she'd looked back and seen that Joni had fallen—but not before she'd crossed the finish line. She'd insisted that Joni should visit the first-aid tent, and at first they'd all wondered if she was going to end up needing stitches, but once the cut was cleaned up, it was agreed that they wouldn't be necessary. Deb and Trina had left them to go and wash off all the mud under the outdoor showers while Eden had stayed.

"Hey, looks like you've already got a scar here on your chin," commented the paramedic. "Don't think this new cut is going to scar, though."

"Ice-skating accident," explained Joni.

"Rochelle MacDonald's fourteenth birthday party," said Eden automatically, almost as though it was a conditioned response.

"That's the one," said Joni.

"Going too fast in the speed-skating round?" guessed the paramedic.

Joni's eyes linked with Eden's. She knew that Eden was remembering what had actually happened that day. Joseph Harris had pushed her over. If she closed her eyes, she could still feel the shove in the center of her back. Could see the ice coming up to meet her face and hear the sound of cruel laughter from Joseph, Luke, and the rest of their mates as the blood from her chin bloomed red on the ice beneath her. Oh God, Trina had been right the other night to wonder why on earth she had ended up kissing Luke in Year Twelve.

"Yeah," said Joni to the paramedic. "Thought I was a better skater than I was."

"Ah well," he said, "they say chicks dig scars, but I can tell you blokes do as well."

"Um, thanks?" said Joni, and then she looked up at Eden and they both laughed.

"Oh, Joni," said Eden then, her voice beginning to wobble, "I'm so, so sorry. I don't know why I got so competitive today. I was being ridiculous."

"No, *I'm* sorry! I was just as bad!" Joni wailed in response.

The paramedic looked back and forth between them. "Okay, now you're totally ruining the tough-girl image."

"Shut up," said Joni crossly, standing up to hug her friend.

"Come on, let's go and find Deb and Trina."

And just like that they'd moved on. Neither of them needing to say what was really going on out loud. And Joni knew that she was going to have to find a way to make her feelings disappear.

Because Eden had won, fair and square.

They weren't planning on hanging around for the mini–music festival that followed the mud run. They had intended on getting cleaned up, piling back into Eden's lemon-yellow Beetle, and heading back to the holiday house for a good night's sleep before the drive back home to-morrow. But there was an intoxicating buzz in the air that came from the exhilaration of hundreds of people having completed a grueling task together despite the shared exhaustion.

The beer was cheap and they were all thirsty after the race. The music was loud and the crowds of people who were drinking and dancing still had dried-up mud caked behind their ears or streaked through the hair on their arms. It was dark and cold, but no one seemed overly bothered by the temperature. They were keeping warm by pushing up against one another as they danced under the stars and, every now and again, a seemingly random set of strangers would start making out—as though this was some sort of sixties free-love festival.

The four girls were now making up for the alcohol-free night they'd had the previous evening. A mixture of dehydration from the day's exer-cise and a lack of food meant they were all far drunker far quicker than they'd even been on the first night they'd arrived at the holiday house.

"'M not going to be able to drive us back to the house, you know?" Eden slurred at Joni and Deb. They were standing at the edge of the crowd, watching Trina, who had somehow ended up on the shoulders of a guy farther up toward the band.

"Nope, def not," agreed Joni. "'S okay, we can sleep in the car or call a taxi, and hey," she said, abruptly switching topics, "is she okay up there? Does she need rescuing?"

They heard Trina let out a loud whoop and Joni said in a posh voice, "I hereby retract my question."

Joni now started examining both Eden and Deb's faces in turn. All of this beer kept making her forget about her mission, and then every now and again she would remember and try once again to figure out who had written that damned letter.

"What?" said Eden, looking back at her. "What's up?"

"How *are* you?" Joni asked. "How are *things*? How are things *going*?"

"Huh?" said Eden.

Joni shifted her focus across to Deb. "What about you? How *are* you? How are *things*?" she said.

"What the fuck?" said Deb.

"Hey," said a voice from behind them, and the three women turned around to see the paramedic who had patched up Joni earlier. "You should probably be taking it a little slower on the drinks. That was a nasty fall you had today."

Joni threw her arms around his neck, making him stumble sideward as he took her weight. "My knight in shining armor!" she exclaimed.

"Oy," said Deb, yanking her by the arm to pull her away, "you already have a knight in shining armor at home."

"Wasn't going to do anything," said Joni crossly. "Just saying thank you is all."

The paramedic laughed and moved off through the crowd, leaving Joni glaring at Deb. "What do you care anyway, you think Kai and I are overrr."

"Huh? No, I don't, what are you on about?" Deb took a large swig from her beer and swayed dangerously on the spot.

"I heeeard you!" Joni said in a singsong voice. "The other night. At the pub. I heeeeard you."

"Fuck," said Deb. She reached out her hands and placed them steadily on Joni's shoulders. "Joni," she said, looking as though it was taking all of her concentration to keep her voice steady and serious, "I'm sorry. I'm soooo sorry. You weren't meant to hear that. I was jus' joking anyway."

"Hear what?" Eden interjected. "Whadidishesay?"

"Ask her," said Joni, suddenly feeling sad and annoyed, and she shook Deb's hands off and turned away from the two of them and started charging through the crowds in the very definite direction of . . . something.

She was pretty sure that at first Deb and Eden had tried to follow her, but there were so many people and it was so dark that she was able to lose them fairly easily. But after a few minutes, she didn't know what she was doing or where she was going or what she even wanted.

Then a thought struck her. There was still one more letter to be read. And it was inside Eden's car. They'd brought it with them because they were planning on heading out to dinner after the mud run and reading the final letter together at the restaurant. What if that last letter held a clue as to who had written the letter she'd found in the fire? She should go to the car and get the letter and read it on her own . . . right now. If only the ground would stop tilting and the world would stop swaying and her vision would stop pulsing.

I am very, very drunk, she thought, and then she chuckled happily to herself. *And one of my friends sort of wants to murder one of my other friends,* she thought. *Or me.* And then she stopped chuckling and started to feel sad again.

"This sucks," she said out loud.

"What sucks?" asked a voice from her left. The paramedic.

"You again!" she said. "You need a name," she added, "so I can stop thinking of you as 'the paramedic.'"

"Sunny," he replied.

"No it isn't," said Joni, looking stupidly up at the sky. "'S dark."

"No, I mean my name is Sunny."

"Ah. Hippy parents?" she asked.

"Yep," he replied. "So, what sucks?"

She spoke carefully, enunciating her words to try to hide the slurring: "I have a problem. I need to get into my friend's car. But I don't have the keys."

"Um, I'm sorry to tell you this. But you should not be driving anywhere right now."

"Not going to!" Joni said indignantly. "I just need something out of the car. I'm on a *mission*."

"A mission?" Sunny asked with interest. "Well, all right, then, as your knight in shining armor, I guess I'd better help you if it's a mission."

Joni wasn't sure at what point it happened, but as they weaved through the gyrating people and then headed across the field to where the cars were parked, somehow he'd taken hold of her hand.

"This isn't . . ." she began, "I mean, I'm not . . . like . . . I'm not coming on to you," she continued as she spotted Eden's car and pulled him toward it. "So I don't really know why we're holding hands. 'Cause I'm married, okay? So nothing is going to happen."

"Scout's honor," Sunny replied.

They reached the car and Joni tried the doors just in case, but all four were locked. "Now what?" she asked.

"Now I break in for you," said Sunny.

"With what?"

"With this." He pulled a set of keys out of his pocket and showed her a small metal tool hanging off the key ring.

"What is that?" Joni asked as she watched him jam the tool into the lock and start jiggling it around.

"Better you don't know," he replied.

"Ooh, Sunny has a dark side."

"Maybe."

It took him less than thirty seconds to jimmy the lock and then the door was open and Joni dove inside and opened the glove box, rummaging around to find the letter that had been stashed inside. Once she had it, Sunny pulled her back out by the hand and for a moment they stood close together, pushed up against the side of the car.

And then Joni realized he was leaning in to kiss her and the face that flashed across her mind wasn't Kai's. It was Ben's. She ducked out from under Sunny and stumbled between the cars, grabbing hold of a side mirror to right herself. "Sorry, Sunny," she said, "but I did tell you I was married." Then she picked up her pace and made her way back toward the crowds.

A guy tried to kiss me, and the first person I think of isn't my husband.

Deb was fucking right. I am in trouble.

And maybe it's going to be harder than I thought to sort out my feelings.

My feelings for Kai. And my feelings for Ben.

She found a patch of grass under a tree off to the side of the dancing and opened up the letter to read it.

Hi,

This is my secret:

   I'm a shit mum. Honestly, I completely suck at this whole mum thing. I don't know what I'm doing, I stuff up all the time, I feel like I'm ruining my kid's life, I feel like I'm constantly second-guessing every single decision I make. If it's a freezing-cold day and I can't get my child to stop pulling off their socks—it's my fault. If my kid won't eat dinner, it's my fault. If they have a tantrum in the middle of the supermarket. Or if I think they're watching too much television or have a bad night's sleep or if they get hurt. It's all on me—and I don't know how to stay on top of it all.

And I don't pay enough attention to my child. The other day I was looking at a video on Facebook. So my kid toddles into the living room, sits down, and starts banging on the xylophone that was in the middle of the rug with this great big grin. Like, "I'm so clever making this loud noise," and all I wanted was for the noise to stop so I could hear the stupid video I was watching. How bad is that? How absolutely, incredibly evil is that? Who does that? Who's more interested in some shit video on Facebook than their own kid exploring their love of music and wanting to share that with their mum? My kid just wanted to show off for me. And you know what I said? I said, "Could you just be quiet for a minute because Mummy is busy." What a bitch. What an absolute and complete bitch.

I was busy. I was busy on fucking Facebook. And when I finished the video, I realized what I'd just done. I'd just shut down my child. When I should have been putting my phone down and enjoying a beautiful moment. When I should have been encouraging and clapping along and laughing and playing and just bloody paying the kid some attention. I mean, seriously, this kid is a complete anomaly in my life: this kid tears me apart and fills me and makes me whole. But that doesn't mean I have a clue how to be a parent!

And here's the worst part: my husband is ready for the next baby. He wants to have it now. And I really, really don't want to. I'm not ready. I'm not even sure if I'll ever be ready. Honestly, I only ever wanted one. Just one. And I thought he agreed with that. But now he's saying this is what he really, really wants. Actually, he's almost demanding that we do it. So if I'm already stuffing up this whole mum thing with one kid, how the hell would I go with two? But I can't seem to get that through to him.

I have no idea what to do about any of this. I don't know how to be a better mum and I don't know how to get through to you-know-who that I don't want another baby. He doesn't realize that I'm failing at being a mum. He doesn't know that I'm so completely shit at it, so he doesn't even get why I don't want another one.

So, who has some sort of magical solution for me? Ha.

From,
Me.

When she was done reading, all that she felt was frustration.

Frustration that this gave her no clue as to who had written the fifth letter.

Frustration that all that these letters had done was make such a mess of everything.

Joni put down the letter and attempted to make a mental stock-take of the letters so far. It was more difficult than it should have been, though, thanks to her state of inebriation. *Right. So the first one . . . the divorced group one . . . that had to be Trin's. 'Cause Josh is a dick and it means they're gonna split. And Deb agreed with me that it was probably Trina's. The second letter was . . . Mine! The second letter was mine. And everyone knows that, but they don't all know that I know that they know. Funny. But do they all know that Ben is my crush? Probably they do. Eden could tell, for sure. The third one, well, of course we all know that one was Eden's. Eden of the infamous teen-age pregnancy. Which leaves . . . which leaves . . . Deb! So this letter belongs to Deb.*

It made sense. It wasn't that Deb was a bad mother or anything like that, but she was hardly the archetypal earth mother, like Eden for instance, so it fit that she would have *felt* like she was a bad mum.

She shouldn't, though, because Joni knew that as much as Deb might not have looked the part, she did love Ruby very much. In fact, Deb knew every single little nuance there was to know about Ruby—Joni knew this because Deb had once listed these things off to Joni when she was whingeing about how unfair it was that it was always the mum's job to be the keeper of such facts. "Strawberry-flavored yogurt gives her a rash on her cheeks," she'd said. "If she has a temperature, she hates the taste of baby Panadol but she'll take children's Dymadon. She loves to be sung the ABC but hates 'Twinkle, Twinkle,' which is crazy, because they both have the same tune. Her favorite toy is the scruffy puppy with the weird, scary sort of grimace. She eats best when she can pick up the food with her hands rather than using a spoon. Anything she can grip in her tiny fists will be demolished in an instant. And do you think Connor knows every single one of these things? Or do you think he just sees her as a cute feminine version of himself?" Deb had asked Joni in an aggressive sort of manner. "No, I bloody doubt it." And Joni had thought, *Yes, that's all well and good, Deb, but why do I have to learn all these things about your kid? I'm not her father!*

Now it made more sense, though. Deb had listed these things off because she'd been trying to prove—maybe even just to herself— that she was doing a good job as a mother.

Great. Yet another thing to fill her with frustration—because the thing was, Joni had *no* idea how to help Deb with any of these sorts of feelings. But God, did she wish she did understand.

"What's that?"

Joni looked up to see Trina standing above her, looking at the letter on her lap.

"Last letter," she sniffed. "You wanna read it?"

"Later. You been crying?" Trina asked.

Joni touched her fingers to her cheeks and felt tears—when had that happened? She hadn't even realized that she'd been that upset.

She shrugged and Trina sat down next to her.

"What's going on?" Trina asked.

Joni felt a lump rise up in her throat and she shook her head and started crying properly now.

"You and Kai have been trying to get pregnant, haven't you?" Trina asked.

Joni kept her eyes on the ground and said, "How'd you know?"

"I didn't. I was guessing. How long has it been?"

"Almost a year now, but it feels like forever."

"Oh, Joni. I'm sorry."

"'S okay. Not your fault."

"Do you know what's going on? Like, I mean, have you been to the doctor to check things out?"

"Yeah," said Joni, sniffing again. "Went to my GP, couple months back. But he wouldn't do any tests until we've been trying for more than twelve months. Said there's probably nothing to worry about. Said sometimes these things just take time."

"But that's a good thing, then!" Trina exclaimed. "That means you just need to keep trying, and eventually, it'll just happen!"

Joni shook her head. "Nope," she said. "I don't believe that. I know it's me, I know I'm the issue. There's something there."

"But, Joni," said Trina gently, "I'm sure they wouldn't—"

"You don't know!" Joni cut her off.

"I just mean that—"

"*Don't* try and fix this. This is something that I know—something that I can just tell."

"Okay," said Trina calmly, "I'm not trying to fix it, but just so you know, I've known at least three different women, two from my mothers' group and one from work, who had similar experiences. One of them took two full years to fall pregnant, and the point is, in the end they were able to have kids. So I'm sure that if—"

"Trina, please," Joni whispered. She couldn't bear to hear about other people's success stories—especially people from Trina's goddamned mothers' group.

That secret fucking society with the most basic membership requirement: the ability to reproduce. Why the hell did any of them even need another group of friends anyway? Weren't the four of them enough?

Eden had been full of girlish delight when she'd found out she and Deb had been allocated to the same local mothers' group. And next thing, the two of them were being kept busy by picnics and coffee dates with their new little circle of mummsy friends. Trina had other friends too, actually. Old uni mates that she still caught up with on a regular basis. Or the girls from her netball team. But not Joni. She'd never had any other friends. Sure, she hung out with colleagues after work sometimes, or went along to dinner with Kai's mates. There was even that old neighbor that she went to the movies with occasionally—but that was only because they both happened to have the same taste in horror flicks. There was no one else who she considered to be as close as her three best friends from high school. They were enough for her. So then why wasn't she enough for them?

"That's why I wanted to win today," said Joni, looking up at Trina. "I just wanted . . . for once . . . to come out on top."

Trina stared back at her, a strange look on her face. "You think the rest of us are on top," she asked, "just because we have kids?"

"Um, yeah," said Joni, unable to stop the note of bitterness from creeping into her voice.

"Joni, you have *no* idea," said Trina.

"Oh, isn't that always the way, Trina? The girl without kids doesn't have a clue what it's like. Well, that's the bloody problem, isn't it? You all think you're above me—you have this special knowledge just because your ovaries do what they're supposed to do."

"No, that's not what I was trying to say," said Trina. "I was just trying to explain that—"

"Besides," Joni cut in, "I guess with me not being able to have kids, I can keep on being the one that always has to make the holiday bookings or arrange the girls' nights out. The one that does bloody everything to keep this group together."

"Hey," said Trina, "that's not true, we don't *make* you do all the organizing."

"Are you kidding me? Of course you do. It's always, 'You do it, Joni, you're so good at finding the great places,' or 'You get the great bargains.' When what you really mean is, 'You have the most spare time—because you don't have kids.'"

"Joni," said Trina, starting to sound like she was losing her patience, "that's not fair. And anyway, how come you never said anything? We always just thought you liked being the organizer of the group—you seem to enjoy it so much. You shouldn't have kept it from us, one of us would have taken over."

"Yeah, like you can talk about keeping things from everyone else," Joni snapped back.

"What do you mean?"

"Those tablets you're taking. The 'multivitamins.' Why did you lie to me when I asked you about them the other day?"

"I . . . I didn't . . ." Trina was fumbling over her words, and for a moment she looked vulnerable and hurt and Joni was starting to regret what she'd said. Why was she always taking things too far? But then Trina's face changed. "You know what?" she said. "Fine. I lied. They weren't multivitamins. But that doesn't make it your business—not everything is about you, Joni. Besides, you want everything out in the open? I was watching from behind when you tripped today. And you know what? Eden saw it happen but she didn't stop. She got herself over the line *first* and then she turned back to help you up. And you want to know why that was? It's because you're not the only one in the world who feels like they need to win sometimes. It's obvious that you have a crush on Ben. And if it's obvious to me, then it's probably just as obvious to her too."

"Really?" said Joni, breathing hard as the anger and embarrassment welled up inside. "Just like it's obvious to the rest of us that Josh treats you like shit?"

"What?" Trina looked like Joni had slapped her across the face. She opened her mouth to speak again, but then the two of them both looked up to see Deb rushing toward them with Eden following her, her expression unreadable.

"What is it?" Trina said, looking up at Deb, but Deb only had eyes for Joni.

"Are you Celine Fletcher?" Deb said, staring down at Joni.

Joni felt her stomach jolt. Celine Fletcher. The pseudonym she'd been using for her articles. *Fuck.* Then she looked past Deb at Eden, whose face, she now realized, was actually a mixture of guilt and triumph. So apparently neither of them had left a damn thing behind after their little competition today after all.

"You told her?" Joni exclaimed. "I told you that in confidence."

"So you are?" interrupted Deb.

"What the hell are you on about, Deb?" asked Trina.

Deb kept her focus zeroed in on Joni as she spoke. "Eden just told me that Joni got a new job and decided to keep it from us," said Deb.

"So," began Trina, "why is that such a big deal?"

"Because the new job is for a parenting website. And she's been writing under a pseudonym and pretending that she's a mum—and her articles are *all* about judging other mums."

"Okay, but, Deb," said Trina, and Joni could tell that she was clearly torn between defending Joni because of what she now knew about her infertility and joining in on Deb's rage because of what Joni had just said a moment ago about Josh. Joni was relieved, though, when Trina's sympathy for her won out and she said carefully, "Listen, before you get angry, you should know what Joni's going through at the moment."

It didn't matter, though. Deb was unstoppable. "I don't give a shit what she's going through," she said. "That doesn't give her the right to say the things that she's been saying all just for the sake of a good story. Do you know that she said if a child was allowed to watch any more than thirty minutes of television per day, then that was tantamount to child abuse? And that it was the mother's responsibility, not the father's, to stay at home with the kids because a child needs maternal love and a man needs to be out providing for his family?"

"No!" said Trina. "There's no way she would write sexist crap like that."

"See for yourself," said Deb, pulling her phone out of her pocket and passing it across to Trina. "Look up parentingdoneright.com. Fucking hell, Joni. I mean I knew—I knew that whoever was writing that crap was doing it for the hits—stirring up controversy with those click-bait headlines. And I knew that I shouldn't fall for it. That I shouldn't let it get to me. But I went to that damn site in the first place to get advice, to get support from other mums. And instead I came across these articles that were being touted as 'expert parenting advice,' and a couple of times, I actually wondered if I was the one in the wrong. Like the breastfeeding one—where you made me feel like the worst mother in the world because I couldn't do it for any longer than six weeks and you said that *my* child was going to be susceptible to all sorts of diseases and that I must not love her enough if I couldn't push through and make it work. Fuck, Joni, you made me hate myself."

"But, Deb, you don't understand. The things I wrote as her—they're not my opinion, I don't agree with the things Celine's said."

"Yes, but you did write them, didn't you?"

"But the articles weren't real! I didn't mean anything by them. I was just trying to keep my boss happy. I didn't expect people to actually take them seriously or hold themselves up to those crazy standards."

"Shit," said Trina as she scanned the content on Deb's phone. "Did you really write this, Joni?"

"Which one is it?" Deb asked, then she said, "Actually, why don't you just read it out loud?"

"Don't," said Joni, but Trina had already started reading.

"'*Fat Mum Lazy Mum,* by Celine Fletcher. Last week I went to my local supermarket to do my week's shopping. As usual, I had all seven days' worth of meals—breakfast, lunch, and dinner—all planned out, because planning ahead is planning for success. DD2 was sitting in the trolley seat, munching on her carrot sticks, and DS4 was walking next to me—staying sensibly by my side as he always does—and helping me complete my list. That's when I saw her walking toward me. A mother with three kids, two of them engaged in a fierce battle like they were possessed by the devil and the third sitting in the trolley—the basket of the trolley, not the seat with the appropriate child restraint—and squealing for chocolate.

"'Now let me just say that it was clear that this mother certainly hadn't seen the inside of a gym in recent days. And look, that's fine, her body, her choice, right? The issue I had, though, was with her kids. Because they were obviously following in their big mama's footsteps. And here's the kicker: in order to get the older two to stop fighting and the younger one to stop screaming, she started handing out donuts. Not just a couple of mini-donuts—oh no, they were giant, cream-filled donuts. Those kids took to them like ducks to water.

"'And I couldn't help but think, *If that's how she gets her kids to behave—by bribing them with sweet treats— well, isn't that just a display of pure laziness?* Because IMHO, those kids should be sat down for a good, firm chat about appropriate public behavior. And as for morning tea snacks—it's not that hard to chop up some carrots, celery, and cucumber sticks and to whiz up some organic homemade hummus, is it? After all, that's what I do for my kids.'"

"Stop," pleaded Joni. "Please, just stop reading it. I'm sorry, okay, but I never thought there would be mums out there that would take it to heart."

"Far out," said Deb. "I feel like my whole world has just been tipped upside down. I feel like an absolute idiot. All this time I'm getting worked up over these articles and you're just there laughing behind my back."

"I was never laughing!"

"Well, you may as well have been."

"Joni, you might think it was okay because you 'didn't mean it,' but to write that stuff, there must have been some truth behind your words," said Trina.

"No! I was following the brief is all. My job was to get mums worked up, that's it."

"You were trying to get mums worked up?" Deb asked, her voice dangerously quiet. "Joni," she said, "do you realize how nasty that is?

And did you really feel good about yourself when you wrote that sort of stuff?"

Joni stood up from the ground so that she could stop feeling like Deb was towering over her. She stared back at Deb angrily. "No," she said. "But I was just doing my job, okay? I didn't think it would hurt anyone. Besides, I wasn't making you read my articles. I wasn't asking you to take them to heart."

"Yeah, well, that sounds like a fucking cop-out to me."

Joni shifted her attention to Eden, who had remained quiet this entire time. "Fucking hell, Eden," she said, "why did you have to tell her?"

Eden shrugged her shoulders. "Because I'm drunk," she said. "It was an accident, just slipped out." But there was no sincerity in her voice, and as Joni looked around at her three best friends—at Trina, who thanks to Joni, now knew that they all hated her husband; at Deb, the woman who had been struggling to trust herself as a parent, an insecurity that had been compounded thanks to Joni's articles; and at Eden, the friend who had chosen to betray her because Joni had betrayed her first—and all Joni wanted to do was cry.

"*So I guess you knew that this was coming, didn't you? That it was all going to blow up in our faces.*"

"*Yes. I figured that's where the story was heading.*"

There was a long pause as Joni fought back tears. Reliving that horrible night—everything that had happened after the mud run—it just hurt. But as much as she wanted to stop, as much as her back was aching and her feet were cramping from being cooped up inside this confessional booth telling this story for so long, she knew she had to keep going. The story wasn't done yet.

"*You got any ideas yet, on who wrote the fifth letter?*" Joni asked.

"*I might. But tell me what happened next first. There's obviously more. You haven't really come to your actual confession yet, have you?*"

"*Are you kidding me?! I've confessed to having a crush on Eden's husband. I've confessed to bagging out Trina's husband to her face and to writing bogus articles that made Deb hate herself! That's not enough for you?*"

"*No. Not when you and I both know that's not the end of it.*"

"*Okay, fine. But first, can I explain something to you about my friendship with these three women? I've been friends with them now for more than twenty years and I thought I knew everything there was to know about them. I knew that when Deb was in primary school, she was the kid that the other kids made fun of—all because she had warts on her hands. I don't know if she even remembers telling me about that. It was right after she gave birth to Ruby. I went in to visit her and she was still high on morphine because she had to have an emergency C-section. So anyway, I'm expecting her to tell me all about how special she feels because she's just become a mother. But instead* she tells me that when she was six years old, none of the other kids in her class would hold her hand when they walked from the classroom to the church for mass. She tells me how it used to break her. She tells me that once upon a time, she used to be a crier. But that, one day, she got hold of her mother's cigarette lighter and she tried to burn the warts off her hand. She ended up with second-degree burns and soon after she swapped schools. I don't know why she chose that moment to tell me that story. Was she worried about what school was going to be like for Ruby one day? I don't know—all I know is that that story broke my damn heart.

"And I know that Trina could have been an artist if she hadn't become a sports teacher. She never took art at school, but once, when we had a sleepover at her house, I found a bunch of drawings in a box under her bed. Charcoal sketches, and they were amazing. I was going to call her out on it, the same way I did when I discovered that Eden could sing. But then it occurred to me—why hadn't she already shown us these drawings? And you know what I realized? I realized that it was the same as when I caught her looking in the mirror trying to see if she had any of her dad's features. She hid her talent because she was afraid that it had come from her dad's side of the family. I don't know how I knew that, I just did. I stole one of the drawings and I keep it in a drawer at home and I've been waiting for the right time to bring it up with her. I'm still waiting.

"I know that Eden crashed her mum's car toward the end of Year Ten—a few weeks after the family had moved back from Adelaide. I know because I was the one that she called when it happened. She didn't even have her learner's permit yet. But she was still so angry with them for making her switch schools twice in one year that she tried to drive herself to the beach while her parents were both out. And I guess now I know there was more to it than that. It wasn't about *changing states or changing schools, was it? It was because she'd just been made to give birth in secret and give the baby away. Makes so much more sense now. Anyway, she called me from a pay phone in tears, asking me what she was supposed to do. I told her to ditch the car and I called her a cab—and I remember that so clearly because it was the first time I'd ever booked a taxi and I was so nervous about how to do it that I nearly forgot to give them the address—and the cab brought her to my house and then I told her not to say a single word to her parents because it would sort itself out, and I was right. They thought the car had been stolen. They reported it to the police, who found it abandoned and assumed the thief had crashed it and dumped it. No one else in this entire world ever knew that Eden had been the one to take her mum's car.*

"So tell me, Father, if I know these three women so well, if I've known them for so long, how could I not have known that one was sneaking around going to support meetings for divorced women? Or that one believed she was completely failing as a mother? Or that the other had a baby when she was sixteen? But more importantly, how could I not know that one of them had those horrible thoughts that I read in that extra letter? How could everything have gone so wrong between us?"

CHAPTER 14

The following afternoon, as Joni took the exit off the freeway and turned left onto Pennant Hills Road to head toward home, she was thinking hard. All the way back from the coast, thoughts of the huge fight with her friends, thoughts of the fifth letter and of her fears about her and Kai had been clamoring for her attention.

She had to sort things out properly with Kai. Both of them needed to stop ignoring the truth.

She needed to talk to her friends. She needed to make everything right again.

Her and Kai should air their feelings, get it all out in the open. She knew what she needed to say: *I feel like you're not attracted to me anymore. Anytime that you turn me down for sex, it makes me think it's because you don't want me.*

And she knew what she ought to say to each one of her friends. *I'm sorry that we fought. I'm sorry that things are all messed up between us, but there's something else that is much, much more important right now. Which one of you wrote this letter? And why? How could you feel that way? When we're all so close! When we all were so close.*

She should tell Kai the truth.

I think that the reason you don't want me is because I am a broken woman. I can't give you a baby. And I think that you might be resenting me because of that.

But also the truth about her crush. Her stupid, stupid crush.

Deb, Trina, Eden . . . Would one of them actually want to hurt someone else?

Would you?

Could you?

Could you follow through with these things you've written?

Kai.

So I need to know. Do you still want to stay with me? Or do you want to leave me for a woman who could give you what you want? Because I don't think I'd blame you.

But was it really that simple? To just sit down and say these words? Any of these words? Either to Kai or to her friends? It should be. Because Kai was her husband. And her friends had been with her since day one of Year Seven.

So she should just tell Kai exactly how she was feeling. Exactly what she was worrying about. And then it would be up to him. Up to him to either affirm her concerns or to reassure her that she's wrong.

And she should just tell her friends what she found. She should confront them. Get to the bottom of this.

How do you even start any of these conversations, though?

After all these months of her and Kai pushing one another away.

After reading those horrendous and worrying words in that letter.

A burst of energy, that's what she needed. She would go to the gym and work out. It would give her the confidence to have the all-important talk with Kai. And to confront her friends next time she saw them.

One big workout and then she would be ready.

Of course she wasn't expecting to run into Ben at the gym.

Although then again, maybe that's exactly what she was expecting.

What Joni didn't know though, was that she wasn't the only one out of her group of friends who wasn't heading straight home. As Joni turned into the driveway of the gym, Deb was turning into the driveway of her local community center. There was a meeting that evening, and after the four nights away with her friends, she wanted something to take her mind off of her problems. Because Joni had been wrong when she'd assumed that the first letter had been Trina's. Because Joni didn't know her friends as well as she thought she did. But Deb had been wrong about something too. Deb had been wrong to assume that Connor wouldn't find out where she was. So while Deb was expressing her deepest feelings to a roomful of strangers, her husband was trying to figure out how a happily married woman could be spending her spare time attending support group meetings for divorced women—and wondering how and when he was going to confront her about it.

And as Joni walked through the front door of the gym, another of her friends was walking through the front door of her own home. She was walking through that door and she was filled with nerves as she prepared herself to see a husband whom she didn't truly love and a little boy who made her feel terrified every single moment as she second-guessed each and every step she took as a mother. Because Joni had been wrong about that letter as well. And as Trina scooped up Nate and hugged him close, she whispered into his hair, "How am I supposed to live like this?" But then the man who had been gradually asserting control over Trina's life came up behind her and said with a smile, "I see Mummy's put on a bit of weight while she's been away these past few days," before prizing Nate back out of her arms and adding as he walked away, "By the way, you missed out on your son's first steps while you were gone." And all that Trina could think of was the packet of tablets in her bag and she didn't want to just take one. She wanted to take fifty.

When Joni sat down at the rowing machine and started adjusting the settings, her third friend waved good-bye to her husband at the door. A husband who had jumped at the chance to take off for the gym the moment she arrived home and could take over with the kids. A husband who she could hardly blame—after all, he'd been taking care of the kids 24/7 for the past four nights straight while she'd been away with her friends. But still, there was a little bit of hurt there because why didn't he want to stay home and spend time with her now that she was back? Hadn't he missed her? And also because she had been planning on telling him the truth about Adelaide. After everything that had happened between her and her friends, she had decided that enough was enough. It was time for the truth. Still, though, she'd waited this long to tell him her secret. What could it hurt to wait just a little longer until he came back home from the gym? The problem with waiting, though, was that it meant thinking about Adelaide. And it meant flashbacks, brutal flashbacks that would hit her without warning. Images that would crowd in on her, jostling one another aside, all of them wanting to be noticed, all of them fighting for her attention.

The pink spaghetti-strap dress.

The sickly-sweet smell of her lilac-flavored Impulse deodorant.

The feel of the table edge pressing and pressing into the small of her back.

Each time one of these images flashed through her mind, her stomach would lurch, just like it did on that first night of the holiday when

Joni had asked her whether or not Pete was the first guy she'd slept
with.

Joni had her headphones in and the treadmill turned up to the highest
speed setting she could manage. Because of the music and her concentration on not losing her footing and sliding backward off the treadmill,
she didn't notice Ben appear on the treadmill next to her at first.

Eventually, though, she started to become aware of a figure out of
the corner of her eye who seemed to keep looking her way. *What?* She
thought with irritation. *What is your problem? Why do you keep looking over? Am I on your favorite machine or something? Or are you
trying to check how fast I'm going? Because if you want to compete
with me, it's pointless, I'm not that great.*

Finally, Joni chanced a look sideways, and when she realized it was
Ben who kept looking her way, giving her silly grins and pulling faces,
she clapped her hand to her mouth.

"Oh my God," she said as she pulled out her headphones and then
jumped both feet onto the outer edges of the running track. "Ben! How
long have you been trying to get my attention?"

"Whole time I've been here. I was just gonna say hi and let you get
on it with it, but then you were so determined not to turn sideways and
look at me that it became a challenge. You realize how stupid I've been
looking to everyone else? Running along next to you making crazy faces
and getting nothing in response?"

"Sorry! I promise it wasn't personal, I didn't even realize it was you."

"Well, I did hope as much. It's all right, you can put your headphones
back in, I'll let you get on with it."

"Nah, that's okay. That song wasn't really doing it for me anyway."

"Oh, good. Because I get way too bored on the treadmill if I don't have someone to talk to. You can keep me company. So how was the big trip? Did you even make it home this arvo before coming here?"

Joni could tell from his friendly tone that Eden clearly hadn't mentioned anything about the huge fight they'd all had the previous evening. Presumably there hadn't been enough time for her to tell him before he'd come out to the gym. She couldn't help but feel relieved. She hated the idea of Ben being angry with her for upsetting Eden. But he was probably going to find out eventually, so she might as well enjoy her last chance to be on friendly terms with him.

"I know," she said. "Pathetic, isn't it? Straight back to the gym."

"Pathetic or dedicated?" he asked.

"Fifty-fifty," Joni suggested.

"I wish I could convince Eden to come here with me," said Ben, then added quickly, "Not that I think she needs to lose weight or anything like that. I just mean it'd be nice to work out together."

"It's okay," Joni reassured him, although inside, she couldn't help but feel a little crushed. She had come to see the gym as her and Ben's place. She couldn't even imagine bringing Kai here! "I know what you mean," she lied. "I would never be able to get Kai here either. He hates the gym. He's always making fun of me for driving to the gym in order to then run on a treadmill. He doesn't believe me when I try to explain that there's a lot more to the gym than treadmills or stationary bikes."

"What are you up to next? Going to do any lifting? Need a spotter at all?"

"Nah, I'm planning on heading down to the pool after this. I've been feeling tense; I think a swim might help me stretch out a bit."

"Mind if I join you? I'm always thinking I should swim more often— good way to unwind after a workout."

"Sure."

In the pool, they didn't talk much. They took a lane each and swam laps, offering one another the occasional nod or smile when their heads both popped up at the same end every now and then. The pool, spa, and sauna were all deserted apart from the two of them. Joni had always found it fascinating how quiet the gym became right in the middle of winter—slowly ramping up as summer crept closer and then peaking right after New Year's Eve with all the determined resolution people. She never judged them for it—once upon a time she'd been the same, sporadic in her attempts at keeping healthy. It was only in the last year, as it had become more and more apparent that she and Kai couldn't get pregnant, that she had become so consistent at the gym. It was something she could control—her health and fitness— which felt good when she seemed unable to control her reproductive system.

Joni had lost count of how many laps they'd done when Ben suggested the spa. They should have sat farther apart really, considering they had the entire thing to themselves. Joni wasn't sure whose fault it was that they ended up sitting side by side, close enough that their knees knocked against one another every now and then as the streaming bubbles from the jets made their legs drift from side to side. Had Ben sat next to her—or she next to him? Either way, neither of them moved apart.

"Can I ask you something?" The idea of asking Ben's advice was completely spontaneous and Joni immediately wondered if she was doing the right thing.

But then Ben's voice was so kind when he replied, "Sure, anything," that Joni plowed on.

"Okay, so I need a guy's point of view. Let's say a husband is always turning his wife down, when she . . . you know, wants to . . ." Joni trailed off, losing her nerve. Why was she asking Ben about this?! It was embarrassing, such a stupid thing to bring up with her friend's husband.

"When she wants to get intimate?" Ben asked, and Joni was relieved that there wasn't a hint of humor or judgment in his voice; he wasn't making fun of her or trying to turn it into a joke.

"Yeah," said Joni. "Do you think it means he doesn't find her attractive anymore?"

Ben hesitated before responding. "I don't think so," he said. "I mean, not necessarily. I'd have to know more about the situation, though. Like, has it been happening for a while?"

"A couple months, I guess."

"And is there something else going on, between this husband and wife?"

"Sort of, yes. There's some problems."

"What kind of problems?"

Joni was unsure how much to say and how to phrase it. "Infertility," she said simply.

"Okay. And have you two spoken about it, you know, had a good chat about how you're both feeling about it?"

Joni shrugged, ignoring the fact that they'd switched from talking about a hypothetical husband and wife and shifted smoothly into talking about herself and Kai. "I guess not. Not really."

"Why?"

"Because I've been waiting for him to say the right thing."

"And what's the right thing to say?"

"That it's not my fault." There was a waver in Joni's voice and she felt mortified. She could not start crying in front of Ben. She should never have brought it up in the first place, they weren't close enough for this kind of conversation. She hadn't even meant for the conversation to take such an emotional turn. In fact, she knew what she had wanted out of the conversation. She'd wanted for another man to just reassure her that she was still desirable. That Kai not wanting to have sex with her didn't mean that she wasn't still fuckable.

"Joni," said Ben quietly, "it's not your fault." Under the water, he reached a hand out to place it on her leg, just above the knee and Joni felt a sharp tingle shoot through her body at the intimacy of his touch.

She turned to face him.

"And you know what else?" said Ben. "I think Kai's a complete dick if he doesn't want to have sex with you, because you're sexy as hell."

There it was. The words that Joni had been desperate to hear. She could feel her heart drumming in her chest, the air frizzing with tension between them. She leaned in, torn between the desire to sob her heart out and to grab hold of Ben and kiss him, hard. Ben was leaning in as well. Their lips were inches apart.

And just like that, they stopped.

Just as it had been difficult to tell whose fault it had been that they'd ended up sitting so close in the spa, it was impossible to tell which one of them was responsible for stopping before it was too late. But next thing they were pulling apart.

"I'm sorry," said Joni quickly, turning away and making to climb straight out of the spa. "I'm so sorry, I shouldn't have—"

"No, I'm sorry," said Ben, reaching out to hold her arm and stop her from jumping straight out. "You were just trying to get something off your chest and I—"

Like Joni, he didn't know what to say next. He let go of her arm and she hopped out of the spa and grabbed her towel.

"Look," said Ben. "It's okay, nothing happened, we were just . . . and then it just . . ."

"We got a bit carried away," Joni agreed.

"So . . . we'll forget about it?"

"Yes. Absolutely."

Joni wrapped her towel around her body and was about to leave but then stopped. "Ben," she said, "will you tell Eden, about what . . . almost happened? I mean . . . about what I *think* almost happened?"

Ben looked uncomfortable. "Shit, Joni, I don't know." He paused. "I don't think I've ever really kept anything from her."

Joni wasn't sure why she said it. It was bad enough that she had just very nearly kissed Eden's husband, so what made her double the betrayal, she wasn't sure. Perhaps it was a way to make her feel better about what had happened, but she blurted out, "Eden's keeping a secret from you."

"What?" said Ben, "What do you mean?"

Immediately Joni regretted her words. What the hell was wrong with her? First she'd almost kissed Eden's husband, and now she'd told him that Eden was hiding something from him. It was like she was simply determined to be destructive. And she'd done it for the benefit of no one but herself. She'd done it because she thought that if Ben knew Eden had secrets, then maybe he'd be more willing to keep what had just occurred between them to himself.

"Forget it," she said quickly. "It's nothing, forget I said anything." She turned and left, heading straight for the female changing rooms so that Ben couldn't follow and ask any more questions.

When she arrived back home after the gym, she headed straight for the shower, barely stopping to acknowledge Kai, which she knew was wrong. He was going to wonder what the hell was up. This was the first he was seeing her after four days up the coast and instead of giving him a big hug hello, she was giving him the cold shoulder.

In the shower, Joni ran through the entire incident over and over. She kept trying to see it from different angles, looking for a sign that her betrayal had not been that bad. Her betrayal of Kai and of Eden. *We didn't kiss, we didn't actually kiss,* she told herself over and over. But she knew that it was more than just a conversation. And the fact that she couldn't seem to get her pulse to slow down no matter how much deep breathing she did meant that there was definitely something to feel guilty about.

And then there was her added betrayal of Eden. Eden had confided in her friends and now Joni had completely broken that trust.

The guilt and the regret were clawing away at her chest.

What was she going to do? Confess to Kai? Or never say a word about what had happened? Either way, she needed to at least talk to him—he was probably hovering outside the bathroom door right now, wondering what was wrong, wondering why she'd come in and headed straight for the shower without a word. Wondering if he'd done something wrong.

Eventually, knowing that if she stayed in here any longer there'd be no hot water left, she stepped out of the shower, wrapped a towel around her body, and opened the bathroom door. He wasn't there, wasn't hovering, worrying. She could hear the sounds of the television coming from the living room and she walked down the hall to find him.

When she stepped into the living room, he looked up at her from the couch and there was no concern across his face at all. "Hey," he said casually, "welcome home, babe. Any thoughts on what we should do for dinner?"

He wasn't annoyed. He hadn't even noticed that she was behaving weirdly. He was in the middle of an episode of *MasterChef*, and she knew that if she didn't say something now then she never would. So she moved straight in front of him, picked up the remote, and turned off the television.

He opened his mouth, obviously about to complain, but then he saw the expression on her face and he stopped.

"What's wrong?" he asked.

Joni dissolved into tears and he reached a hand out to grab hold of her and pull her down onto the couch next to him.

"Hey," he said, wrapping his arms around her, "hey, hey, hey." His voice was tender as he spoke into her hair. "What is it, hon? What's the matter?"

"It's everything," she replied. "It's us."

"Joni," he said, pulling back from her and tipping his head to the side in an attempt to catch her eye. "Joni, just talk to me, what's going on?"

She fell forward, pressing her face against his chest, and it all came tumbling out. "How can you not know what's going on?! We can't get pregnant and we've stopped even trying and I'm pretty sure you're just waiting for the right moment to tell me you don't want to be with me anymore."

"What? No! What are you on about? You said you went to the doctor and they said it was normal for it to take a little while sometimes. They said it would happen eventually—I didn't even think this was an issue anymore, I thought that news made you happy."

"Happy? Are you kidding me? It just means that they're delaying the inevitable because there *is* something wrong and the something that's wrong is me. I'm fucked up inside, and if you want kids, you may as well find someone else to do it with."

"Joni! You're not making any sense!"

"You haven't wanted to have sex with me for months—how is that not an obvious sign that you don't want me? Every time I try to start something with you, you turn me down. Just say it, you're not attracted to me anymore."

"No. Nope. Not true." Kai placed his hands on Joni's upper arms and pushed her away from him again so that they were face-to-face. "Joni, you're gorgeous. Stunning. Especially right now, seeing as you're all naked and wet under that towel. I'm still just as attracted to you as I was the day I met you. I've just been busy with work and I thought you were too. We're both so tired every night when we get home and you've been stressed about those new articles you've been writing. Babe, I've just been trying to be 'sensitive New Age guy'—I've tried to give you some space, let you focus on your new job.

"And look, I interpreted what the doctor said as a sign that this whole having-a-baby thing was a complete nonissue—that we could pull back on it a bit; we could just let it happen when the time was right. I most definitely haven't been sitting around thinking that I need to go and get someone else knocked up. Joni, when it comes to having kids—well, I've never been that desperate to become a dad anyway. I mean, I was happy to do it when you said you wanted to start trying because if it was something that you wanted, if it was going to make you happy, then it was something that I wanted."

Joni felt a flicker of hope start to ignite inside. Had she really been misinterpreting everything all this time?

"But, why've you been turning me down . . . anytime I've tried to . . . you know?"

"*When,* though? Because I swear to God, I wasn't aware that I was turning you down! Tell me something: all these times that you tell me I've said no, on any of these occasions, did you ever actually come right out and say, 'Hey, Kai, I want to have sex with you'?"

"No . . . I guess I didn't exactly . . ."

"So what exactly has been happening, then?"

"I don't know. I guess I've just been giving you . . . hints. Um, there was that time when I invited you into the shower with me."

"When? I promise I don't even remember that. Wait, was I brushing my teeth? You know I can never hear you when you try to talk to me over the top of my electric toothbrush! And hints? Really? Are you serious? Did any of these hints consist of you actually placing your hand on my dick or putting your tongue down my throat? Joni, I'm a guy. I don't do subtle. You should have just *said* something. Besides, we're married adults! Not high school kids trying to guess whether or not we like one another! Why did you even need to hint at it?"

"So . . . you do . . . still want me, then?"

"Of course I still want you, you goose. Jesus, I can't believe you could have thought that. You're insane. Quite possibly certifiably. Has it really been that long since we last had sex?"

"Eighty-four days."

"Really? Joni, I'm sorry, I didn't even realize we'd let it get that long, I promise it wasn't intentional."

"You don't need to be sorry," whispered Joni. "I do."

"No, you don't." Kai pulled her back in close again for another hug, "You don't have to apologize for what was just a silly mix-up."

Joni hugged him back tightly, thinking to herself, *But I do have to be sorry. Because I almost kissed another man.* But did she need to say it? Because that's all it was really—an almost kiss—nothing more. A result of her getting carried away, and now that she knew the truth about what was going on between her and Kai, now that she knew he still loved her, still found her attractive, those feelings for Ben were starting to subside. She wasn't naive enough to think they could simply vanish altogether with the snap of her fingers—but some of that sheen was beginning to fade. So then why bring it up? Why add another burden to their marriage when they'd just sorted everything out and there was nothing behind it anyway? Actually, maybe it was time to switch her gym membership to another branch. Out of sight, out of mind.

"Hey, Joni," said Kai. "I would very much like to have sex with you right now. You see how easy that was? I just came right out and said it. Or, if you don't want to use your words, here's a great example of how you can hint at it in a not so subtle way," and he slipped his hand under the towel to cup one of her breasts, brushing his thumb across her nipple, making her senses alight with desire. With his other hand, he lifted her chin and then he leaned in and kissed her. With his lips still pressed against hers, he whispered, "If this is what you want, then let's go make a baby."

The sex that night was slow, sweet, and emotional. There was lots of gazing deeply into one another's eyes and then cracking up laughing because they both felt silly about being so serious. Usually when they made love, Joni always came first and then they would switch positions to Kai's favorite and Kai would follow her several minutes later. But tonight they climaxed together, and when they came, it was hard and fast and intense. They fell apart, both of them breathing hard, then Kai propped himself up on his elbow to look down at Joni.

"I adore you, Joni Camilleri. Don't you forget it."

"So that's it. My final confession. I almost kissed Ben. I almost cheated on my husband. But I didn't. And I think that means it doesn't count, and please don't tell me that I'm wrong about that because everything is so much better between Kai and me now and I don't want to mess it all up just because I need to get something off my chest."

"That's why you're here, then? Because this is the best way for you to get it off your chest?"

"Yes. Well, that and also the fact that I still don't know who wrote the fifth letter and I still don't know just how worried I need to be about the letter. It's been three weeks since the holiday and none of us has even seen each other, so I do at least know that everyone is safe—for now. You see, Eden texted us all the other day. She's invited the group around to her place this Saturday night for a dinner party. Partners too. Which tells me that Ben hasn't told her what happened either. And I'm guessing she's organized this dinner party as a way to get us all back on speaking terms after the night of the mud run. That's why I decided I needed to come and talk to someone, that's why I came to see you.

"So. Expert opinion, please, Father. Who do you think wrote the fifth letter and what do you think my next move should be?"

CHAPTER 15

"W" e need to talk."

Four simple words.

Four different voices.

Four different meanings.

Four different reactions.

It was ironic that Joni had always been so intent on making sure she and her three best friends followed the same path when now, here they were, all having conversations with their partners that started out in a more similar way than she ever could have imagined.

Trina was first. It was the morning of Eden's dinner party and she couldn't handle the idea of facing her friends that evening without having done something. Without having taken the first steps toward making a change.

"We need to talk."

Josh looked amused by the seriousness in her voice.

"Oh, do we?" he asked.

"Yes. I want a divorce."

But his response wasn't at all what she was expecting.

Deb was up next. But she wasn't the one speaking, though; it was Connor, and she was so very afraid of what he was going to say next.

"We need to talk. I know about the meetings."

She felt a mixture of anxiety tinged with relief. Because at least now he knew. At least now she wasn't hiding secrets from him. But how was she supposed to explain the true reasons behind what she'd been doing?

For Eden, it was Ben who spoke those four words. It was late afternoon and she was rushing around, trying to get the house ready for the guests they were expecting that evening as well as making sure the kids were all packed up ready to be picked up by their grandmother, when he stopped her still, his face sort of gray, a tremble in his hands, and puppy-dog eyes imploring, and she knew, just knew, it was going to be something bad.

"We need to talk. I need to confess. I almost kissed Joni."

When he told her it hurt—but not the way she would have thought—it wasn't a clean and pure moment of heartbreak. No. Instead it was a twisting of her guts.

Joni was last. When she spoke those four words to Kai, she knew that he was worried at first. His face had that "oh God, what now?" expression. Probably he thought she wanted to have yet another DNM about their relationship.

But then she smiled and held out the small, white stick with a shaking hand. "No way?!" he'd asked. "No. Fucking. Way!" And then he'd lifted her off the floor and spun her around when he hugged her.

CHAPTER 16

J oni was carrying the news, tucked away inside like a warm hot-water bottle. Somehow, everything else seemed to pale in comparison to this special, delicate secret that Kai and she now shared together.

The fifth letter stopped seeming so threatening. Yes, she was still going to confront her friend this evening—she would ask her about it gently, just as Father O'Reilly had suggested—just to make sure she was okay. Just to be certain that there was nothing more to it than simply words. She knew who had written the letter now. Talking it all out with Father O'Reilly, sifting through each and every event of the holiday, had finally led her to the answer.

Trina.

Trina was the one who had an unsupportive husband.

Trina was the one who was a bit off-kilter because of whatever secret medication she'd been taking.

Admittedly, Father O'Reilly had had a different view on who it was. But Father O'Reilly didn't know her friends as well as Joni did.

She felt silly now for worrying so much about it. It was probably nothing, just Trina's private thoughts. Obviously due to some catharsis Trina had needed at the time. Once she'd written about them, she'd gotten it all out of her head and that's why she'd burned the letter. Because she was going to get over it and move on. She wasn't dangerous! Didn't they all have moments when they felt annoyed or angry with someone close to them? Weren't there times during high school when one or the other of them would have a bit of a bitch or a moan to each other about someone else in the group but then next thing they were best friends again?

And perhaps now that so much had been aired among the four of them on that holiday, then Trina's anger would be dissipating even further. It was just something that their friendship circle had needed to go through. A way to get all their cards on the table. Now they could all start moving forward again. She wasn't one hundred percent certain of *who* it was that Trina had been so angry with when she wrote that letter. But as long as Trina really was getting over it, then it didn't really matter.

Apart from receiving the text invite from Eden, Joni hadn't spoken to anyone since the holiday, so she didn't know how things were going with any of them. She did feel a bit guilty about that, that she hadn't checked in to ask if anyone had dealt with any of their problems.

But she would fix that tonight. And Trina, as the fifth letter writer, would be the first one she would pull aside at some point to see how she was doing. She would tell her that she knew about that letter, that she had no need to feel inferior toward one single person within their group, regardless of how well they were doing at work or how lucky they were to have a good-looking, supportive husband or bright, happy children or whatever it was that she was so jealous of.

And Joni was going to go about it the right way as well. She wasn't going to tell anyone else about the letter behind Trina's back. She would talk to Trina and Trina only, and as long as she was okay, as long as she was making changes or doing whatever it was that she needed to do to get past this secret obsession, then there would be no need for anyone else to ever know that Trina had once felt that way about them.

So it was time to put those worries about that letter to rest. It seemed so silly now that she'd been so concerned that night back at the holiday house when she'd first read those words. That she'd watched each of her friends so closely the next morning at the mud run, trying to catch someone out, acting like a private investigator as she carefully scrutinized every move, waiting to see if someone did something suspicious.

And Joni's own issues were getting fixed now too. That moment with Ben at the gym: it was a wake-up call. It was a realization that she loved Kai, more than anything. That they'd just been struggling a bit through a difficult time. It had been a make-or-break situation. And it most definitely hadn't broken them. She didn't need to feel worried about the almost kiss with Ben because it hadn't actually happened. There had been no betrayal, and therefore there was no reason to feel guilty or uncomfortable around Eden and Ben.

Everything was coming together. Everything was fixed. Eden and Kai would never need to know about what almost happened. She and Ben could just be normal friends again. Trina would be fixed. And she and Kai had a new path ahead. Plus, she'd switched gyms—the one that was closer to her work made way more sense anyway. The future looked good.

As they pulled up to Eden's neat little single-story red-brick home, with the pink and white rosebushes out the front and the warm, yellow light illuminating the front doorstep, Kai reached out for her hand and gave it a squeeze. "You going to tell them tonight?" he asked.

"Maybe," she said, and the hot-water bottle warmed her once again. "Probably," she admitted.

"Guess you'll be driving us home, hey?" he joked.

"Looks like," she replied. And she didn't mind one bit.

Joni hung back and let Trina and Josh head inside first when Eden opened the front door. They'd all arrived at the same time and Deb and Connor were heading up the front path as they filed through the front door.

As much as she thought that everything was going to be fine now, Joni was still a bit unsure about facing Ben for the first time. She caught Eden's eye on the way through the door and tried to tell if there was any sign that Ben had told her what had almost happened. At first, the expression on her face was indiscernible, but then she gave Joni a big welcoming smile and Joni felt her body relax. *It's all okay; she doesn't know and she will never need to know.*

Deb and Connor stepped in behind them as they all crowded in the entranceway, removing their jackets.

"We brought wine!" announced Josh, and Eden took the bottle gratefully, even as she was reprimanding him for bringing something when they'd all been instructed not to bring a thing.

"So did we, actually," admitted Deb, handing over the second bottle of wine. And then Kai laughed as he presented a third and fourth bottle. "Great minds and all that," he said.

Ben appeared from the kitchen and waved at them all down the hall. "Come on," he called. "She'll be here any minute, come and make conversation while we still can."

At first, Joni was too busy paying attention to the look on Ben's face, checking to see if he was likely to give anything away. But he was keeping his face straight, completely impartial. And then she caught up and started to wonder about the same thing the others were all looking puzzled about.

"What do you mean, Ben?" Deb called as they all trooped through the doorway to the kitchen, "Um, this is it. We're all here."

Trina was the first to pick up on the look on Eden's face, though. "Eden?" she asked. "What's going on?"

Eden and Ben looked at one another and then Ben's mouth dropped open. "You didn't tell them?" he asked.

"Tell us what?" Deb demanded. And the penny dropped for Joni. Of course, the Thermomix dinner party that Eden had mentioned back on the first day of the holiday; that's what this was.

"Well," said Eden slowly, "I didn't think it was really relevant."

She looked around at the others and was opening her mouth to explain when the doorbell went. "Hang on," she said. "Let me just bring her in and then I'll explain."

Joni stood in the kitchen with everyone else, being careful to keep her face as nonchalant as possible. She didn't want to give away the fact that she knew what was going on. A moment later, Eden was back, leading a friendly-looking woman with short blond hair and a smart navy skirt and jacket ensemble into the room.

"So!" Eden announced. "This is Aimee, and she'll be cooking our dinner for us tonight."

"You hired a chef?" asked Connor, confused.

Aimee giggled at him. "Oh, I'd hardly call myself that!" she said. "The Thermomix is the real chef here."

Connor stared back at her in confusion. "The thermo-what?" he asked.

But Deb was glaring at Eden and spoke next. "You fucking tricked us again, didn't you?"

"Deb!" exclaimed Connor, while Aimee looked slightly aghast at her language.

"No," said Eden carefully, "I didn't . . . trick you. I invited you around for dinner . . . and that's what you're here for . . . dinner."

"Um," said Aimee, "do you all need a minute?"

"No, no, we're fine," said Eden. "Come around here," she added, guiding Aimee around the other side of the kitchen bench. "Ben will show you how everything's set up. He's got all the ingredients ready."

Ben was looking between Aimee, Deb, and Eden, and then Joni saw him fix his gaze on Kai and his face became rigid, while Kai grinned back, completely unaware that anything was amiss.

"Maybe we should all get out of the way while you're getting sorted, Eden," said Trina. "We'll wait in the lounge."

"Fine," said Deb, "but someone better bring the wine."

The six of them all filed back out of the room and through to the lounge, leaving Ben, Eden, and Aimee behind in the kitchen. Kai, Josh, and Connor all sat themselves down on the couches to make awkward "we're the husbands, so we're supposed to be mates" conversation while Trina pulled Deb aside and Joni automatically followed.

"Deb," hissed Trina as they all huddled in a corner on the far side of the room next to an oil heater that was failing miserably to warm anything further than a one-meter radius around itself. "Honestly, it doesn't matter. You know what Eden's like, she loves this stuff. Just go along with it, okay? At least it's not like the Nutrimetics one where we had to put up with the guided meditation."

Deb rolled her eyes, but then she turned her focus on Joni. "How's *work*?" she asked, placing such emphasis on the second word that Joni wouldn't have been surprised if venom had shot out of her mouth.

But Joni still had her hot-water bottle for protection, and nothing, not even Deb's disapproval of her, could stop her inner glow now.

"Yeah, all right, Deb, I get it, you're still pissed with me. Well, guess what? A few days ago I told my boss I wanted to transfer back to my old role, and if she didn't let me, I was going to quit."

"Oh," said Deb, looking completely taken aback. "Wait, does that mean you'll lose your pay raise as well?"

"Not if my boss doesn't want me to start spreading rumors about the fact the Parenting Done Right has been publishing fabricated articles."

"Wow, Joni," said Trina. "That's some hard-core negotiating, good for you."

Joni grinned back at her and was glad to see that Deb was wearing a look of admiration on her face. "Nice one, Joni," she said. "Sorry," she added, "I shouldn't have pounced on you like that straightaway."

"All good," Joni replied. "Hey, Deb, do you mind if I have a quick word alone with Trina?"

Despite the fact that she was clearly curious, Deb gave Joni a begrudging nod and then joined the guys over on the couches.

"Listen," said Joni, keeping her voice as low as possible. "There's something important we need to talk about. There's no easy way to put this, so I'm just going to say it." Joni paused to take a deep breath. "I know your secret," she said.

Trina's eyes widened. "You know? How?"

"Well, it's a long story, but on the last night of the holiday—" Joni began.

"Wait," Trina interrupted. "What do you mean on the holiday? I only did it this morning."

"This morning? What did you do this morning?" Joni looked back at Trina with dismay. Had she been wrong to think that there was no serious danger around that letter? Had Trina done or said something to whoever it was that she hated this morning?

"I asked Josh for a divorce. Isn't that what you were talking about?"

"Shit! You did? No, that's not what I meant at all. But what do you mean, why the hell is he here with you tonight, then?"

"It's complicated." Trina looked across the room at the men and Deb sitting on the couches and Joni followed her gaze, and they both saw Josh staring straight back at them, a dangerous glint in his eyes.

"Fuck," hissed Trina. "He knows we're talking about him. We need to do this later."

Trina moved swiftly away from Joni and over to join the others on the couches, squeezing herself in between Deb and Kai, who had struck up a conversation about a tech company that Kai was suggesting Deb should get her team to investigate for insurance fraud because it would totally help him steal a new client away from them.

"So there's absolutely no basis to your accusations at all, then?" Deb was asking as Joni followed Trina and perched herself on the arm of the opposite couch all while trying hard not to look at Josh and not let her face give away the fact that Trina had just dropped that news on her.

Eden's head appeared through the door. "Five minutes," she told them all brightly. "Did you guys get wineglasses out yet?"

"I'll grab them," said Josh, hopping up from the couch and turning to the cabinet behind him. "How many do we need, two, four, six . . ." he started to count.

"Don't worry about me," said Joni. And all three women swiveled their heads at once to look at her.

"What do you mean, don't worry about you?" asked Trina.

"Designated driver," she replied quickly.

Eden's head vanished back through the kitchen door and Josh started handing glasses around while Connor unscrewed the top of the first bottle of wine.

"You know you should probably take it easy yourself," said Josh as

Trina took a glass off him and then held it out for Connor to pour her wine for her.

"What?" she asked. "Why?"

"Oh, you know, just in case." He smiled significantly around the room at the others while Trina's face turned white. Between Josh's manic grin and Trina's look of terror, no one else seemed to know how to react. But then Ben came through the door and cut through the silence.

"Oh, I'll take one of those," he said.

Unfortunately, it was Joni who was now holding the spare glass after Josh had passed it to her when he was sending the glasses around the group. She looked down at the glass in her hand and then held it out to Ben. As he reached across to take it from her, his fingers brushed against hers, and in an involuntary flinch, Joni's hand sprang open, letting the glass fall straight to the floor, where it smashed on the floorboards.

Joni chanced a quick look at Ben's face and saw the horror in his eyes. She tried desperately to send him a mental message: *It was nothing! Just an accident! I don't have feelings for you, I don't, I truly don't!*

But he'd already crouched down to start picking up the broken pieces and Kai had sprung up from the couch to help. "No, no," he said when Joni started to bend down to pick up the glass as well, "I've got it."

"Dinnnnner!" trilled a happy voice from the kitchen then, and the others all obediently sidestepped their way around the mess and trooped back out from the lounge room and through to the kitchen. Joni hovered awkwardly above Ben and Kai for a moment, not wanting to leave the two of them in there on their own, and then she realized she looked silly just watching them gathering up the broken glass, so she headed through to the kitchen as well. Everyone had placed their wineglasses down at the dining table that had been set up so that they could all sit in a semicircle facing the kitchen counter, but Trina immediately picked her glass back up as she took her seat and downed it in one.

"Cheers to that!" said Deb, clearly delighted that the dinner party was transitioning into a drinking night, and she followed suit, skolling her glass of wine.

Aimee looked back and forth between the two women with a look of alarm on her face. "Well that's . . . that's . . . different," she said eventually.

"Trina," said Josh in an aside that was still loud enough for everyone else to hear, "didn't you hear me before? I said I thought you should take it easy."

"And I disagreed with you," Trina replied evenly. She turned to face Connor, who was still holding the wine bottle. "Fill 'er up, please," she said.

"No thanks, Connor," said Josh. "She doesn't need another one."

The whole room fell silent and Trina pushed her glass toward Connor. "Fill it up, please," she repeated.

"Ah," said Connor, looking between Trina and Josh as Ben and Kai returned from the lounge, both of them holding handfuls of broken glass, "Sorry, mate, the lady's spoken." He tried to laugh as he poured Trina's wine for her, but now Josh was glaring across the table at him while Deb was simultaneously looking like she was torn between thumping Josh and macking Connor. The guys tipped the broken glass into the rubbish bin and everyone took their seats quietly. Eden gave Aimee an encouraging nod.

"So, I guess I'll . . . I'll just get us started, then," said Aimee in a stilted voice. "You're all here to experience the extraordinary cooking ability of this sleek-looking machine right here, the Thermomix . . ." Her voice began to rally as she got into her spiel, but then she made the mistake of asking the group a question. "And who's already heard of the Thermomix?"

Deb gave a great guffaw. "You mean who's heard of the world's most overpriced blender?" But then Eden's shoulders slumped with disappointment and Deb stopped short, a guilty look on her face. "Sorry," she said. "Just a joke."

Aimee gave a forced titter of a laugh and then smoothly continued on. "Well," she said, "I can assure you it's much, much more than a blender. The Thermomix is capable of doing everything from—" She stopped midsentence, though, her eyes on Trina, who was steadily downing her second glass of wine. Trina slammed it back down on the table like it was a shot glass and then slid it across to Connor. "More, please," she said.

"Oh," said Connor, "okay, just let me grab the next bottle, this one's empty."

Joni looked down the table at Josh, and saw that his face was twisting with fury. She decided to step in, temporarily remove Trina from the situation. "Trina?" she asked. "Could you just come and help me with something for a second?"

"With what?" Trina asked shortly.

"Um, I need to . . . borrow something. I forgot to bring any . . ." Joni tried to give her a significant look. "You know?!" she hissed.

"Tampons?" Trina asked loudly. "I don't have any with me."

"Can we please just go and check your bag," said Joni desperately.

"Oh! I have some!" said Eden, but then realized her mistake and fell quiet. "Ah, no actually, no, I don't," she said.

"Oh, all right, fine," Trina huffed, and got up from her chair to follow Joni, who waved at Aimee to continue on with the demonstration without them. They walked right back down the hall and stopped near the front door.

"What is it, Joni?" Trina asked. "Can't you see I'm trying to drink my troubles away?"

"Yes, I noticed. And I also noticed that Josh is behaving like a complete asshole. Finish telling me what happened today. So you told him you wanted a divorce. Clearly, he didn't take it well."

Trina stared back at Joni. "How come none of you ever said anything sooner—about how you all felt?"

Joni squirmed on the spot. "I don't know, Trina. I suppose because it's not that easy—to tell a friend that you're worried about her relationship with her *husband*. With the father of her child. Like, where do you even start with a conversation like that?"

"Well, you seemed to manage it fine the night of the mud run."

"Yeah, and look how well that went. None of us has even spoken since that night. Admittedly, there were several other factors at play, though."

"Have you told anyone else, by the way, about your issues conceiving? I'm sorry that we didn't get to talk more about that. It wasn't fair that right after sharing that sort of a secret, you then had to endure everyone grilling you over your work. I should have stuck up for you more."

Joni wondered if she should tell Trina her news right there and then. Tell her that there was no need to worry about any of that anymore. But now wasn't the time. Trina was changing the subject and they needed to get back to the matter at hand.

"Forget about that for now," she said. "Talk to me about Josh."

Trina stayed silent for a moment. She looked up at the ceiling, pretended momentarily to be fascinated by the extremely ordinary light fitting above them, but then she took a deep breath and looked back at Joni. "So it was a mixture of things that got me there," she began. "It might surprise you to know that I've always been well aware of how badly he treats me. I've always known, but I've always made excuses for it. And it wasn't until you said something on that holiday that I started to really take a closer look at my life."

"When I told you we all think he treats you like shit?"

"Nope. Not that. When you told me that you lied to me about the girls on the basketball court."

"What? How does that have anything to do with Josh?"

"Because it got me started on a path of what-ifs. What if you hadn't lied to me that day? What if I hadn't become friends with you, Deb, or Eden? You remember how I met Josh? It was through Deb's brother. They weren't close friends, but that was the connection. So, if I wasn't friends with Deb, I never would have met Josh."

"You mean if I never lied to you, you wouldn't have ended up with a horrible husband?" Joni was feeling terrible. Trina was tracing everything back to her and she couldn't bear to be the reason that Trina was so unhappy and being treated so badly.

"No, that's not a bad thing, though," argued Trina. "Because if I hadn't met Josh then I never would have had Nate, and I adore that kid so much with everything I've got. So it's for the best, okay? No—the point is—it just got me thinking about fate. About the parts of your life that you can and can't control, and it made me realize that I wasn't taking control when I should have been. I was going with the flow. I was doing what I thought was the right thing—following this path that's been laid out for me and making decisions based on avoiding my mother's life and I wasn't stopping to think about what I wanted. And what I want is my son—and not my husband."

"Wow," breathed Joni. "Big stuff."

"Yep," said Trina, and now her voice was sounding forlorn and Joni realized her attention had been drawn by something behind her. She turned to see what Trina was looking at and found herself face-to-face with a framed black-and-white photo of Eden and Ben on their wedding day. The two of them both had their heads thrown back, their mouths open wide with surprised laughter. Joni remembered that moment, it was right after the flower girl—one of Ben's nieces—had tripped and put one hand right through the top layer of their wedding cake. Another bride might have been furious, but not Eden—Eden had thought it was hilarious.

"What's it like, Joni?" Trina asked. "What's it like to be married to someone *normal* like Kai or Ben or Connor?" Then she screwed up her face and reached out to touch Joni's arm, "Oh no," she said. "I'm so sorry, I forgot about the crush thing. Is that . . . is that still happening? Are you still . . . ?"

"No, no," said Joni quickly. "It's all good. I'm over it and everything is great with Kai and me again, honestly. It was nothing more than a stupid crush. And I promise, you're going to get to experience what it's like to have someone great now too, okay? When you're through all of this and you're ready to move on, you're going to meet that someone out there that you actually deserve and who actually deserves you."

"Yeah, well, small problem with that. You see, I *tried* to take back control, yet Josh is still here tonight, isn't he? I mean how many husbands do you know that would want to go out to a dinner party with his wife's friends right after she's asked for a divorce? And there he is in there with *my* friends, acting like everything is fine. Pretending like there's a possibility I could actually be pregnant where there's no chance in hell. Just to mess with me. Mind games—that's his thing, that's his way of controlling me. God, do you know how hard it was for me to actually say the words, to actually tell him? And yet his reaction was to act like I was a silly little girl throwing a hissy fit. It didn't matter what I said, he wouldn't take me seriously."

"So what are you going to do?"

Trina threw up her hands. "What the hell else can I do? I have to leave, right? I have to pack my stuff and just go."

"Go where?"

"Mum's. It's the only way to show him that I'm serious."

"What about Nate?"

"Well, obviously I'll take him with me! I'm not planning on abandoning my son, Joni!"

"No, that's not what I meant . . . I just mean, how are you going to deal with . . . like, the custody stuff?"

"Hopefully we'll be able to find a way to come to a fair arrangement, once he's got the message that it's over. Maybe even without getting courts involved or whatever. Truth is, he *has* always been a decent dad to Nate. The guy's a misogynistic prick, but he's good to his son. Jesus, who knows? Maybe I'm lucky we didn't have a little girl? Or maybe it's just me that he's an asshole to? Fuck, I don't know. The point is, I'm done with him. And I'm done with those damn tablets he's been making me take."

Joni felt a jolt. "He's been making you take the tablets? Trina, can you please tell me what kind of tablets they are?"

Trina shrugged, "No reason not to now. I'm not going to be taking them anymore. They were a type of appetite suppressant. Main ingredient is phentermine. It's usually prescribed by doctors to people who are overweight or obese . . . if they need a bit of a kick start, you know, if they're having trouble losing the weight. But the ones I've been taking . . . Josh ordered them through the Internet."

"What the hell? You're not overweight, not even a little bit," said Joni. "In fact, I'm pretty sure you're underweight. And so they're not even properly prescribed by a doctor for you?"

"Nope."

"And what exactly is phentermine anyway?"

"Basically, it's the main ingredient in speed. And I think when you get it legally from your doctor, it's a lot more, um, watered down, I suppose you could say? But the stuff that Josh gets is strong."

"Why did you take them at all, though, Trina?"

"I don't know! I know I shouldn't have, but you have to understand, that's Josh's way. He gets under your skin. He would just make these comments all the time. Things like how he never thought I'd have a stomach on me—right after I gave birth—and how desperate I must be to get my prebaby body back or that my jeans were looking a bit tight. Then one day he starts talking about these tablets he's heard of, and how it might just give me the little bit of help I need to get back into shape again. So I said I'd go to the doctor and have a chat about it. But before my appointment comes up, the next day out of the blue he has the tablets. At first he tells me it's a free sample he got from the chemist. Made out like it was no big deal, and I thought, 'Well, if the chemist is handing them out, then there can't be any harm in taking them.'

"Anyway, the first couple of days that I took them—you don't understand how much of a boost this stuff gave me, obviously I understand now why—but at the time I just thought it was this amazing, completely legal wonder drug. All of a sudden I had all this extra energy. I could run—further and faster than I could before. I could get four loads of washing done and vacuum and mop the floors and change all the sheets and I still didn't feel like I needed to collapse on the couch like a slob. I wasn't sleeping great, but I could get by on much less sleep now, so it didn't matter. And my appetite was pretty much cut in half. You wouldn't believe how fast the baby weight dropped off me."

"Oh my God," said Joni. "That's not the right way to lose weight after you have a baby. Aren't you supposed to do it gradually?"

"Yeah, well—I know that now, don't I? But like I said, I didn't know I was going about it the wrong way. I was trusting Josh. When the tablets ran out, he magically had another pack waiting ready for me. I guess if I thought about it, I would have known that the chemist wouldn't keep handing out free samples, but you have to understand how good it was making me feel. I felt so amazing on that stuff, like I was able to be my best self. Like I had the energy to be the mum I should be to Nate. You know that stuff I wrote about in my letter? When I said I didn't pay attention to him because I was on Facebook? That happened when I'd run out of tablets for a couple of weeks. When I wasn't my best self anymore. That's what I was like when I wasn't on the drugs. I'd become sluggish and unmotivated and basically just a shitty mum. But when I was taking the tablets, that's when I would shine! I'd have all the energy in the world. I could keep up with Nate, I could stay on top of things. I could stop failing."

"Wait a minute. That was your letter? I thought Deb wrote that one. I thought you were the one going to the divorced-women-support-group meetings. I mean, that's sort of why I mentioned how we all felt about Josh, because I figured it meant divorce was already in the cards for you."

"Nope, but I might have to ask Deb for the details of those meetings, hey? Ha. Anyway, the point is, I get it now. The tablets were just another way that Josh was controlling me. And once again you were the one who helped me to see that."

"Me? How? I didn't even know what the tablets were."

"Yeah, but you called me out on it. It made me realize that I must have known I was doing the wrong thing considering the fact that I didn't want to tell you what they were when you asked about them. Afterward I was thinking to myself, 'Why am I being so defensive about this? Why don't I just tell her what they are?' But I knew why. When I got home, I took a look at the computer and I found the sites where Josh had been ordering them for me. Dodgy sites. And God, the money he was wasting on the damn things as well. Anyway, it all combined together to make me realize I needed to get out."

Joni wasn't sure that now was exactly the perfect time, but as long as Trina was in the mood to share, it was probably her best chance to confront her as well. "Trina," she said as gently as she could, "all of this stuff, everything that's been going on with Josh and the tablets—is that why you wrote that extra letter? Is that why you were feeling so resentful toward one of us?"

"What?" Trina asked, her face creased with confusion. "What extra letter?"

"While we were up the coast. The one you wrote on the first night and then replaced with something new and tried to destroy in the fire. I found it."

"Joni," said Trina, "I have no idea what the hell you're talking about."

Joni started to lose some of her conviction. "But . . ." she said, "but I was sure it was your letter. It fits, you're the most likely."

"The most likely what?"

Joni looked back at Trina, confused. "Someone wrote two letters," she said. "They said that they hate someone else in our group. That they were . . . obsessed with them . . ." Her voice started to falter.

"You think I hate one of our friends?" Trina asked, looking stung. "You think I'm obsessed with them?"

"I'm sorry," said Joni. "I just thought that . . . with everything you had going on, and then the way you're downing the wine tonight as well . . . I thought you made the most sense."

"Well, thanks a lot," huffed Trina.

"Shit, Trina," said Joni, "I'm sorry, I didn't mean to upset you . . . well, more than you already were anyway."

"Hang on," said Trina. "So you're saying while we were away, someone typed up two letters?"

"Yes."

"And so that person might have crept back in to use the computer in the middle of the night, in order to write a new letter after she got rid of the first one?"

"I guess so," said Joni. "I didn't really think about how they did it, like, the logistics of it."

"Someone came in to use the computer in the middle of the night while I was asleep in there," said Trina. "That first night after we'd all written our letters. Normally I'd be dead to the world and I wouldn't have heard a thing. But because I was on those tablets, I wasn't sleeping well, so I heard them come in and type something up. But I didn't really think that much of it, I just figured someone had cold feet about what they'd written and they were maybe changing it a bit, you know, deleting a few lines or something."

"Who?" asked Joni. "Who was it?"

"Well, that's the thing," said Trina. "I couldn't really turn to look and see who it was because I didn't want them to know I knew they were there. But just from the corner of my eye . . . from the way they moved around the room . . . well, to be honest, I thought it was you."

"Me!" said Joni. "No, it wasn't me. I think I'd know if I wrote a letter about hating someone and wanting to hurt them."

"The letter talks about wanting to hurt someone?" Trina asked. "Bloody hell, that's bad."

"Yes. But I don't know who."

"And so . . . you're sure you didn't write it? You were pretty drunk . . . we all were. And, well . . . aren't you sort of . . . the most likely candidate anyway? You know . . . because of the whole not-having-a-baby thing?" Trina looked nervous about saying it, but Joni wasn't offended.

"No, Trina," she said firmly, "I am one hundred percent certain that I didn't write an entire letter and then completely forget doing it. I was drunk, but I wasn't catatonic."

The doorbell rang then, making them both jump. "For fuck's sake," said Trina, "who else are we expecting? Don't tell me there's some other sales rep coming? What else has she signed us up for?"

Joni opened the door and she and Trina both looked out in surprise to see Eden's mother, Jan, standing at the door.

"Oh, hi, girls," she said stiffly. "I just popped over to get one of Maisie's toys. Apparently it's her favorite and she won't be able to sleep without it."

Eden came down the hall from the kitchen. "What are you doing here?" she asked, her voice sharp. "Is there something wrong with the kids?"

"No, no, nothing's wrong. Apparently we just need the 'floppy tiger.'" Jan pronounced the words carefully, as though she had been under strict instruction from Maisie to make certain she got the exact right toy.

"Oh my God, I can't believe I forgot to pack it," said Eden, her hands beginning to flutter at her side. "I knew this was a bad idea. This is why I didn't want them to have a sleepover with you."

"It's fine, Eden," said her mother. "Not a disaster, I'll get the 'floppy tiger' and take it back to her and everything will be fine."

"I'll go and grab it," said Eden.

"No, you should go back to your guests," said Jan. "I can find it in her room. She described it down to the very last detail."

"Yeah, you go, Eden," said Joni. "You too," she added to Trina. "I'll help find it."

Eden looked reluctant but turned and headed back to the kitchen, with Trina following.

"I'll give you a hand, just in case it's hiding or something," said Joni, walking with Jan into Maisie's bedroom.

"Thank you," Jan said in an overly polite, formal sort of voice.

They were searching through Maisie's bedroom, pulling back bed-covers to check underneath and sifting through the toy box when Jan spoke in a brisk, clipped voice. "You girls had an interesting holiday away, I hear?"

"Oh," said Joni, "Eden told you . . . about the letters we wrote?"

"Briefly. She said some old secrets had been shared. But that's all she would say." They both stopped searching and stood, staring at one another across the top of Maisie's bed.

"Did she?" Joni watched Jan's face carefully. What was her motivation here? What was she trying to get from Joni?

"Look, Joni. I know you're all aware of the fact that my daughter and I don't have the best relationship. For goodness' sake, tonight is the first occasion she's let me have my grandchildren stay the night with me. But I'd very much like to know what exactly it was that she told you on that holiday. I didn't appreciate the way she was trying to taunt me by suggesting she'd shared something with you three but refusing to say what it was."

Joni stared at Eden's mother, completely taken aback. This was probably the most the woman had ever even said to her.

"Mrs. Chester," she said, "maybe you should ask Eden."

"I'm asking you, Joni," she snapped.

Joni stayed quiet, trying to figure out what to say. It was funny that despite the fact that she was an adult now, one of her friends' mothers could still make her feel like she was a kid again, in trouble for breaking her favorite vase or for running too noisily through the house.

Jan spoke again. "She told you what happened in Adelaide, didn't she?"

Joni didn't need to reply; clearly the look on her face gave Jan the answer she was after.

"You realize there's more to the story than what she's told you?" Jan continued on. "Another side to it? I bet she didn't tell you she was drunk, did she? Or that she was the instigator? I bet she spun her lies—that little tale that she made up to get herself out of trouble."

Joni twisted her face in confusion. What was this woman on about

now? What did she mean? Eden was drunk when she got herself pregnant, is that what she was saying? What did that have to do with anything? Still Joni didn't need to speak, though, Jan kept plowing on.

"You realize she's been holding this against me all this time? Like it's
all my fault!"

Joni couldn't help herself. Maybe it was the guilt from having betrayed Eden with Ben that made her want to stand up for her now. Or
maybe it was the hard edge to Jan's voice that was making her feel so
protective toward her friend.

"Well, of course she blames you!" Joni exclaimed. "You and her dad!
You two were the ones who made her give him up! Didn't you even stop
to consider whether or not you were doing the right thing? How could
you be so callous about it? Surely you must wonder about him?"

"Wonder about him! What on earth are you on about? Why would I
wonder about him?"

"Because he's your grandson! Why wouldn't you wonder about him!
Why wouldn't you want to know! He's not just a part of Eden, he's a part
of you as well."

"Joni," said Jan angrily, "what the hell are you talking about? What
grandson?"

Joni stared back, completely mystified by the unexpected turn in the
conversation. What did she mean "what grandson"?

"The . . . the baby," she said, faltering. "The one that Eden had in
Adelaide, that you put up for adoption—after Eden got pregnant in high
school."

Jan glared at her, her voice full of derisive scorn when she spoke
again.

"Eden never had a baby in Adelaide," she said firmly. "And she most
definitely didn't get pregnant in high school."

CHAPTER 17

It's a funny truth that you can never fully know everything there is to know about a person, regardless of how close you think you are. Because people will always have certain secrets that they will keep to themselves, for as long as they can.

For instance, Joni never knew that in 2015, when she was out at an expensive harborside restaurant for dinner with Kai and his parents, with a view of the opera house and a $46 main of roast-duck-and-sweet-potato mash and a $130 bottle of Cab Merlot, Trina was standing by her hospital bed, cradling her tiny newborn baby in her arms, whose face was illuminated by the streetlamp that filtered through the window as she ran the tips of her fingers from his forehead to his cheek, and quietly cried while she whispered her secrets to her son.

Because Joni had been right to think that Trina had been just about to break up with Josh when she found out she was pregnant.

Trina's back was stiff and her arms ached. She was at that stage of exhaustion where you were sort of delirious and running on pure adrenaline because every time she tried to put Nate down in his cradle, he would scream and Trina would scoop him straight back up again and continue pacing the room.

"You're mine," she whispered as she looked down at his now peaceful, sleeping face. "All mine. My baby. My responsibility. There's something I need to tell you, though, something that if I say it now, then I can get it off my chest and you won't ever need to know, because you won't remember me saying this and I'll never say it again. But you were an accident. You're not actually supposed to be here right now. And, here comes the worst part. Your dad . . . he's not the best husband. He's, um . . . he's a bit . . . tough on me. At times he can be . . . cruel; judgmental of me and my choices. But I decided to give it a go anyway. Because it's important to me that you get to grow up in a nice, stable environment, with both a mum and a dad. And I believe that if I give him the chance, he might be able to change. And I do know that he'll be good to you. I'm hoping that by the time you're old enough to be aware of what's going on around you, I'll have been able to fix things, and all you'll see is two happy parents who love you. Because it's what you deserve. And you'll never know that you were an accident, because you were the best accident ever. The most wonderful surprise. But my second promise to you is that if I can't fix things, if I can't make him be a better man, then I *will* leave. But I need to give him that chance first. I need to give both of you a chance."

And in 2016, when Joni was snuggled up next to Kai on the couch in their living room as they watched an episode of *CSI,* and wondering why he didn't seem to be noticing the fact that she was tracing her fingers up and down his thigh in what she thought was a very suggestive manner, Deb was walking into her second support group meeting for divorced women. While Deb might have brushed it off in her letter as this silly, naughty, voyeuristic thing that she was doing—going along to these meetings to hear the juicy details of other people's lives—that wasn't true. It was much more to her than that. In fact, it had very little to do with the other women in the group and even less to do with her husband. But it had everything to do with her own parents and with their divorce.

When she entered the room, she grabbed hold of a plastic chair and dragged it across to join the circle, letting it make a high-pitched squealing noise as its metal legs scraped against the linoleum floor. She squeezed in between two women, gave the woman who was speaking a quick smile, and waved at her to continue. "It's all good," she said. "Keep going, I'll catch up." She glanced around while she waited for her turn, at the rest of the chairs stacked at one end of the room and at the kitchenette along the back wall. At the plates of biscuits, the kettle, the basket of tea bags and the sugar sachets, and the jar of instant coffee with a stack of Styrofoam cups.

The woman who was speaking was explaining how her ex had yet again stood her up for a custody hearing. ". . . I knew he wouldn't show up. I just knew it. He bloody never does. He's the one who pushes for these hearings. I get these demanding letters from his solicitor. I blow-dry my hair and I put on makeup because I can't stand for him to see me looking anything other than my absolute best. I catch a bus to Quakers Hill train station. I sit in the freezing cold on the platform and I get myself to Parramatta by five forty-five A.M. And then I wait. And I wait and he never bloody shows. You would think that would be enough for them to see that he doesn't actually care, wouldn't you?"

Deb nodded along with the other women in the group and made the appropriate tsk, tsk noises at the right times. And then it was her turn to speak and she launched into her prepared story about the day she had to sit her children down and tell them that their parents were getting a divorce. Only in truth, in this scenario she had been one of those children, sitting side by side with her brother on the couch, knees together, hands on their legs, prim and proper like primary school kids posing for their school photo. "It was strange that they ended up sitting that way," she said. "Normally, they both would have been slouching. My son would have had his legs spread wide, taking up as much room as possible, the way tall boys do, and my daughter would have had her feet curled up underneath her, even though she knew she wasn't supposed to put her feet on the couch. Even though she knew it drove her mother . . . me—even though she knew it drove me crazy. But I guess it was something about the way we told them we needed to talk to the both of them together. Something about the tone of our voices—that made the both of them want to sit up straight-backed and pay attention."

Joni also never knew, though, that on a warm Saturday in March of 1997, as she was sitting cross-legged on top of her purple-and-white-striped quilt, in the middle of her bed, listening to her Spiderbait CD and hunching over a long letter to Eden, in which she was explaining in great detail just how annoying Mr. Lawson was being in science lately, especially now that she didn't have Eden sitting next to her, keeping her sane, Eden was 1,300 kilometers away in Adelaide, feeling self-conscious in her pale pink, spaghetti-strap dress as she followed her parents through the front door of a sleek, contemporary home with an oversized foyer and cavernous ceilings.

Eden had wanted to wear jeans and a T-shirt, but her mum had insisted she dress up for the occasion. She had her mini candy-striped backpack slung over one shoulder. Her Velcro Billabong wallet, some Impulse deodorant spray, and her brand-new Olympus camera were inside.

Dinner at her dad's new boss's house. This boss was apparently the reason that they'd had to pack up their life in Sydney and move to Adelaide for half a year. He liked Dad's work on the something-or-other job and he needed his help with a similar something-else-or-other job.

Eden knew very little about what her dad did. She just knew it all came down to her having to leave her school and her friends behind for six long months.

When she first spotted Clarke, her stomach actually did a small flip. His good looks were nothing short of extraordinary. One of those boys who was tall and well built with great cheekbones and a neat short-back-and-sides haircut. Not to mention the piercing blue eyes. He was older and he gave her a great, big welcoming smile that made her melt inside. The crush was instantaneous. She was already imagining what it would be like to touch his hand, to brush her lips against his fingers. Her designs on Clarke didn't extend much further than that. She hadn't really had much experience with boys back in Sydney before this. Just a short-lived "relationship" with a boy named Jared. She wasn't even sure if you could call what happened between her and Jared her first kiss. A clumsy pressing of their lips together that resulted in her cheeks glowing bright red in embarrassment.

It was supposed to be an innocent game of table tennis. Clarke offered to show her around the house so that they could "stay out of the way" of the adults. She found out that he was nineteen—already out of high school. But he didn't act like he was annoyed at having to look after some "little girl," as Eden might have expected (especially with her in this stupid damned dress her mum had made her wear). In fact, he treated her like she was his age. Rolled his eyes at her about how annoying were *parents*?! Made jokes that she didn't get, but she pretended to laugh anyway. After showing her all the way around the house, they ended up in the downstairs games room, where he suggested a game of table tennis. She'd snapped a photo of him standing behind the table, grinning at her and holding out the two paddleboards, ready for her to grab one.

Eden was nervous. As she stashed the camera back into her bag, she wondered what would happen if she was absolutely terrible at table tennis. What if she couldn't even return the ball back across the table and it turned into this horribly one-sided and pointless game and eventually they had to give up and concede that she was useless? Or what if she got this stupid look on her face when she hit the ball—maybe a slack-jawed grimace or a tongue poked out in concentration? How was she supposed to play against this model-like Adonis and not completely embarrass herself? As it was, she kept fumbling over her words—not that she'd said much, because what could she say that would possibly be cool enough to impress Clarke?

He said he just wanted to help her with her technique. When he moved around behind her and placed his arms around hers, her body convulsed with two simultaneous reactions: a shiver of delight, he was touching her! He liked her! This was her wildest dream come true! Sure, it was a wildest dream that she had only just conceived fifteen minutes prior when she'd met Clarke for the first time, but still—this was unbelievable! But then that second reaction: *But his touch is too much. He's all around me . . . and so sudden. I don't know him, I just met him, he didn't ask if this was okay, and now his hands are becoming firmer and his body is pressing up against me and I'm feeling . . . I'm feeling . . . suffocated!*

At first Eden was frozen. What was she supposed to say? How was she supposed to disentangle herself from his touch? Would he be offended? What if she was overreacting? What if he laughed at her or said, "What the hell are you talking about, I was just trying to show you how to hit the ball!"

But the more he pushed his body up against her back, the more she knew this wasn't a misunderstanding.

And so she tried to pull away. That's when his arms wrapped around her even tighter and his mouth was on her neck, wet lips and hot breath—

and all pretense of correcting her technique had vanished. His hands crept their way up her arms and then slipped around in front to clutch at her breasts and Eden quivered with fear.

"I don't . . . I don't want . . ." she tried to whisper.

"Shh," was his response, not a gentle whisper but a harsh whoosh in her ear. "I know you want me. I saw the way you've been looking at me. You've got a little crush, haven't you, Eden?"

"No!" Again Eden tried to pull away, but she was still trying to be polite. Still attempting to disentangle herself without offending.

"It's okay," said Clarke. "I won't tell. Let's just have some . . . fun." And now he reached down to the hem of her dress and started to lift it, sliding the material up her thigh, his hand creeping around between her legs, and all the while still pushing, pushing against her with his entire heavy body.

"Stop," she said, her shaking voice followed by a tiny sob. "Please, I don't want to."

"Yes, you do," he insisted, his hands continuing to scrabble clumsily at her body.

And finally Eden stopped being polite. She jammed her elbow into his ribs, forcing him backward. It wasn't enough to push his body completely clear of her own, but it was enough for her to get the leverage she needed to then spin around on the spot, place her hands on his chest, and push him away with everything she had.

They both stood still for a moment, the two of them breathing hard, Eden with her back against the table-tennis table and Clarke just two steps away from her, staring at her with this smirk on his face and a greedy look in his eyes. He made to lunge for her again and Eden tried to sidestep him. Her hip banged painfully against the corner edge of the table, slowing her down, and he caught hold of her arm and yanked her back toward him.

"Stop!" she tried again. But Clarke wasn't used to being told no. He threw her down onto a couch behind them and then climbed straight on top of her, squeezing his thighs tight to hold her in place and holding on to her wrists to pin her arms at her sides.

"I'll scream," she whimpered. "I'll scream for my parents."

"If you scream, I'll punch you so hard that you'll pass out and then you won't even know what I'm doing to you," he replied.

"But I don't want to," she tried again, and now she was sobbing outright, the tears streaming down her cheeks, her chest heaving, her entire body shaking. The fight-or-flight instinct was kicking in, but right now she didn't know how to do either, he had her entire body locked down underneath him.

He let go of one wrist in order to start tearing at her dress and her hand flew up to stop him, fighting him with everything she had, pushing, scratching, hitting. Suddenly he leaned right back away from her and there was just a flicker of relief—*he was going to stop*. He was going to listen to her. He was going to let her go—and then she saw his head flying toward her, his face about to crash into her own.

It was strange just how many thoughts could tumble through her mind in that split second before he head-butted her and knocked her out.

What's happening?

What's he doing?

Is he crazy? He's going to crash right into me!

And then the realization.

He's going to knock me out.

Then nothing but darkness and a blank mind.

When Eden woke, she was alone. She tried to sit up fast, but she got dizzy and fell back. Her hands reached for her clothing next and she was relieved to find that she was still fully dressed. Pink dress, bra, underpants—all in place.

Nothing had happened! He'd stopped. He'd decided to leave her alone. But then she shifted slightly as she tried once more to sit up and she felt a searing pain between her legs and she knew that she was wrong. He hadn't let her be. He'd violated her body and then re-dressed her like she was a life-size doll.

There was a strange taste in her mouth—a taste she couldn't seem to understand, but before she had the chance to examine it any further, she heard footsteps. She prepared to cower in fear from her attacker, but instead of seeing Clarke appear in the room, she saw her mother. Her mother who was now striding toward her, a furious expression of rage across her face.

She knew! Her mother knew what had happened to her. She had come to save her. Come to comfort her, to tell her it was all right, to make everything okay again.

Instead, though, within seconds, her mother was above her, glaring down at her. "Eden Elizabeth Chester. I cannot believe that you would do this! And here of all places, at your father's boss's house! I mean, we knew you were angry about moving to Adelaide, but I never thought you would do something like this!"

The fog in Eden's brain from having been concussed was making it impossible for her to understand what her mother was saying to her. Why was she so mad? Surely she couldn't blame Eden for what Clarke had done to her?

And then Eden's mum reached down and picked up a bottle from the floor.

"Scotch?" she exclaimed. "And how much exactly did you drink?"

"Mum," Eden pleaded, "please, what are you talking about?" The words came out thick and wobbly, as though her mouth was full of marbles, and her mum shook her head disapprovingly. "For God's sake, Eden," she said. "You're drunk!"

"No, Mum, no! I didn't . . . I wouldn't . . . I haven't had anything to drink!"

"Oh please, Eden. I can smell it on your breath. Clarke already came and told me that you drank so much that you passed out. He said he hadn't realized you were sneaking it, otherwise he would have stopped you sooner."

Now Eden understood the strange taste in her mouth. "Mum! No. He must have poured some in my mouth!"

"Don't be ridiculous. Why on earth would he do that when he was the one who came and told me what had happened? And he was nice enough to pull me aside so that both your father and his father don't know about this. Heaven knows what Mr. Arlington would think if he knew you'd done this right here in his house. Come on; up. You're going outside to get some fresh air and sober up and your father is never going to find out about this."

Now Eden was crying again. Her head ached where Clarke's head had smashed into hers and she didn't know how to explain to her mother that she had it all completely wrong when everything looked so bad.

Her first mistake was waiting so long before she tried once again to convince her mother of the truth. Maybe if she'd pushed, maybe if she'd demanded that her parents take her straight to the police or to a doctor— maybe they could have seen the evidence, the truth, for themselves, like those damp, dark red-brown spots on her underpants that she discovered later that night. The underpants that she had immediately stuffed inside a plastic bag, tied up tight, and thrown straight in the bin so she would never have to look at them again.

Instead she let her mum drag her outside and deposit her on a white wooden swing around the side of the house, among the beautiful flowering hedges and neatly manicured garden beds. Eden was to sit there and stay out of sight until she felt sober.

Eden spent two hours on her own on that damn swing. Despite the warm sun, she was shivering uncontrollably. Any sound made her entire body jerk, her insides flip.

When they finally went back home, Eden got straight into the shower and scrubbed away all traces of Clarke, letting her endless tears mix in with the water. And then later, she finally tried yet again to explain to her mother the truth.

The problem was that Clarke had already taken Jan aside for his own little talk that afternoon. Apparently he'd explained that there had been a bit of a silly misunderstanding—an unfortunate "incident" downstairs in the games room.

"I'm so sorry, but I think your daughter has a little bit of a crush."

"No, Mum, that's not true. I mean, at first, I thought that he was cute and stuff, but that's not what—"

"This is a bit embarrassing to be honest, but well . . . she tried to kiss me."

"I didn't! That didn't happen, I never . . ."

"So of course I tried to let her down easy. I tried to explain that I was just too old for her. I think that's when she started sneaking the scotch from behind the bar in the games room. And then she got angry and told me she was going to make up a story to get me into trouble."

"No! I didn't say that! I'm not making this up!"

"Look, I'm sure she's a lovely girl. But to be honest, I have a girlfriend—she's at uni with me . . . so you can only imagine how it makes me feel to have her make up this awful story about me. And if my girlfriend ever heard it, well, she's from a very prominent family. It just wouldn't be good—these kinds of untrue accusations. Not good for me or for my family."

"No, Mum! He started to touch me, he . . . he put his hands . . ."

"And perhaps I'm a bit to blame for the misunderstanding. I was

trying to make sure she felt at home, trying to be friendly. I made the mistake of giving her a little bit of a hand with her table-tennis technique and I think the wires must have gotten a little crossed. She misinterpreted, you know what girls that age can be like."

"That's NOT true!"

It simply didn't matter how many times Eden tried desperately to tell her mother what had happened down in that games room. Clarke was older. Clarke was charming. Clarke was Dad's boss's son. Clarke was polite and apologetic for the misunderstanding, and perhaps, worst of all, he *forgave* her for her apparent faux pas. When Eden tried to use the lump on her forehead as evidence, her mother told her that Clarke said she'd tripped and bumped her head after drinking too much. When Eden argued further, her mother said she'd been warned by other parents that Eden might try to act out in retaliation for being made to move away from her school and her friends.

And the worst part was not knowing whether Eden's mum ever would have believed her, even if Clarke hadn't had the chance to spin his story before Eden explained what had happened.

Maybe she never would have believed Eden's words. Because maybe she simply didn't want to. She didn't want to jeopardize her husband's career. She didn't want to know that there was something wrong. She just wanted to get through these six months, support her husband as was her role as the dutiful wife, and then get back to Sydney with the knowledge that his faithful service of the company would cement the upward trajectory of his career path. It was easier to believe Clarke's version of events because that meant fewer difficult questions.

It was the beginning of the end for Eden's relationship with her mother. They had always gotten along well enough—as well as teenage girls got along with their mums. But for Eden, her mum's breach of trust could never be forgotten and it could never be forgiven.

Eden took to that stupid pink spaghetti-strap dress later that night with a pair of kitchen scissors. When she was done there was nothing but torn strips of material left.

Six months later, when the family moved back to Sydney and Eden had her first day back at her old school, she had been so full of relief to see her friends waiting for her right there at the school gate, five minutes before the bell was due to ring for homeroom.

Even though all three of them had written to her so regularly throughout her six months away, she'd still been terrified that they would treat her differently when she got back. That she might not be welcomed straight back into the group. The fact that she hadn't really replied to any of their letters didn't help her fears. She knew she should have, and that they would have every right to be angry with her for never replying. After all, receiving their letters had kept her sane while she'd been in Adelaide. But she couldn't reply because she just didn't know what to say.

She desperately wanted to tell them the truth. To share what had happened to her in that very first week when she arrived in Adelaide. But how did you write something like that down in a letter? Although, then again, she wasn't sure that she'd ever be able to speak those words out loud either. Knowing the reaction she'd received the first time she'd tried to tell the truth about what had happened.

Her own mother. The one person who was supposed to believe in her. The one person she should have been able to trust.

But then Joni, Deb, and Trina had all hugged her so tight as they welcomed her back, treating her like she was no different, like she'd never even left, and Eden had decided then and there that she would tell them the truth.

They were her friends. People said blood was thicker than water, but they also said you choose your friends, not your family. So she started to plan what she might say. How she might ask them to take a walk with her at lunchtime, across to the other side of the oval, away from eavesdropping ears and prying eyes.

They would believe her.

They would take her word for it. Wouldn't they?

But then at recess, Joni had asked to see her photos from Adelaide, before Eden had the chance to bring up her horrible story.

Eden hadn't even realized that there was one of him in there. This was back in the day when you took your rolls of film into a camera shop and had them developed. Back when every single click of the camera cost you money—money in film and money in developing. She'd had them all developed at once after arriving back home in Sydney. All seven rolls. And she hadn't looked through them properly before bringing them into school with her. She should have, though. She really, really should have. If she'd seen that photo, she would have burned it on the spot.

"Who is *that*?! He's cute!" Joni had exclaimed as she leafed through the shots.

Eden had looked up and then leaned across Trina to see who Joni was pointing it. Her voice caught in her throat when she saw his face.

"He's—he's just the son of my dad's boss," she had said shortly. But unfortunately, Joni hadn't picked up on Eden's discomfort at all.

"Ooh! Boss's son! How hot is he?!" she'd persisted, full of girlish excitement. "Oh my God, can you imagine being his girlfriend? Can you imagine getting to kiss him? Can you imagine getting to . . ." She'd trailed off and given the others a significant look while comically raising her eyebrows, and then they'd all fallen about laughing while Eden had to stop herself from vomiting right then and there.

She'd taken that photo of him before she knew his true self. Back when he was just a handsome older boy. A boy who seemed cool and smart and funny. A boy who she was developing a bit of a crush on—even as she knew it was pointless. He was out of her league. There was no way he'd have any interest in her.

She shouldn't really have blamed Joni for thinking he was cute. After all, Eden had thought he was cute at first too, so why shouldn't Joni point out his good looks when she saw that photo of him?

But at that moment when it happened, Eden hated Joni. Hated her with every fiber in her body. And she knew that she couldn't tell them the truth after all. They wouldn't understand. In fact, they probably wouldn't even believe her! Because why would a guy who was that good-looking want to even consider touching her?

Maybe they would all laugh again and say, "Oh yeah, sure, Eden, of course the nineteen-year-old uni student wants to have sex with a high school kid." But the worst part might be if they added, "And even if he did want you—why on earth wouldn't you want him right back?"

So she didn't tell them what had happened. And all this time, she hadn't told another soul what had happened. She'd kept it locked up inside until that night of their holiday, when everyone had started talking about sharing secrets and she had wondered if this was her chance.

Truth or lie?

Truth or lie?

Joni was on her way back to the kitchen when Ben appeared in front of her. She was still reeling from Mrs. Chester's revelation.

Eden lied in her letter. Eden lied when she said she'd had a teen-age pregnancy. And if she thought about it—it all made sense: Eden's discomfort when they'd asked for details about the adoption. The way she'd looked panicked when Trina had asked who the father was, but had latched on to Deb's answer on her behalf.

So, her letter was a complete fabrication.

Which meant that Eden was the one who had written the fifth letter. Eden was the one who hated someone within their friendship circle.

The only thing Joni didn't know, though, was *who* it was that Eden was obsessed with. She had to find out. For some reason, the idea that Eden was behind those words in that letter worried her a lot more than when she had thought it was written by Trina. It was just that Eden came across as so harmless, so to know that she had these hidden feelings deep inside, it was somehow more shocking.

Joni tried to step past Ben; she had to get in there and find a way to take Eden aside and talk to her about the letter. She had to find out who it was that Eden hated so much.

But Ben stepped sideways and blocked Joni's path.

"Joni," he hissed. "I need a word."

"Huh?" Joni had been so engrossed in her thoughts that she barely registered the look on his face, but then she focused and she saw just how panicked he looked.

"What's wrong?" she asked.

"Not here. I don't want to be overheard." Ben guided her back down the hall and into Maisie's bedroom, where she'd stood just five minutes earlier and heard the truth about Eden from Mrs. Chester. Eden's mum had left immediately after their conversation, carrying Maisie's floppy tiger and muttering something about the fact that Joni was insane and that she didn't appreciate practical jokes. She hadn't given Joni the chance to explain why she'd thought Jan had an extra grandson somewhere out there in the world—although that was probably for the best.

Now Ben sat down on his daughter's Strawberry Shortcake bedspread and looked up at Joni.

"I had to tell her," he said, a miserable look on his face. "I had to tell Eden what happened with us."

"What? You told her? But why? Ben, nothing actually happened!"

"Yes, Joni. It did. It might not have been an actual physical indiscretion, but it was still something. Joni, we almost kissed!"

"But we didn't!" Joni was about to argue further, to explain that honestly, it hadn't meant a damn thing because it was all just based on her own feelings of inadequacy due to a complete misunderstanding between herself and Kai—but she stopped short as the look on Ben's face swiftly changed. He'd stopped looking miserable, and instead, he looked terrified.

"What?" she began, but then she sensed it. Someone else was right behind her, standing in the doorway of Maisie's bedroom. She swung around, praying that it wasn't who she thought it was going to be.

It was.

Kai was staring at her with an expression of shock and hurt across his face. And now his focus shifted to Ben. "You almost kissed my wife?" he asked, his voice dangerously quiet.

"Mate," said Ben.

"Mate? Are you fucking kidding me? You're going to call me your mate?"

"It's not what you think."

"How the hell do you know what I think?" Kai stepped into the room and Joni moved to block him. She grabbed his hand and started to pull at him, trying to guide him back out of the bedroom. "Let me explain," she begged as his rigid form continued to hold steady. "Please," she said again, "come outside with me." She let go of his hand and instead placed her hands on either side of his face, making him look into her eyes. "Kai," she whispered, "just let me tell you properly, please."

Something in his face changed. A flicker of compassion maybe—or curiosity—he needed to know more. So he relented and he let Joni push him backward out of the room. But the look he threw at Ben as they went out into the hallway was clear—this wasn't the end of his conversation with Ben.

Joni led Kai through the lounge and then out into the backyard, trying to stay out of sight of the kitchen windows.

"Okay," said Kai as they stopped under the pergola, the two of them hardly noticing the chilled night air. "Talk."

"Right," said Joni, realizing that now she actually had to find a way to explain. To make him understand that it was nothing, nothing at all to worry about. "We were at the gym together—and this was before, before we had our big talk, before I knew that I'd stuffed up, that I'd misunderstood everything that was happening with us—"

"Wait. Is this why you were crying that night when you came home? Is this why we even *had* that big talk?"

"Yes, but . . . look, the important thing is . . . the thing you have to understand . . . the thing you have to know—"

"For fuck's sake, Joni! Spit it out!"

"Nothing happened! We didn't kiss!"

"Goddammit, Joni, something happened! I mean, hey, I didn't kiss Leah or Andrea at work yesterday either! I didn't kiss some random woman on the train the other morning. I didn't kiss Deb or Eden or Trina earlier tonight! But I don't usually have to come to you in tears and confess to you that I didn't kiss them because I don't end up in a position where there's any possible chance that I *could* kiss them. So, please, Joni, explain to me what happened."

"Okay! Okay. I'll explain." Joni pulled back one of the chairs from the outdoor dining setting and sat down; she dropped her hands between her knees and slumped forward, staring down at the ground. Then she spoke.

"I never meant for anything to happen between us. It's not what I wanted, I swear. It was just that . . . in my mind, I was failing you. Like I told you that night after the holiday, I was so sure, so, so certain that you didn't want me anymore." She looked back up at Kai again. He'd remained standing and she tried to reach out for his hand, but he wasn't ready to take it just yet. She searched his face, trying to find a sign that he understood. That he still trusted her.

"Please," she pleaded, "you need to know that I believed these things. I was sure that they were true. This was before you fixed all that for me. Before I knew how wrong I was, how stupid I was being."

Kai pulled back another chair and sat opposite her.

"Okay," he said. "You thought everything was imploding with the two of us. But how the hell does Ben come into any of this?"

"He was just someone to talk to, babe. I guess . . . I guess we'd flirted. But I thought it was completely harmless. I mean, everyone flirts, right? I've seen you do it with the waitress at that Indian restaurant you love!"

"Joni. I'm friendly with her. I don't try and kiss her."

"Yes, I know, I just mean that. That's all I thought I was doing. Being friendly! But then he started to make me feel . . . desirable again. And on the spur of the moment, I confided in him, about our problems."

"You confided in *him*? Before coming to me?"

"I know. I know. It was a mistake. But like I said, it was spur of the moment. I thought I couldn't talk to you. I thought everything with us was all messed up. And then, he complimented me and it made me feel special, and all that happened was we both started to lean in and then . . . nothing. We stopped! That was it. That was the whole thing. Over. I promise."

Once again, Joni reached out for Kai's hand. This time he let her take it.

"I'm sorry," she said. "I'm so, so sorry."

"So," Kai said quietly, "nothing physical actually happened between you and Ben. *Nothing*."

"No," she said. "I promise, nothing happened."

"But you wanted it to?" he asked.

"No," said Joni. "I guess for just a second, just a split second . . . I *thought* that I did. But *not* because I wanted it from him, just because I was wanting to feel something . . . from someone."

"Do you have feelings for him?"

"No," she said again. "Not even a little bit. I swear to you. I love you. I love you so, so much, and I hate that I've hurt you and I hate that I've made you doubt my feelings, but I promise, I absolutely one hundred percent promise—it was nothing. Nothing happened at all."

"Nothing *physical* happened," Kai corrected her. "But I do believe you when you say you don't have feelings for him. You were never any good at lying. The truth has always been easy to read with you—all I have to do is look at your eyes." He squeezed her hand gently and then pulled her out of her seat and across to him, sitting her on his lap and wrapping his arms around her.

"Look," he said, "obviously I'm not thrilled about what happened . . . but I think I get it. I saw how devastated you were that night when you told me how you were feeling. I saw how much you truly believed that I was going to end up leaving you. And I do still trust you, Joni. I know you. You're not a cheater."

"So . . . we're good?" Joni whispered, pulling his arms around her even tighter. "We're okay?"

"Yes, Joni. We're okay. I feel like shit about the whole thing. And don't expect me to have a beer with that asshole in there anytime soon. But we're okay." Then he dropped one hand to her stomach and stroked it gently. "Besides," he added, "we have other things to focus on now."

"Kai . . . this might be a bad time to tell you this . . . but can I make one more confession?"

"Oh, fuck," he said, throwing his head back, but not letting her go. "Right. What else is it?"

"I've been smoking. Not since I found out our news, obviously. But before that, when I thought we couldn't get pregnant."

Kai laughed. "You thought that was a secret?! Joni, I knew you were smoking! In fact, I didn't even realize you thought you were hiding it from me. I thought you were just trying to do it away from me because you knew I don't like being around cigarette smoke. But I didn't comment because you're an adult. Your body, your choice."

"Oh."

"So how come?" Kai asked. "What was it that made you take it up?"

Joni shrugged. "I think I was trying to punish my body. A bit of a fuck-you to myself. If you can't conceive, then I'll screw you over with nicotine. Stupid, hey?"

"Yeah—but you already knew that. Hey, you think we can ditch the rest of this dinner party and just go home?"

Joni thought about the revelation about Eden and her secret. But could she really confront her about any of that tonight? Now that she knew Ben had told her the truth? Probably not. And anyway, it was more important that she focused on her relationship with Kai.

"Sure," she said. "We can come up with an excuse."

"You came back!"

"Hey, I thought you weren't meant to know who was in here, you know, I thought there was supposed to be a certain level of anonymity."

"Yes, that's all well and good, but when a person sits there talking to me for almost half the day, you get to know their voice. Anyway, I've been wondering about you. Wondering what happened when you went to the dinner party. Did you confront her? What happened?"

"Well, if you thought the story was long and complicated before . . . Ha, where do I even start? You know what? The thing is . . . if we'd just left the dinner party when we said we were going to, maybe things could have gone differently. But we didn't—we got stuck and then . . . okay, I guess I need to fill you in on the in-between stuff first.

"You were right, though. I was wrong. Trina didn't write the fifth letter."

CHAPTER 18

Back in the kitchen, Joni was waiting for a pause in the demonstration so she could make their excuses and get her and Kai out of there. But then Aimee pounced on Kai. "Oh, good!" she exclaimed. "You two are back just in time to help me out. I need a volunteer to chop these onions for me. We're going to have a bit of a competition!"

"Oh, um, sorry, Aimee," Joni tried to intervene. "We were actually about to—"

"No, no, it's okay, you can sit down and watch. It's just your lovely man here that I need. I've already got my other volunteer," said Aimee. Kai shrugged at Joni, giving her a look that said, "Don't worry about it, I'll just do it quick and then we'll be gone."

But then Ben appeared from inside the walk-in pantry and Aimee smiled widely and said, "Ah, here he is, our other volunteer! I've got you your competitor!"

Oh shit!

Ben and Kai locked eyes and Joni looked helplessly between them, wondering how she could stop this from escalating.

"Kai!" she said desperately. "You have that thing with onions, they always make your eyes water so bad. Maybe someone else should take your place! How about Trina?" Then she looked at Trina, who was swaying in her seat and she realized that she must have been continuing to down the wine like it was water and she strongly doubted her ability to hold a knife steady.

"It's fine, Joni," said Kai steadily. "I don't have any issues with eyes."

Deb caught Joni's attention and mouthed at her, *What's up?*

But there was no way Joni could explain just with facial expressions everything that had transpired in the past ten minutes.

"Lovely!" said Aimee. "Right, gents. Which one of you would like to do it the old-fashioned way, and which one wants to chop their onion with the Thermomix?"

Wonderful. This wasn't going to turn into a pissing contest between the two of them, was it? But there was no stopping it now. Joni took a seat next to Deb and prayed that no one was about to lose a finger to that extremely large butcher's knife Aimee had just handed across to Kai.

Joni realized Deb was now nudging her under the table, trying to get her to tell her what was going on.

"Not now!" Joni hissed.

Eden shot a look across the table at them, and when Joni looked back at her, the look that passed between them was one of knowing.

I know and I know that you know and you know that I know.

Meanwhile, Ben and Kai had taken their positions at the kitchen counter. Ben was poised with his hands hovering in the air above the bowl of the Thermomix, two onions in each hand. Kai's onions were in front of him on a chopping board, the knife pressed against the first onion, ready to start.

"All right!" said Aimee, "and we'll start in three, two, one . . . chop!"

Onion was flying everywhere. Ben had dropped all four of his onions into the Thermomix at once and then switched it straight on, not bothering to check the settings, not bothering to place any sort of cover over the top.

Kai's hand was a blur as he started chopping wildly.

"Bet you weren't expecting them to take it this seriously, were you, Aimee?" Trina shouted happily.

"Okay . . . okay," said Aimee with a nervous laugh. "Yes, they are taking it quite seriously, aren't they? Ah, maybe just take it easy a bit there . . . we don't want to see anyone lose a finger!"

"Lower your voice a bit, Trina," said Josh loudly. "You sound absolutely sloshed."

"Fuck off, Josh," said Trina.

"You know what?" said Aimee. "I don't usually do this at demonstrations, but would anyone mind . . . could I perhaps get one of those glasses of wine?"

"Sure, you can take my wife's glass," said Josh.

"Give it a rest, Josh," said Deb.

"Oh shit!" interrupted Connor. "Is that blood in your onions, Kai?"

"What? No, don't think so." Kai was continuing to chop in a crazed frenzy while Ben had stepped back from the Thermomix and was picking bits of onion off his shirt and out of his hair.

"I did warn you!" said Aimee as she reached across the table for the wine and started pouring herself a large glass. "I warned you to take it easy. You can't sue me for this!" And she started gulping her wine at a speed that would give Trina a run for her money.

"No, seriously, mate, I think you need to stop. Ben's done anyway. His onions are all chopped."

Kai threw his knife down, grabbed a tea towel and wrapped it around his cut finger, and then stormed out of the kitchen. Joni made to chase after him, but Connor had already followed and Deb grabbed her arm. "Let Connor go," she said. "They've always got along well. You, come with me."

"Right," said Aimee. "How about we take a break before we serve up our potato, leek, and onion soup. I'm not sure that this onion is exactly . . . usable."

Joni let Deb drag her back outside again.

"Are you sure we should leave Trina and Josh in there?" Joni asked worriedly.

"It's okay, Eden and Ben are with them and we'll get to their issues. I'm just glad to see Trina standing up for herself with him for once. Although I can't believe how much the two of them air their stuff in public. I mean you don't see Connor and me shouting at each other in there, do you? And we weren't even speaking with one another this morning."

"Wait, what? What's happening with you two?"

"Oh, he found out about the meetings. Someone from the group called and left a message for me and he was all like, excuse me? Why is my WIFE going to divorce group meetings? It all blew up in my face, hey? But that's okay, we're good at putting our shit aside. We're going to have it out tomorrow. So tell me, what's going on with you and Kai?"

"Um . . . long story," said Joni.

"I gathered that," said Deb. "So start at the beginning."

Joni opened her mouth to speak but the door opened behind them and they both turned to see Eden heading out to join them. "Deb," she said, "I think Trina needs you, you're the best at intervening between her and Josh . . . do you mind?"

Deb looked back at Joni. "Hang on, let me just see what's happening with Trina and then we'll continue, okay?"

Joni was making to follow Deb back inside, not wanting to be left on her own with Eden considering everything she now knew. But Eden caught her arm. "Joni, can we have a word, please?"

Fuck. This was happening. Joni considered refusing. She could just say, "Not now—I need to go and check on Kai." But the conversation was going to have to happen eventually. And it wasn't fair to Eden to brush her off. So why not just get it over and done with now?

Joni obediently followed Eden as she led her away from the back door and through the gate to stand by the pool for their chat, each step just delaying the inevitable conversation that was to come.

The water was sparkling with the bright blue pool lights and the ripples were casting speckled shadows across their faces. For a moment they just stared at the pool, no one speaking. But then Eden said quietly, "Joni, I'm trying okay. I'm trying to be okay with you. I do want to forgive you . . . because there's nothing really to forgive, right?"

"Oh gosh," said Joni. "We're jumping right into it, are we?"

"Well, yeah. I mean, what do you want from me? You want me to dance around it or make this big revelation where I tell you that I know, which is pointless because it's clear that you know that I know."

"Yeah, okay, fair enough. Sorry, you just took me by surprise, that's all. And I guess I wasn't expecting you to be so . . . nice."

Eden gave a small laugh. "That's me, isn't it? Nice Eden. Calm Eden. The one that's always easygoing. The one that can't hold on to her husband or keep him satisfied enough that he doesn't want to go around kissing one of her best friends."

Ah. Maybe not so calm about it all, then.

"But, Eden, you know that nothing actually happened between Ben and me, right?"

"That's what Ben kept saying," said Eden, and her voice started out low, but as she spoke it was rising, steadily rising, louder and louder. "Over and over and over. Nothing happened, nothing happened, nothing happened. It was just some kind of natural connection, some kind of a bond the two of you formed together at the gym. All that sweating and heavy lifting and hot skin. Something was bound to grow between the two of you, right? But if nothing happened, you both wouldn't look so bloody guilty, would you?"

"No! It wasn't like that at all—"

"You know what the worst part is?" Eden interrupted. "The fact that not only did you share some sort of a special 'moment' with my husband. You also told Ben I was keeping a secret from him. Yeah, he told me that part too. This afternoon when it was all weighing on him so much that he couldn't stand it anymore. And then he had the gall to ask me what my secret was! As if that was the time for me to share. Jesus. You were trying to make yourself feel better, weren't you? By telling him I'd hidden something from him. Trying to convince yourself that if I had secrets, then I'd somehow already betrayed him, so what you two did wasn't so wrong?"

"Eden, I'm sorry! I really am, I never meant for it to get like that. And no, that's not what I was doing . . . I don't know why I told him that . . . I guess I was trying to . . . trying to . . ."

"Trying to what?"

"Well, it sounds bad . . . but I was trying to stop him from telling you about me. Trying to give him a reason to just let it go and forget about it because as soon as we even got close to kissing, we both realized it wasn't what either of us wanted and it seemed like telling you or telling Kai would just mean hurting you both for no reason."

Joni hesitated for a moment and then she plowed on. "But look, Eden, the thing is, it's not like you did have a secret from him anyway, right? Because the baby in your letter . . . your secret . . . it was a lie."

"What do you mean?" she asked sharply.

"Eden, I *know*. I spoke with your mum, while I was helping her look for Maisie's toy. She told me that you were never pregnant. That you didn't give up a baby for adoption in Adelaide."

Eden stared back at Joni. For a moment she looked like she might try and argue it, but then her whole body seemed to slump, as though she'd been holding on to this lie for too long and she was finally able to let it go.

"Yes," she said. "You're right. I lied in my letter. But you're also wrong, Joni. You're wrong when you say that I don't have a secret, that I haven't been keeping something from Ben, because I do. I have the secret of what really happened to me in Adelaide. Something that I was planning on telling Ben all about when I was ready. Actually, I wanted to share it with him after I got back home from the coast, but instead he got all weird with me. And then he decided to let his confession out first, before I had the chance. So thanks for that. Thanks a lot. Because of you—I've still got this horrible, horrible secret locked up inside and I feel like I'm never, EVER going to be able to get better."

"Look," said Joni, "I'm sorry, okay? I'm sorry, I'm sorry, I'm sorry. I fucked up. I did something awful and it meant that you didn't get to get something off your chest to Ben, and I know that sucks." Her voice was starting to get louder now as the frustration welled up inside. Because now it was obviously time to get down to the truth. Time to put all that shit with Ben to the side and find out who it was that Eden hated and deal with it. "But why didn't you just tell us whatever it was that you were hiding?" Joni continued. "Why make up this crazy story if you really did have something you needed to say? We're your friends!"

"Really, Joni? You're my friend? Gee, I don't know. If we're all such *great friends,* then how could one of us make a move on the other one's husband?"

Joni groaned with frustration, she felt like tearing out her hair. "Nothing! Happened! And I need you to forget about that for now! Because that letter you wrote, that was before all of this, and we need to get to the bottom of it all. So come on. Tell me! That's what the whole letter-writing thing was supposed to be about in the first place, wasn't it? It was a chance to get some shit out in the open. Tell me!"

"It's not that easy to just come out and say!" Eden's voice was now matching Joni's in volume and anger.

"Isn't it, though? Because you managed to say the truth once, didn't you? When you wrote it in your letter!"

"What the hell are you talking about?"

"I found it! I found your other letter—it didn't burn completely in the fire. So, you've said it once before, now say it again. Tell me who it is that you hate! Who is it, Eden? Who is it that you're so jealous of? Who is it that you're so obsessed with?" Joni was outright shouting now. Shouting at her friend as she tried to coax the truth from her. She needed to say it; if they were ever going to move forward from this, then she needed to say it.

"Is it me?" Joni yelled. "Am I the one that you can't stand? Am I the one that you hate so much, to the point that you want to hurt me? And do you really expect anyone to believe that you actually could hurt them anyway? Sweet, calm Eden—could you ever really hurt someone?"

Their shouting had grown so loud now that it had finally attracted the attention of the others inside. The back door slid open and the rest of their friends all spilled out onto the back lawn to see what all the yelling was about. Joni was vaguely aware of their presence as she continued to shout.

"TELL ME!! Tell me the truth!"

And that's when Eden lost it once and for all.

"Who do I hate?" she screamed. "Right now? YOU, Joni! You're the one that I hate! But I have NO FUCKING IDEA WHAT LETTER YOU'RE TALKING ABOUT!"

On the last word, Eden placed her hands on Joni's shoulders and pushed her hard.

Joni had a moment of complete confusion as she lost her balance and started to fall backward. And just like when Clarke had head-butted Eden all those years ago in Adelaide, a surprising number of thoughts rushed through Joni's mind. First: disbelief, Eden had actually pushed her! She'd actually put her hands on her and pushed her backward. Like they were kids in a schoolyard fight. Then, fear—was she going to hurt herself? Followed closely by relief; no, she wasn't going to get hurt because there was a pool right there behind her, a soft landing!

But as she balanced for a moment at the edge of the pool, arms comically flailing, she realized that she wasn't going to have a soft landing after all. Because . . . well, why was her ankle twisting like that? And why was her body shifting, causing her to begin her descent at such a strange angle. They'd been having their conversation right down near the end of the pool, which meant that where Joni was about to fall wasn't just open water—it was the corner of the pool. And so that's why when she finally landed, instead of her body becoming completely encased in cool water, her head missed. And instead, it hit the hard, concrete edge of the side of the pool, with a horrible crack mixed in with the sound of the splash.

Right before it hit one more thought crossed Joni's mind.

Did she just say, "what fucking letter?"

Then nothing.

While Joni was sinking beneath the surface of the pool, there was a flurry of movement around her. Friends running toward the pool area, shouting, panicking. But before they were through the gate, Eden had already dived in. She grabbed hold of Joni's body—a deadweight in the water—and heaved her over to the side, where several hands were waiting to pull her up and out of the water.

Voices spoke over one another.

"Is she breathing?"

"Is she conscious?"

"Joni, can you hear us? Open your eyes."

"Someone call an ambulance."

"Is she going to be okay?"

Eden stayed in the water, her head above the surface and her arms sculling to keep her afloat as she watched the drama unfold.

"What the hell happened?"

"She pushed her, I saw it."

"Yes, but why, why were they fighting?"

"Does it matter?"

"Someone should get her out as well."

And then those same friends were pulling Eden out of the water as well. Rough hands heaving her up and over the edge. Cold air hitting skin. Goose bumps appearing up and down arms and legs. But Eden's eyes stayed fixed on Joni. And Joni remained unaware of a single thing that was going on around her.

Someone had called triple zero and was explaining the emergency over the phone. "She fell into the pool, hit her head, not responsive, not sure if she's breathing . . ."

"She didn't fall! Tell them she was pushed!"

"Why! What does that have to do with it, why do the paramedics need to know that?"

"I don't know! Aren't details important?"

"I don't think that detail is relevant, I mean, unless we're getting the police involved."

"The police? Don't be ridiculous. Why would we be getting the police involved?"

And then Kai's voice cut clear across the others. "Tell them she's pregnant as well."

The clamoring voices fell silent collectively as everyone thought the same thing.

Joni's pregnant?

Joni's pregnant, and right now, she's not breathing.

CHAPTER 19

When the ambulance was gone, taking both Joni and Kai away to the hospital, the remaining six friends were left standing awkwardly around Eden and Ben's backyard. Eden wrapped in a blanket, shivering and silent. Ben, ashen-faced and grim. Deb and Connor holding hands, both lost for what to do next. Trina and Josh resolutely avoiding one another's gaze.

Inside the ambulance, Joni was oddly simultaneously aware but not aware of what was going on around her as she drifted in and out of consciousness.

Trina was still drunk, but as the sound of the wailing siren died down in the distance, she took charge anyway. She sent Connor inside to see Aimee off. She instructed Ben to take Eden upstairs for a hot shower and fresh clothes. And she told Josh to just go home. Strangely enough, he listened.

Trina and Deb were left alone in the backyard.

Joni came to again. Her thoughts flew back through the streets to her friends. *Who is it? Who is it? Who is it?* she wondered.

"What the hell do you think happened out here?" Deb asked.

"I'm not entirely sure, but I think I have an idea. Did Joni say anything to you about an extra letter that she found?"

Deb frowned and shook her head. "No, what do you mean?"

"Well, I think maybe that's what this was all about. Joni told me she found an extra letter while we were away on holiday. A letter that someone wrote and then tried to get rid of—because they changed their mind about sharing it with us. She thought that it was mine. Anyway, the letter apparently talked about hating someone in our group. About wanting to hurt them. I think Joni must have figured out that the letter was written by Eden. Obviously, she confronted her and things got heated. And look, I don't know, I don't think Eden really did intend for Joni to get hurt when she pushed her. I think she thought she'd just fall in the water and that would be it. But the point is, she did get hurt and Eden's got some sort of issues that we need to sort out. So when she's done in the shower and all dressed, I think we should sit her down for a talk, right? I mean, do you agree we're better off dealing with this now? Tonight? While everything is still fresh? Or . . . or am I wrong?" Trina's voice was starting to falter but Deb nodded.

I have to get back there. I have to tell them I was wrong. I have to find out who wrote it.

* * *

"No, no, you're probably right. Although . . . maybe it's better if we don't both go confronting her over this? What if I just talk to her on my own, you know, so she doesn't feel like she's being ambushed."

"Maybe. Although Joni tried to talk to her on her own and look how that turned out."

"Yes, but obviously that's because Joni was the one that Eden was so obsessed with, right? So it's not like she's going to act out with me, is she?"

"I suppose," Trina conceded.

"God, this is so crazy, isn't it? I hope Joni's okay. Did you know she was pregnant?"

"No, but I did wonder when she talked about being designated driver tonight. You know she told me while we were away that she thought she was infertile? I told her it would happen, if she just relaxed and let it. But you know Joni, never one to be patient, is she?"

Trina or Deb? Trina or Deb? Did Trina lie to me when I asked her? Or was I wrong from the beginning?

"Totally true," said Deb. "So typical that she'd be the one to find the letter in the fire as well, isn't it?"

There was a pregnant pause.

Trina stared at Deb.

Deb stared back at Trina.

"I never mentioned the fire."

"What?"

Trina spoke carefully, an edge to her voice. "I didn't say anything about the fact that Joni found the letter in the fire."

"Yes, you did, you must have. How else would I have known that?"

"No"—Trina held firm—"I didn't."

"Well, then I guess I must have assumed, because . . . I don't know . . . that would just be the most obvious place, wouldn't it?"

"Deb. Don't lie to me."

Deb's face slowly changed.

She smiled at Trina.

Joni slipped back into the darkness and the ambulance officer continued to work on her as they rocketed around the corners on their way to the hospital.

"Can't get anything past you, can I?"

"You wrote the letter."

"Yep. I sure did."

"Fucking hell. So . . . who then? Who is it that you hate? Who is it that you wrote about in this letter?"

Deb gave Trina a funny look, then said, "You don't remember me, do you?"

"Remember you?! What are you on about? Remember you from when?"

"From almost thirty fucking years ago. When we went to the same primary school together."

Trina shook her head resolutely, "What are you *on* about? You didn't go to my primary school! All four of us went to different places before high school. You went to Saint Bernadette's! I went to Gladesville Public."

"Yes, but *before* that you were at Our Lady of Lourdes, weren't you? For two years, same as me. Then we both changed schools."

Trina was stunned, but she still didn't understand what any of this had to do with Deb's anger. "Deb!" she exclaimed. "I didn't know you went there as well. I mean, yeah, I was there just for kindy and Year One before my mum decided to swap me over to a public school. But are you sure about this? I don't remember you being there at all."

"Well, do you remember this? Do you remember that there was a girl in your class who had warts all over her hands?" And now Deb was stepping closer to Trina, holding out her hands for Trina to see. "A girl that everyone used to tease because of those warts? And do you remember being the one who came up with that horrible chant that everyone used to sing at me? *'Eenie, meenie, miney, moe, catch miss warty by the toe, if she touches you, let her go, and run home to the doctor.'*"

The ambulance pulled up outside the hospital. Kai tried not to get in the way as they expertly transferred Joni out of the back of the ambulance and in through the automatic doors.

Joni woke once more.

"Oh God. That was you? I felt awful for years about that, I've always hated that I teased that girl, I had no idea it was you."

"You felt awful for years? How do you think I felt?"

"But why didn't you ever say anything? Why did you even become my friend in high school if you hated me so much?"

"Because I didn't recognize you at first. In fact, I didn't know for a long time that you were the same person. Not until one of our holidays, a few years back, when we were all sitting around drinking and you mentioned something about going to a different school for kindy. You mentioned OLOL and I was just about to say, 'Hey, I went there too!' when all of a sudden I could remember you. This little girl that I'd hated all those years ago—her face merged with yours and I knew you were the same person. The kid who tortured me. Who got all the other girls *and* the boys to go along with it as well.

"And I was sitting there wondering whether or not I should say something. Whether or not I should confront you, but then the conversation changed and I'd missed my opportunity and I thought: '*Later.* I'll bring it up with her later, once I've figured out exactly what I want to say.'"

"But you should have! You should have just said something! I would have tried to explain."

Joni was being wheeled down the corridor. The paramedics gave clipped instructions as they handed her over. Kai tried to ask, he needed to know—but no one was paying him any attention. Joni tried to speak.

"At first I thought I would be able to just forgive you for it. I thought, 'As soon as I get this out in the open and clear the air, she'll say sorry for being such a little bitch and I'll be able to move on.' But the longer I let it fester, the harder it was to bring it up. And I felt so silly about the whole thing! I mean, it seemed so stupid that there was this insignificant thing from so long ago that was pressing down on me. I kept thinking, 'Well, but it doesn't even matter anymore. Because I'm a changed person now.' I mean, I know you and Joni and Eden have always thought of me as the coolest one within our group. The prettiest. The most assertive, independent, and sure of myself. So the idea that *I*—that someone like *me*— could be worrying about something like that, it just seemed laughable. It made me wonder if I wasn't really all of these things. If I was just conning the world into believing that I was this confident, strong-willed woman when instead I was just as fucked up as everyone else. And then I started to worry about what I would do if I brought it up and you reacted the wrong way! What if you weren't even sorry? What if you didn't give a shit, if you hadn't given it a second thought all these years? God, that made me crazy, imagining these different ways you might react. I even started picturing you singing that stupid chant at me again, expecting me to laugh along with it."

"Deb, please—"

"Let me finish! From there, I guess this rift started to form between us. A rift that you had no idea even existed. All of a sudden little things that you did seemed to just annoy me beyond belief! Things that I used to love about you—they just drove me crazy instead! The way you spoke, the way you acted, the jokes you made.

"But I kept pushing it deep down inside. I don't know why, for some reason it became my own dirty, little secret. This strange, palpable hatred I had for you. I was a good actress, though, wasn't I? And yeah, I know, that probably wasn't the right thing to do. Probably what I should have done was let myself drift away from this group of friends altogether. I should have distanced myself from you. Because if I was never going to work up the nerve to confront you, I really shouldn't have kept spending all that time with you—with someone I'd learned to hate so deeply.

"But can I tell you something? The hatred started to become sort of enjoyable. Like not being able to look away from the scene of an accident. I just couldn't look away. I found ways to provoke myself. Ways to get you to do the things that I knew would irritate me the most.

"Did you know that at the end of Year One I actually tried to burn the warts off my hand with a cigarette lighter?" Deb shoved her hands right under Trina's face, showing her the silvery-white scars and then she pulled them away again and stepped back, turned to look over at the pool, at the spot where Joni had hit her head, where there was just a smear of blood on the edge.

"And did you know that years later, when my mum sat me down to tell me that her and dad were getting a divorce, she cited that as one of the reasons?" Deb asked, keeping her gaze fixed on the water. "I mean, of course she wasn't trying to blame me, but she used it as an example. She stood in front of me and she said, 'Deb, it broke my heart when you did that to your poor little hands. And all this time I've thought, if I wasn't so focused on my own problems, on my issues with your dad, then maybe I would have been a better mother and I would have realized how much you were hurting before you took matters into your own hands.' Ridiculous, isn't it? She was trying to make me feel better, trying to tell me that they were getting divorced because she wanted to be a better mum—but instead she made me feel a million times worse! Because all I heard was 'Deb, if you didn't burn your hands, your dad and I wouldn't be getting a divorce.' Oh, she said other things, sure, other reasons. And I know now that it's not fair to blame one thing on the other especially considering it took nine years for them to go through with the divorce after I did that to my hands. But still, it hurt! It hurt just as much as it hurt back when you and the others made up your horrible rhymes and made those disgusted faces and made me feel like I had leprosy."

"Jesus Christ, Deb, stop! So for the past couple of years, ever since you found out I made fun of you as a kid, you've been blaming me for . . . for everything? For any kind of insecurity you've ever experienced? For your parents' divorce?"

Joni finally managed to make her voice work. "Father O'Reilly," she whispered.

"What?" said Kai. "No, Joni, honey, no; you're going to be fine. You don't need a priest."

Finally, Deb turned back from the pool and looked at Trina again. "Don't make it sound like I'm being unfair, okay! Because I'm not. Those kinds of things from someone's childhood—they can shape a person; you realize that?"

"Sure they can! But only if you let them!"

"You can't talk about that. You're the one who married a guy who's a complete asshole just because you grew up without a dad! How's that for letting things from your childhood shape your future? And that man has never been good enough for you, never. Always treated you like shit."

"Oh yeah? And why would you care about that anyway? I mean considering the fact that you hate me so much. I would have thought that would make you happy!"

"No! It doesn't. It frustrates the fuck out of me. You deserve better than that. And yes, I do hate you, but I also . . . God, I don't know, I sort of idolize you—and don't you dare laugh at me about that—but, you have to understand that when I was in high school, always acting like I didn't give a shit about anything and being so fucking cool, it was because I was always trying to be just as popular as you—or the you I remembered anyway, the little girl who'd picked on me, but who also had tons of friends and people who followed her and loved her. So like I said—once I put two and two together and worked out that you were the same person, I had these weird love-hate feelings for you. I was obsessed with you and I've been obsessed with you ever since. That's why I call you out on being too skinny and tell you straight when I think Josh is being unfair to you, because even though I hate you, I still need for you to be . . . to be . . . God, I don't know, I need you to be the queen bee I know you once were."

"But you also want to hurt me?"

"What?"

"Joni said the letter mentioned you wanting to actually, physically hurt somebody. So, is that part of this whole weird obsession as well, then? I mean, should I be worried that you're about to push me in the pool like Eden did to Joni?"

But Kai didn't understand what Joni meant. She didn't mean she wanted to see a priest. She meant that Father O'Reilly had it right. He'd picked

Deb as the fifth letter writer, and Joni had a strong feeling that all along, he'd had it right and she should have trusted his judgment in the first place and she'd just realized that it must have been Deb who had let Trina fall when they went abseiling.

"No! Yes! Jesus, I don't know. It's all messed up in my head. I'm so confused. Yes, I've had thoughts, horrible thoughts that I can't control where I think I just want to get back at you, but no, I don't think I'd ever actually do anything. They're just thoughts, that's all they are."

Trina closed her eyes, blocking Deb out, gathering her thoughts. And then she saw it. The image of the sky and the ground all tumbling and twisting into one around her as she fell. Felt her body slamming into the rock face when the rope pulled taut again, jerking her to a halt. The pain from the sharp knock to her head.

And she knew. Her eyes flew open again. "The abseiling accident," she said, her shoulders and back rigid, her hands clenched shut. "That was you, wasn't it? You were the one who was supposed to be hanging on to my rope. It wasn't a mix-up with Brett, you let go on purpose!"

"No!"

"Don't lie! You were shakier than I was when I got down to the ground—I'd never seen you look so afraid. I just thought it was because you cared about me, but it wasn't, was it? It was because you were feeling guilty about what you'd almost done."

"No, no, I didn't mean for that to happen. I just . . . I had one of my moments . . . one of my moments where I start to wonder about how it would feel if something ever happened to you . . . but I didn't really mean to let it go . . . Brett was readjusting something for me and all I did was just loosen my grip the tiniest bit, and the next thing, the rope was flying through my hands . . . but I didn't truly want you to get hurt, I didn't!

I grabbed hold again straightaway. Brett had to help me gain control again, but I was doing it, I was definitely doing it."

Deb was moving toward Trina again, trying to get close to her, a desperate look on her face, and Trina was backing away, shaking her head. "Stay away from me!"

"What the fuck is going on out here?" Josh was striding across the lawn toward them. "I came back because I forgot my jacket and the first thing I hear is you two out the back yelling at one another like hysterical schoolgirls. What the hell is wrong with the both of you? Trina, you need to come home with me."

"No."

"What do you mean, no? I should never have let you stay here in the first place. I thought I'd be nice and let you have your little chat with your messed-up friends and sort our shit out tomorrow. But now I see I was wrong about that. Get in the car."

Deb stepped forward, ready to argue with Josh, but Trina shoved her roughly to the side. "I don't need you to fight my battles for me and I don't want you to either. You want to see me be the tough bitch I once was? Watch."

And Trina turned back to her husband.

"Josh, you can't speak to me like that and you can't pretend like I didn't tell you today that I want a divorce, just because it's not something that you want. It's over between us. I tried to give you the chance to change, and to be honest, I gave you more time than I should have, but that's just because you made it harder than I thought it would be to find the strength to actually go through with it. But I'll tell you something, I have that strength now, I have all the strength I need and more. We're getting a divorce and you're going to have to deal with it."

Now Trina switched her attention back to Deb. "And you," she said.

"I'm sorry I hurt you all those years ago, I really am. But we're through. We're not friends anymore, Deb. Don't ever try to call me."

You have to call someone, Joni thought—because she'd lost her voice again—you have to call someone, Kai, you have to call them and warn them that Deb is dangerous. But then she was being wheeled through two large doors, away from Kai, and the doctors around her were talking about relieving some sort of pressure on her brain. And it was then that her thoughts shifted away from her friends as she realized that through- out all of this obsession around who wrote that damn letter, she hadn't spared a single thought for her unborn baby. *I'm sorry,* she thought, *I'm so, so sorry little one. Please hold on.* And then the darkness swallowed her up once again.

As Trina turned her back on both her friend and her husband, it was in- stinct that made her swing back around again—because she didn't even see Deb start to lunge at her from the corner of her eye, nor did she hear anything—she just sensed it. And next thing Deb was coming at her, arms outstretched, a crazed look on her face and one clear objective: revenge. She wanted to cause Trina pain. Her hands were aiming for her throat. Trina felt Josh start to move in as well. *Oh, that's sweet, he does care about me, he wants to protect me.*

But I don't need your help, buddy.

And she punched Deb right in the face.

By the time Ben had brought Eden back downstairs, dressed in warm tracksuit pants and a jumper, hair still damp from the shower, their guests had all vanished.

It was for the best, though, because it meant the two of them could finally have an honest conversation. And Eden was able to tell Ben the truth about Adelaide. When she was done, he gave her the reaction she'd been waiting for all these years. He reached out and pulled her into his arms, holding her tight and letting her cry into his chest for as long as she needed.

Kai didn't want to let her in when they heard the soft knock at the door. But Joni gave him a nod and he conceded, opening the door and allowing Eden to hurry into the hospital room and straight across to Joni's bed. She stopped short then, though, and Joni knew why. It was the shock of Joni's appearance. The bandage wound around her head and the large patch of her hair that had been shaved away.

"Joni," Eden began, "you have to know . . . I'm so, so sorry. I never meant for you to get hurt, I just . . . I just lost it, and all that I thought would happen would be you falling into the pool and then you'd climb back out and be annoyed with me for getting your clothes wet and that would be it. I didn't want you to get so hurt," she said again.

"I know," said Joni quietly. "I know you couldn't have predicted me hitting my head like that."

Joni saw the question on Eden's lips, knew what she was about to ask next, but she couldn't bear it, so she delayed it a little longer and got in first with her own question.

"You heard about what happened with Deb and Trina?" she asked.

"Yes. How did you know?"

"Trina's already been to see me."

"Oh."

"You know the only reason I thought it was you was because I found out your letter was a fake. It just seemed then like you were the most logical. Why *did* you write a fake letter, Eden?"

Eden sat down on the end of Joni's bed and shrugged. "It was a weird thing to do. I know that. And I should have used those stupid letters as my opportunity to share the truth. But I sat down in front of the computer and all I could think was—'This isn't the right way to tell you all about what actually did happen to me in Adelaide.' It's almost as though the truth was too . . . too grimy to share as a part of this whole girlie truth-or-dare-style secret-sharing thing. And then you guys were all banging on the door, telling me to hurry up so the next person could write their letter, and so I panicked. And I knew I had to come up with something to write about. Something worthy of what we were doing. A teenage pregnancy! It seemed like the perfect lie to tell and the time I'd spent in Adelaide meant I'd been away just long enough for the lie to be feasible.

"I regretted it as soon as the letter was read aloud by the bonfire that night and you all started asking questions. All I could do was keep my answers short and simple, and thankfully, eventually you all stopped questioning me and I thought, 'Okay, that's it, I got away with it.' But I knew it would catch up with me before too long."

"Do you want to tell me what really happened in Adelaide?"

"Yeah, I do. And I will, but not right now. Please, Joni, I need to know . . . Have you . . . have you lost . . . the baby?" she asked. Joni could see that Eden was holding her breath as she waited, praying that Joni would say no. And Joni wished she could give her the answer she wanted.

Joni turned to look out the window, and Kai, who had been sitting quietly on a chair on the other side of the room, stood up and came to hold Joni's hand.

"I'm not pregnant anymore," said Joni. "But the thing is, the doctor says she's not one hundred percent sure about whether or not I actually ever was pregnant. It was so early; you know? So there's a possibility it was really just a false positive. Sometimes it happens, she said—for instance, if maybe the egg was fertilized but it was never really viable in the first place. And most people who have that happen to them don't even know that anything actually occurred. They just get their period a little late. At the same time, if I *was* pregnant, if it was a true positive, then yes—the accident could have made me lose it. Or more so, the surgery they performed afterward to reduce the swelling of my brain."

Joni watched as Eden's face fell, her lip trembled, and the tears started to fall.

"I was lucky, though. They got to it quick enough that there was no long-term brain damage," said Joni. "So that's good, right? And the other thing is, the doctor that's looking after me here did say it's highly unlikely that I would have been pregnant. I knew all along that there was something up with my body, that there was a reason it was taking us so long to conceive, and I knew that my GP was being too blasé about it all. I didn't have any symptoms—apart from the fact that we were having trouble conceiving—so he wasn't willing to investigate it for me—he wanted me to be patient and come back after we'd tried a little longer.

"Anyway, turns out I was right. The doctor here, she did an ultrasound to check things out for me, and it turns out I have something called fibroids—these growths on my uterus. Funny thing is, most women who get these can still get pregnant, but apparently I'm a special case, because I have them both on the inside of my uterus *and* on the outside—and one of them is distorting the shape of my uterus. She said surgery is a possibility but then there's the risk of scarring in the uterus, which comes with its own issues. Basically, she said the odds of me having fallen pregnant naturally considering the state of my uterus at the moment were very slim. So you don't need to blame yourself, Eden, because I can't lose a baby if there was never any baby to lose."

Eden put her hand to her mouth and began to sob. "But you could have been, Joni. That could have been your miracle chance and I might be the reason you lost it."

Eden's devastation was palpable and it tore at Joni's heart, because what if she was right? What if that had been her one chance and it had been ripped away from her?

"Eden," said Joni then, "I'm sorry to do this, I know you feel awful . . . but could you please leave now? I just need to be alone."

After Eden had left, Kai squeezed her hand. "Do you want me to leave you alone as well?" he asked.

Joni shook her head. "No," she said. "I need you right here." And she let the fresh wave of sobs engulf her.

CHAPTER 20

J oni and Kai sat side by side at the airport, holding hands as they waited for the boarding call for their flight. Her short curls sat close to her scalp. The area they'd needed to shave was too large for her to cover up, so she'd had to cut it all off. But she was kind of starting to like her new look.

It was quite remarkable how quickly and easily they had made all the decisions and then the arrangements to make this all happen.

Should we sell the house or rent it out?

Do we both quit our jobs or just me? And can you take a leave of absence for this long if you don't quit?

Do we start with Italy or Spain?

Do you think our families are going to forgive us for taking off for so long with so little notice?

Backpacks or suitcases?

Can we really afford to just travel for this long without working?

And the most important question:

Do we still keep trying for a baby? Or do we just stop?

In the end, though, the answers had come so easily to them because they had both realized that there were more important things in life than worrying about what might or might not be.

And Joni had to really reassess why it was that she had ever wanted to get pregnant. Did she actually want to have children? Or was it all just a part of her whole, keeping-up-with-her-friends obsession?

"I heard that Deb's pregnant," said Joni, her voice a little tight.

"Oh, really?" asked Kai. "Is that a good idea? Considering everything she's, ah . . . going through at the moment?"

"I don't know. Maybe it'll be good for her. I know she's been seeing a psychiatrist. And I think now that she got everything out in the open, it made it easier for her to start getting over her whole thing with Trina. Plus, the fact that Trina's now out of her life, so I guess it's like there's no trigger anymore."

"Are you . . . how do you feel about that? I mean about the fact that she's pregnant?"

Joni shrugged. "I feel . . . okay, I guess. But I'm glad we're going to be out of the country for the next little while. I don't know," she said then. "Maybe you're just not meant to stay friends with people from high school for so long after school. Maybe it just doesn't work."

"Maybe," said Kai, giving her hand a squeeze.

Before they'd headed to the airport, Joni had taken the time to make just one more trip to see Father O'Reilly.

"So it was Deb all along, then?"

"Yep, crazy Deb we all call her now."

"Oh, well, I don't think that's going to really help with her recovery."

"I'm just kidding, Father! No, to be honest, the four of us haven't really seen each other since I got out of hospital. I've spoken a little with some of them, here and there—you know, just caught up on the latest— but mostly it feels like we're all drifting apart."

"How does that make you feel?"

"A bit shit. Sorry—I mean a bit bad. But then again, also kinda good, like we need this. I do know that Trina's moved in with her mum and it seems like the separation with Josh is going pretty well. I mean, he's still a dick, obviously. Sorry, but he is. But they did at least manage to sort out custody and they split up their assets as well, all without too much trouble. And she joined her new basketball team, so I guess she's out there making new friends now. Good for her, right?"

"Absolutely."

"I heard that Eden and Ben are doing great now too. I guess the positive thing about her pushing me in the pool was that it kinda made us even—you know? She forgave me for the whole almost-kissing-her-husband thing because she was so desperate for me to be okay with her about my fall."

"Are you okay with her about that?"

"Yes. I am. Because the more I think about it, the more I believe that I never was pregnant in the first place. You might believe in miracles Father, but I'm more of a realist. Besides, traveling the world child-free is looking pretty damned good right about now.

"Anyway, I'm hoping that Eden might have confronted her mum

about how badly she let her down in Adelaide. I still can't believe she didn't trust her own daughter, that she let that slimy bastard sell her that piece-of-crap story. Insane. You know, I did get the chance to ask Eden why she didn't tell us what had happened as soon as she got back to Sydney, though. I mean, we were her best friends! We would have believed her; we could have helped her! She said she was going to. She said she wanted to tell us the first day she came back to school. But apparently someone said something that made her feel like she couldn't. I don't know who it was or what they said, but God, it's such a shame that she was stopped in her tracks when she could have started healing so much sooner."

"Hey, tell me something. Did she ever explain why she reacted that way with the guy in the pub when you were on your holiday? You know, the one where you thought she randomly lost it."

"Yeah, she did actually. Apparently, it was the words he whispered in her ear: 'Let's just have some fun.' She said it was the exact same phrasing that asshole back in Adelaide used on her. Sent her right off the edge, poor girl."

"That's awful. I wish that bloke from Adelaide turned up to see me for confession. I'd give him more than a few Hail Marys."

"Father! You can't say that! Anyway . . . he might have already got what was coming to him . . ."

"Is that right? Okay. Out with it. What did you do?"

"Okay, so . . . I may have tracked him down on Facebook. And I may have discovered that he'd moved to Sydney. And that he works at a pretty big accounting firm in the city these days."

"And . . . ?"

"And . . . it's probably best I don't tell you any more than that. You don't want me to start confessing all over again, do you?"

"Probably not. All right, then. We'll leave it there. I'm trusting that *you didn't cross a line, though. Now, what about the third friend? Crazy Deb, as she's now known. How's she doing?"*

"Better. She got help and I know she hates the fact that she ever felt that way about Trina. But Trina won't take her calls, and I don't know if she ever will. And I can understand that. Although then again, Trina is the one who gave her a bloody nose and two black eyes when she punched her in the face—I told you that, right? On the flip side, though, Deb professed to having murderous feelings for Trina, so, you know, tit for tat, right? Ha. Connor's kept Eden and me updated via e-mail, though. Told us he'd become a stay-at-home dad—firstly so that he could help Deb out during her, ah . . . mental health recovery, but then, even when she was ready to go back to work. He decided he liked being home with Ruby. And now apparently she's pregnant, and the plan is, she'll just take six weeks off work with the baby and then he'll take over and keep being a stay-at-home dad. He said Deb loves it. Said she really struggled with the transition into motherhood. Loved Ruby beyond belief but felt like she was losing herself. She's much happier now. I think she'd love the chance to make things up to Trina, though. I'm just not sure that will ever happen.

"Anyway, I should get going. We're leaving for the airport soon and Kai's going to think I've turned into some sort of religious nut—no offense—with all these long visits I've had here at the church. I'll miss talking to you, though. Maybe I'll send you a postcard?"

"A postcard would be great. You take care, okay?"

"Will do."

CHAPTER 21

—————

Two and a Half Years Later

Joni was the first one to arrive at the café. She looked around for a familiar face, but after realizing there was no one else there, she chose a table in the corner and sat down to watch for the others.

She didn't know for sure who had written the letter asking her to be here. But if she had to guess, she thought she had a pretty good idea of who it would be. And the letter was pretty damn convincing.

It felt strange that an entire two years could have passed without her having really seen any of her group of friends whom she had once been so close to. In the early days, there had been the odd phone call or e-mail here and there, but it hadn't taken long for communication between the four of them to dry up. Too much history. Too much bad blood.

She had to admit, she was sort of looking forward to telling them all about her life of late. How great traveling the world had been. How she and Kai couldn't wait to start planning their next trip. At the same time, though, she was feeling extremely peculiar—just the thought of seeing her three closest friends after what felt like such a long, long time. And the fact that they'd been separated by oceans for the last couple of years made the divide seem even wider. She felt like she'd become a different person while they'd traveled. Reinvented herself a bit—because she could. Tried things that would probably make Deb scoff—like meditating in mountaintop temples, hiking through rain forests, and jumping down waterfalls—and so she was feeling somehow . . . aloof from the others. As though she'd grown apart from them, experienced things that they would never experience. And then she remembered that Trina, Eden, and Deb had all experienced motherhood, the one thing Joni never would—and she was brought back down to the ground a bit.

They'd made their decision, though, her and Kai. While they were traveling they'd come to the final realization that no, they didn't want to keep trying for kids—for them, it wasn't meant to be.

Joni looked up then to see Trina standing in front of her—she hadn't even noticed her come in. She was looking lean and fit, but at the same time, she'd definitely put some weight on since Joni had seen her last. Divorce was agreeing with her. She looked well.

"Was it you?" Trina asked.

"Not me," said Joni, knowing exactly what she was talking about.

"Then I guess that just leaves . . ."

"Eden or Deb," said Joni—and as she spoke she saw a second familiar face approaching the two of them. Eden wound her way between the tables and chairs and then stopped and stood next to Trina and gave them all a hopeful smile.

"So this is a nice surprise, isn't it?" she said.

"A surprise? Really?" asked Trina. "Don't try and tell me it wasn't you."

"I have no idea what you're talking about," Eden said sweetly.

Joni and Trina both tipped their heads to the side to examine Eden's stomach. "Is that . . ." began Joni.

"Yeah," agreed Trina. "Is that what we think it is?"

"You'll be in so much trouble if it isn't," sang a waitress who was passing their table.

Eden laughed. "They're safe," she said. "Yeah," she continued, looking back at Joni and Trina, "Ben and I decided to go for a third. Wow, Joni," she added then, "I can't believe how tanned you are. And your hair is so blond now. Where exactly have you been traveling?"

Joni shrugged. "Just wherever it's summer really," she replied, and instantly realized she sounded like a complete wanker. "Just all over," she said. "But hang on, you both know the rules, no talking until we've ordered. I'm going up to the counter, you guys want me to order you something?"

"A coffee, please?" asked Trina.

"Extra-hot latte?"

"Yep."

"Eden?"

"Hot chocolate for me, please. Double marshmallows."

They all turned then when they heard the café door open once again. Joni looked quickly at Trina. "You ready for this?" she asked.

"Yep."

They all three watched as Deb picked her way through the café across to their table, and all three sets of eyes were on the bundle in her arms. When she reached them, Joni started doing the math. That looked like a newborn baby in Deb's arms. But she was pregnant more than two years ago when Joni and Kai had left for their trip! That baby should be one and a half by now!

"Okay," said Joni, standing up to take a closer look. "I'm breaking the no-chatting rule. Did you have two babies in a row, Deb?" she asked. "How did we not know this?"

Deb shook her head. "No," she said. "I wondered if any of you had heard. I lost my little one in between Ruby and Sage here. I had a mis-carriage."

"Oh, Deb," said Joni, "I'm sorry. I'm so, so sorry."

"No," said Deb as tears started to slide down her cheeks, "I'm sorry. I'm sorry for what I did to this group. I'm sorry that I tore us all apart," and now she turned to Trina: "And I'm sorry for what I did to you," she said, "for the way I treated you."

Trina carefully pried the baby out of Deb's arms as she continued to cry. "It's okay, Deb," she said. "We all tore this group apart, all four of us. So let's put the past behind us, hey? I think it's time for us all to move on." Trina looked down at Sage. "She's gorgeous, Deb, absolutely beautiful."

After that, they all started hugging. Hugging and crying and then laughing and then crying some more. The waitress watched the four of them with complete, unadulterated, and unapologetic fascination.

Then they starting talking.

They learned that a couple of months back, Eden had been singing at one of her regular restaurants when a scout had approached her and asked her if she would be willing to audition for the next season of *The Voice*. At first she'd turned him down, but then Pete, the head chef at the restaurant—and also her ex-boyfriend—had confessed that he had been the one to call the scout and so she promised him she'd at least think about it, and now . . . well, she was thinking that she might actually go through with it. Although if she got through to the show, the timing was going to be a little tight with this next baby, but she was just going to play it by ear and see what happened.

"That guy totally still holds a torch for you, Eden." Trina laughed.

They found out that Deb had recently finished up with her psychia-trist and that she was also starting to develop a better relationship with her parents, having finally forgiven them for getting divorced and for making her feel like it was her fault. She told them how, while the second pregnancy, the one that she'd lost, had been completely unplanned, she and Connor had decided a little while later that they wanted to try for another. And now that she had Sage, the whole thing of being a mum had finally started to click into place for her. All of a sudden she got it.

She understood how to divide her love—and she understood how to prioritize. "It's like that thing where on an airplane you're always supposed to put your own oxygen mask on first before assisting children," she explained. "It makes sense, right? If you're not okay, then how can you take care of your kids? So now I do all the things that *I* need to do to make sure I feel sane—like letting Connor be a stay-at-home dad while I keep working. And like taking my antianxiety meds. Taking care of me means I can take care of my kids."

At one stage, Deb hopped up to order another round of coffees and she swiftly passed Sage across to Joni without asking, and Joni found herself looking down at this squishy little face with deep blue eyes and she thought to herself, *This is all I need. Cuddles with my friends' babies. This is enough.*

They heard how well Nate was doing at preschool, how Trina was currently tossing up whether he'd be ready for school next year or if she should hold him back until the following year. And that the nice thing about that was that she and Josh were discussing it together like proper, mature adults. Josh had recently started dating a woman from work and Trina was perfectly fine with that. Happy in fact, to see him moving on. Although she was planning on keeping a bit of an eye on him. Watching for any sign that he was back to old habits and behaving in that spoiled, controlling way. She didn't want to see another woman go through what she had gone through.

Trina also told them about the new apartment she'd rented so that she could move out of her mum's place. It was small, but it was filled with sunshine, and most importantly, it was all hers. And she'd just recently started dating herself.

"Oh, that's so exciting," Joni said when Trina paused to take a sip of her coffee. "So who is he? What's he like? What's his name?"

"Well, he's a psychologist now, but he actually used to be a priest! Apparently he discovered through taking confession from the congregation that he missed his old life where he used to be able to talk with people and help them solve their issues. Well, that and the fact that he was a Catholic priest and he also missed sex. So he decided to ask to be released from his vow and the Church let him go. His name is Matt O'Reilly."

EPILOGUE

——————

Dear Girls,

I know you probably don't want to see anyone from our old group anytime soon, but I'm asking you to meet up for maybe just one last coffee. One last chance to see one another ... to maybe reminisce, catch up—and I don't know, maybe even mend some bridges?

If you're willing, meet me at the Coffee Bean Hut on Wallace Street at 2 P.M. this Friday.

If you need more convincing, take a look at the attached photocopied pages.

Love
From Me

This is the official diary of Joni Camilleri, Eden Chester, Deborah Camden, and Trina Chan. The purpose of this journal is to share secrets and pass hidden messages in class. All information recorded in this diary stays between the four of us. Feel free to write whatever you want in here, whenever you want to.

My turn first! Joni Camilleri reporting for duty!! So! I was just in math and you won't believe what happened. Greg Henderson threw a salad sandwich at the ceiling fan and it totally exploded. I mean, it went everywhere. I got a piece of tomato down the back of my neck. So gross. He is such an idiot. Anyway, that's all I have to say for now. See you at lunchtime!

Hi, this is Deb. I am being made to write in here by force. I have absolutely nothing to say. Except that Chad Forbes is the hottest guy in school. But that is IT. I will not write in here again. It's silly.

P.S. Love youse.

Hi all,
Guess it's my turn, then, seeing as Deb just shoved this into my arms as I was on my way to design and tech class. So what are we supposed to write in here again? Hang on, let me just read the instructions at the top. Oh yeah—we share secrets and stuff . . . riiiight. Um, I hate design and tech, does that count? Probably not, 'cause I guess it's not really a secret, is it? You all already know that I hate D and T, right? Oh, crap, Mr. Gallea is looking over at me and I think he's wondering what I'm writing in . . . gotta goooo!

—Trin

Hi everyone,
My turn. I mean, Eden's turn . . . me.

I actually do have something to tell you and it's KILLING me. This is the all-time WORST news ever. Okay, so please don't hate me . . . but . . . Dad is making us move to Adelaide because of his STUPID JOB. Apparently we have to move there for an ENTIRE SIX MONTHS. I am devastated. Please, please, please promise me you will *all* write to me, *all* the time. Every day. You have to. No take-backs. We have to stay friends forever. Swear it.

Love, Eden

I solemnly swear that I will write to you every day (or, okay, at least every week) and that we will stay friends forever.

—Joni Camilleri

I don't promise to write all the time. But I will write *sometimes* and we can stay friends. Okay? That good enough?

—Deb Camden

I hereby pinkie promise to be your friend forever, Eden. And Joni and Deb too.

—Trina Chan

Thank you everyone. I promise it right back too. Friends forever and for always.

—Eden Chester

ACKNOWLEDGMENTS

Writing this novel has been a wonderful roller coaster of an adventure with all sorts of people to thank along the way. To my astonishingly fabulous editors, Carrie Feron, Anna Valdinger, Maxine Hitchcock and Mary Rennie, along with every other person on the Australian, U.S., and U.K. publishing teams: my heartfelt gratitude for all the hard work you put into this book to coax the final story out of the original manuscript.

To Pippa Masson, thank you for continuing to be such an extraordinary agent (and thank you also to Tara Wynne for stepping in while Pippa is otherwise engaged!). I'm also very grateful to Sheila Crowley and Kate Cooper for being equally wonderful agents across the ocean. To Diane and Bernie Moriarty, Madeleine and Arthur Menasse, Liane Moriarty, Jaci Moriarty, Kati Harrington and Fiona Ostric—I'm forever grateful for all of the advice, the babysitting, the cappuccinos, and goodies and, of course, an extra special thank you to those of you who were kind enough to read early drafts and offer invaluable feedback.

Several people helped me out with various content-related questions (including but not limited to, horse riding queries, medical advice, and rock climbing tips), thank you Simone Monaghan, Kerry Lockwood, Colin Macdonald, and Bosco Tan. To Emilie Martin, thank you for allowing me to use your brilliant lasagne analogy and to everyone on Facebook that answered my inane questions regarding names of bands and songs from the 90s, you're all brilliant! I'm also extremely appreciative of all of the wonderful readers who kindly reach out and let me know when they enjoy my writing along with all of the book bloggers and Facebook friends and Twitter followers I've connected with along the way. Youeni Café, thank you for allowing me to sit at your counter for several hours at a time while I was working on this book and for always remembering my coffee order.

Finally, a gigantic thank you to Steve, Maddie, and Piper Menasse for being the best and most supportive family a Nicola could ever dream of.

About the author

About the book

Read on

Insights,
Interviews
& More...

Meet Nicola Moriarty

NICOLA MORIARTY is a Sydney-based novelist, copywriter, and mum to two small (but remarkably strong-willed) daughters. In between various career changes, becoming a mum, and completing her BA, she began to write. Now she can't seem to stop. Her previous works include the novels *Free-Falling* and *Paper Chains,* and the novella *Captivation,* as well as contributions to two UK anthologies. She was awarded the Fred Rush Convocation prize from Macquarie University, along with "Best Australian Debut" from Chicklit Club. She blogs (occasionally) at her website here: www.nicolamoriarty.com.au.

Behind the Book

I'm sitting in a café, and I'm supposed to be writing. In fact, I was writing, and it was going pretty well. But every now and then I found myself looking up to watch a group of middle-aged women who are sitting having coffee. When they first arrived, there were just two of them, but they pulled extra chairs up to the table and, eventually, the others arrived. Seven women. One of them was having a birthday, as a few of them had handed her gift bags as they arrived.

The more I glance across at them, the more I wonder about their lives. How do they all know one another? How did they become friends? Do they always all get along? They all seem so different. One has closely cropped, gray hair, thick, square glasses, and a sleeveless black top. Another looks motherly, with her shoulder-length bob and three-quarter pants. One is tall, thin, and businesslike, another looks to be the youngest—long hair, wide belt, shorts.

When the last one turned up, I realized something. That might be us one day. I have a group of girlfriends who have been a part of my life now for around twenty years. There are seven of us. Seven girls who became friends in high school and stayed friends despite all the constant changes throughout our lives.

We used to see each other at least five times a week. Now we can easily go five weeks without meeting up. When we see ▶

Behind the Book *(continued)*

each other, our voices all start tumbling. We talk about our days, our weeks, our kids, our partners, our parents, our parents-in-law. We give advice—whether it's wanted or not. We reminisce and we usually start laughing at some point, loudly enough to annoy the people at the next table.

I'm looking over at these women again, and I'm wondering if they've ever been drunk together. Have they ever cried over the phone with one another? Have they ever threatened to punch a boy because he broke their friend's heart? Have they held each other's hair back when they were sick? Have they shared secrets and fears? And have they ever nearly broken apart?

Because there were times. There were moments when we nearly fell apart. Moments when we fought, when boyfriends came between us or religion or politics or values caused a disagreement. And in that moment of wondering, an idea is sparked. And I'm thinking, what if one of those disagreements that nearly tore us apart had been bigger? What if there had been a long-held secret that someone in our group had kept locked away—and one day, it erupted between us and caused our group to implode?

And all of the sudden I knew—I had the seeds of my next book.

I'm just lucky that, for me, it's only fiction. Although, then again, we do have a girls' weekend away booked for next month. ∽

Reading Group Guide

1. The book's narrator, Joni, is disappointed to learn that her childhood friends don't share everything like they used to. Do you think she's being dramatic? How many of your secrets do you share with your friends?

2. Do you believe Joni as a narrator, or do you think her point of view is skewed?

3. Even in her letter, Joni didn't share what was happening in her quest for a child. Why do you think she held that back, even as she was hoping for greater connection with her girlfriends?

4. One of the secrets revealed is that someone has a crush on another woman's husband. Is this sort of feeling better kept private or discussed openly? Would you have shared such a secret?

5. It was Joni who pulled Deb, Trina, and Eden into a friendship on that first day of school, and Joni who brings them together in the cottage years later. Does everyone have a role in a friendship group? Discuss the consequences of this and how these roles change over time.

6. For years Eden kept what really happened in Adelaide a secret from her friends. Even when given the ▶

opportunity to share her secret in
the letter she backed out of spilling
the truth. What did you think when
you learned her truth? Were you
surprised?

7. Drinking is a recurring topic in the
novel, from Deb's drunken escapade
at school to Eden's horrific attack in
Adelaide to Trina's behavior at Eden's
dinner party. Do you think the story
would be different if these women
hadn't overindulged?

8. Are friendships with those you
meet in childhood different from
ones formed later in life? How does
meeting at a young age change your
relationship?

9. Joni and Eden are both desperate
to win the Dirty Thirty Challenge.
Is competitiveness healthy within
friendships? When does it become
too much?

10. In one of the letters, a woman reveals
worries over being a bad mother while
her husband is ready for a second
child. Reading the examples given in
the letter, are the concerns legitimate?
Why do you think these pressures still
concern women more than men?

11. Were you surprised when you learned
who wrote the fifth letter? Who did
you think wrote it while you were
reading? Discuss the ways in which
the author toys with the reader. ∽

Excerpt from
Those Other Women

Prologue

She wrapped it up in a blanket and she walked. She walked and walked until her heels were rubbed raw and blisters appeared on her soles. She left the city and she continued on through the suburbs, past darkened red-brick bungalows with neatly mowed lawns and curtains drawn tight. She put one foot in front of the other until she found a national park. Hectares upon hectares of dense bush. Towering scribbly gums and wattle trees spread wild. She pushed her way through shrubs that scratched at her ankles and branches that lashed at her cheeks. Distant howls mingled with the honeyed sounds of owls hunting possums and snakes. Deep inside, she chose a spot near the slow-moving waters of a thin creek. The ground was hard but she raked at the claylike soil with her fingernails, scraping and digging and pushing the dirt aside until a small cavern was formed. Serenaded by a chorus of frogs and cicadas she placed the small bundle inside and covered it over with dirt and twigs.

    And then she ran. ▸

The Imposter

The exhausted mother stole five minutes to creep into the bathroom and lock the door. It was the school holidays and the kids seemed to want every bit of her attention at every single moment. So this was the one place she could demand privacy. Although she knew some mothers couldn't even find peace in there. Recently she'd seen a photo on Facebook of a toddler's fingers wriggling under the bathroom door, vying for its mother's attention.

But she'd laid down the law from day one with her kids. *You don't need to watch me poop. I don't care how lonely you are. I don't care if you want a Vegemite sandwich right this second. I don't care if you're desperate for me to see the exact scene of the* Trolls *movie that's on at the moment—a scene I've already seen fifteen times before. Right now, in here, it's Mummy's time.*

She leaned against the toothpaste-smeared sink, signed into her secondary account on Facebook, and flicked across to the group. Just being logged in under the fake persona made her breathe a sigh of relief. A gentle calm washed over her. She may have joined with an ulterior motive in mind, but now, this was her alternate reality. Here she was someone else. Here she could shake off everything that defined her. Mother. Wife. Constant caregiver. Her surrounds melted away, the soggy bath mat underfoot, the plastic toys stacked on the edge of the bath, and the streaked glass of the shower screen that beckoned to be wiped cleaned.

Did she feel a level of guilt about the fact that she was lying to these women?

Yes, of course she did. But it didn't last. ▶

PART ONE

Poppy

Chapter 1

December

Poppy pulled into the driveway of the tall, gray, Harris Park town house she rented with her husband. It was a gorgeous summer's evening, and as much as she was loving the warmer months, she wasn't enjoying the way the back of her blouse was sticking to the car seat. It was too hot to cook, so she'd picked up Chinese takeaway on her way home from work. Wontons instead of spring rolls because they were Garret's favorite. Steamed rice instead of fried because she was "making an effort" to choose healthier options. Beef in black bean sauce plus battered honey chicken because she wasn't making *that* much of an effort. Harris Park was only twenty kilometers west of Sydney's center, but the drive home from her office in North Sydney usually took more than an hour thanks to traffic. She was ravenous.

She climbed out of the car and immediately realized that the beef and black bean sauce had spilled out of the container and soaked through the paper bag. Poppy carried it carefully out in front, trying not to get the sauce on her white shirt. On the way to the door she noticed that the leaves on the row of hedging lilly pillys they'd planted down the side of the driveway had shriveled and turned a burned crispy brown in the summer heat. She wondered if they would be salvageable.

She struggled to get the keys in the door while holding the leaking bag of Chinese and she was momentarily irritated with Garret for not hearing the jangling sound and coming to give her a hand. When the lock finally yielded, she stepped inside and felt an odd sense that something was different. She ignored it, though, she needed to get the Chinese food through to the kitchen before it dripped.

"Hope you didn't start cooking," she sang out as she stepped out of her heels and padded through to the kitchen in stockinged feet.

Poppy stopped short at the doorway. Garret was sitting at the table, staring up at her, hands clasped in front of him. Beside him was her best friend, Karleen, ▶

hands identically clasped. The two of them looked like they were on a panel ready to interview her.

Poppy grinned at them. Her birthday was approaching next month. They must have been planning something special for her. Later, she hated that she could have been so naive.

"Karleen! I didn't see your car out front. There's enough if you want dinner," she started to gabble, holding the soggy paper bag out in front, "provided I haven't lost too much from the split container."

"Poppy, sit down, would you?" Karleen motioned toward the bench seat opposite.

Poppy wasn't overly taken aback. That's what Karleen had always been like. Abrupt and commanding. But Garret's silence started to worry her. Plus, the fact that he didn't seem to want to meet her eyes.

Poppy dumped the food on the table and sat. "What's up, guys? Is something wrong?"

"You have to understand, Poppy," Karleen said, her voice even more emphatic than usual as she reached across to put one hand over the top of Poppy's, her curly hair bouncing around her face, "we're not doing this to hurt you."

"Sorry, what is it that I'm supposed to understand?"

Karleen continued as though Poppy hadn't spoken. "And that's why we want to be as up-front and honest as possible with you."

"Sorry," Poppy repeated, "what exactly are you telling me?" She looked to Garret for clarification, because so far he'd remained quiet, had let Karleen do all the talking.

But he continued to stay silent.

"It's not the kind of thing we can control, Poppy," Karleen went on. "We didn't mean for this to happen. We just fell, you know?"

A cool burning sensation was making its way up Poppy's arms. It crept up her neck, it flushed her face.

"You fell?" Poppy tried again to catch Garret's eye, but he wouldn't look at her, refused to meet her gaze.

"Yes," said Karleen. "We fell . . . in love."

"What? Don't be ridiculous! This is a joke, right?"

"No, Poppy, this is very, very serious. We've been sleeping together. We can't lie to you anymore."

Poppy snatched her hand out from under Karleen's. She glared at her friend, willing her to tell her that it wasn't true, that it was all a joke—a nasty practical joke—but a joke nonetheless. But instead Karleen simply held her gaze unflinchingly and Poppy was the one who had to break eye contact. She looked down at her trembling hands and saw black bean sauce under her fingernails. She stood and walked over to the sink, turned on the tap, and started scrubbing at her fingers, digging under her nails with the dishcloth. A large black blowfly landed ▶

on the draining board next to her, twitched its wings, and inched toward some crumbs left behind from breakfast. She automatically crouched down to fetch the flyswatter from the cupboard under the sink and then stopped. An image of her chasing a fly around the kitchen while Garret and Karleen waited for her to react to their news crossed her mind and she couldn't tell if she was on the verge of tears or laughter. It all just felt so absurd. She straightened and saw that the fly was gone.

Karleen and Garret.
Garret and Karleen.

Her best friend and her husband, announcing that they were in love. But Garret didn't even like Karleen that much. Sure, they got along okay, but more as a matter of convenience, the way any husband gets along with his wife's best friend. But he also whinged about her to Poppy. Complained if she talked too much when the three of them went to the movies together. Said she had terrible taste in restaurants when she booked dinner for them at the new Mexican place on Arthur Street.

So what, now Poppy was supposed to believe he'd all of the sudden fallen in love with her? It didn't make any sense. Or had his complaints about Karleen been a ruse?

Karleen appeared behind her then, wrapped one arm around her shoulder, and reached out the other to flick on the kettle. "Here, Poppy, I'll make you a cup of peppermint tea," she said, as if tea was going to fix everything.

Poppy squirmed out of Karleen's hold and backed away from her, placing one hand on the smooth rounded edge of the laminate bench to steady herself. Inside, she was tumbling. Tumbling and rolling and falling and crashing. Inside, she couldn't breathe.

But on the outside, she remained still. She couldn't find the right words, didn't know what to say. So instead she simply watched as Karleen casually went through her cupboards to grab the mugs and tea bags. In truth, Poppy understood that the only reason Karleen knew her kitchen so well was that she was her best friend, but now it felt like her familiarity in Poppy's home was a result of her relationship with Garret, and that betrayal felt much, much worse than the sexual deception.

For a moment, Poppy saw herself spinning around on the spot, snatching hold of one of the blue-and-white herringbone-patterned mugs Karleen had pulled out of the cupboard, and swinging her arm as hard and as fast as possible to crack that mug against Karleen's skull.

Of course, she wouldn't actually do that. But God how she wanted to. Poppy turned away in case Karleen could somehow guess the violent thoughts she was harboring, and she caught sight ▶

of her own reflection in the window above the kitchen sink. Her neat blond hair, parted in the middle and scraped back into a short, low ponytail—the same way she wore it every single day. *Boring. I look like a boring, middle-aged woman who gets up every morning, does her hair the same way, wears the same smart office wear, goes to the same job, comes home in the afternoon, watches the same television shows, goes to bed at the same time only to get up and do it all again.* Now she wished she could smash the mug against the head of the woman in the window instead.

She felt irritated then. Irritated that she was directing all her anger at Karleen or inward at herself when Garret was the one who'd cheated. When Garret was the one who'd betrayed his marriage vows. And she felt frustrated. Frustrated that she didn't get to tell him it was over. That she didn't get to throw his clothes on the front lawn. It was all too much to take in. Too much to process in one hit.

Maybe it would have been easier if it had happened like a scene in a movie. If she'd sprung them in bed together. Found them with the sheets a tangled mess around them. Karleen scrambling to find her bra. Garret gathering the bedclothes around himself, covering up his junk self-consciously. The telltale sticky wet patch between the two of them. At least that would have given her some satisfaction—the chance to be self-

righteously indignant. The right to yell
and scream and kick him out. It would
have spurred her into action, instead of
this weird, polite, tea-drinking
confrontation they'd concocted.

Poppy gripped the benchtop harder.
She looked over at Garret, who was staring
resolutely down at the table.

"How long?"

Karleen didn't hesitate to step in with
an answer. "Four months."

"I'm not asking you, I'm asking my
husband," Poppy snapped.

"He'll only tell you the same thing."

She kept her back to Karleen. "Here?"
she asked, her voice rising as she spoke.
"Did you fuck her here in this house,
Garret? In our bed?"

"Poppy, please," Garret whispered.

She pushed past Karleen and strode out
of the room. She took the stairs two at a
time, opened their bedroom door, and
stood still at the foot of the bed.

There were no rumpled sheets. No
indents in the pillows. She leaned down
and touched her fingertips to the covers,
and then she realized. These were fresh
sheets. They'd had sex here, today, and
afterward they'd changed the sheets.
Made the bed with neat hospital corners.
Was she supposed to be appreciative?
She looked across at her bedside table,
saw the open novel facedown where she'd
placed it last night when her eyes had
become too tired to continue reading. ▶

Excerpt from *Those Other Women* (continued)

It was a thriller, which Garret had read first, and she'd rolled over under the covers and prodded him in the arm. "I'm up to the bit where you realize the guy from the coffee shop is the same one the girl is dating but she hasn't figured it out yet."

"Getting to the good stuff," he'd said sleepily.

"You want to get up to some good stuff right now?"

"Rain check, babe? Half asleep already."

She wanted to reach back through time to the previous evening, grab hold of her own shoulders, and shake. How many times had he asked for a rain check? How many times had he avoided any kind of physical contact with her, turned away from her at night? And she'd had no idea there was anything wrong. She'd thought it was a normal part of marriage. You went through dry spells. Things became complacent, you took your relationship for granted. How many warning signs had she missed?

She backed out of the room and headed down the stairs. But on the bottom step she grasped hold of the banister, sank to the floor, and let the tears fall. She cried silently, desperate that Garret and Karleen not hear her.

A moment later, a pair of feet appeared in front of her. Neatly painted toenails in a demure dusky pink. She looked up to see Karleen staring down at her, her face filled with pity. Pity that Poppy didn't want. Pity that Poppy couldn't bear.

"I really am sorry, Poppy. We never wanted to hurt you like this."

But her tone belied her words. She might have felt pity, but there was no guilt and no kindness. Why was she doing this? They'd been friends for more than thirty years. And while Karleen had never been the overtly affectionate type, had never been the friend who you giggled with late into the night or shared long lingering cuddles with—she *had* always cared for Poppy. So what had changed to turn her against Poppy in this way?

Once again, Karleen reached out to touch her but Poppy recoiled. "Don't. Why are you doing this? Why are you acting this way? Why are you being so . . . so mean?" It felt like such a juvenile question, but she didn't know how else to put it. Karleen shook her head. "I told you, that's not what this is about. We're not trying to hurt you."

Poppy looked up at her friend. "But you are! You are hurting me."

She stood and walked back to the kitchen, scrubbing at her cheeks with the sleeve of her shirt as she went. Karleen followed close behind.

Garret was still in the same place. Still staring down at the table.

Poppy sat opposite him once again.

Look at me, she begged him silently, her eyes boring into the top of his bowed ▶

head. *Just look at me.* He kept his head down, low enough that she was staring right at the golf-ball-sized bald patch on his crown. Recently she'd been trying to talk him into shaving his head so he could go bald gracefully, beat his hair at its own game. He hadn't been ready to, though, he worried that his face was too round for a buzz cut. Now that would be Karleen's problem.

And just when Poppy thought none of this could hurt any more than it already did, they delivered their ultimate blow. Karleen picked up the cup of tea she'd made earlier, placed it in front of Poppy, and said, "Poppy, the truth is, Garret *does* want children."

Poppy's head snapped back. "What are you talking about?" she asked. "No, he doesn't. Garret's never wanted kids. *Never.*"

Karleen slipped around to the other side of the table and placed one hand possessively on Garret's shoulder. "Yes, Poppy, he does."

"Stop! Using! My fucking name!" Poppy screamed back at Karleen, and now her anger did shift across to Garret. Because for God's sake, the absolute sack of a man still hadn't looked at her. *Tell her she's wrong, tell her you don't want kids. Tell her you don't want her.* She kicked her leg out under the table and caught Garret in the shin, hard. She knew it would hurt him quite a lot. He'd had shin splints over the previous few months, which meant even the slightest bump was agonizing. She was right. He let out an anguished shout and finally he did look up at her. To his credit, his expression was full of guilt rather than reproach.

Karleen, on the other hand, wasn't so understanding. "Oh, Poppy," she admonished. "There's no need for that." And her hand snuck its way from Garret's shoulder to stroke the back of his neck.

"No need? The two of you are liars. Garret doesn't want children. Garret never wanted children."

"Poppy," Karleen began, but Garret finally cut in. "Give us a minute, would you, Karls?" He shifted sideways, letting her hand fall from the back of his neck while reaching down to massage his shin under the table.

"We agreed we would do this together, as a team."

Poppy snorted. A team? Karleen couldn't stop digging the knife in.

"I know, but I need to talk to Poppy . . . alone."

Karleen huffed and left the room. A moment later the front door slammed and Poppy could imagine Karleen standing out on the front porch, arms folded, foot tapping as she waited. Karleen had never been patient.

At long last, Poppy's husband held her gaze. His eyes were kind and somehow they were full of sorrow without the ▶

condescending pity that Karleen's eyes offered. "I feel awful. This isn't how I meant for this to go."

Hundreds of questions swirled through Poppy's head.

Oh yes? And how exactly did you expect it would go?

How did this happen?

When did things go wrong between us? Why now? Why *her*?

But the one that came out of her mouth was unexpected.

"Since when do you call her Karls?"

"I . . . I don't know."

"She's always hated nicknames. Aren't you something special, then?"

Even when they were kids no one was allowed to shorten Karleen's name. She'd given one of her ex's the boot for no other reason than the fact that he wouldn't stop calling her Kazza.

Garret reached across the table and took hold of one of her hands between his own. Poppy knew she shouldn't let him touch her. He didn't deserve to ever feel the warmth of her skin again. But somehow she couldn't make her body react, she couldn't pull away. He stroked her wrist with his thumb.

"I hate seeing you like this. I hate hurting you and I never intended for this to happen. I swear to you I didn't. Karleen and I falling for one another, it was so far out of the blue, I don't think anyone could have predicted it. She wasn't lying when she said it just happened."

"And what about the other stuff? About you all of a sudden wanting kids now. Is that true too?"

Garret hesitated and then he nodded. "It is. At least, it's what I think I want."

"When did that happen? When did you change your mind? Or were you lying all along?"

"I didn't lie and it's not that I've suddenly changed my mind either. It was more gradual. It's like this, when we first got together you knew straight out what you wanted and it wasn't kids. To be honest, I wasn't fussed either way, but I loved you and I was happy to go along with what you wanted."

"But you—"

Garret silenced her with a small shake of his head. "Let me get this out. I know, I *know*. I said it was what I wanted too. And I believed I was happy. But over the years, I started to wonder, I started to have doubts."

"You never said."

"That's true and I should have told you, I should have voiced my thoughts, my fears that one day I was going to regret not having children. But I didn't, because like I said, you've always been so sure. Tell me, babe, had I brought it up with you, would you have honestly considered changing your mind?"

Everything that Poppy wanted to say clamored to have its turn. Where did she start with something like this? The blowfly returned, landing on the table between ▶

them. Poppy fixed her gaze on it and eventually she spoke.

"But how am I supposed to answer that? How am I supposed to know what I might have said, what I might have done? When you never even gave me the chance?"

"I didn't ask because it wouldn't have been fair for me to put you in that position. Especially when I was still trying to figure it all out for myself. To expect you to reconsider when you made it clear from day one that you never wanted children. Babe, it was a deal breaker for you, I knew that."

Poppy finally wrenched her hand out of Garret's grip and slammed her palm down on the table, killing the fly. She wiped the remains of the dead insect on her gray suit pants. "Stop calling me babe! You don't get to call me that anymore. And you want to talk about being fair? You didn't want to put me in that position, so instead you cheated on me with my best friend! That's fucking absurd!"

"I know, but like I said, we didn't mean for it to happen. We started out just talking. That time we were all meeting for a drink after work at Platinum's Bar and you ran late. It was awkward at first, usually Karleen and I would need you to be the icebreaker between us. But she'd just had that terrible blind date with the IT guy. She was feeling down and we both put a fair few drinks away and got chatting. She told me how she was ready to start a family and she was scared she was running out of time—"

"STOP! I don't want to hear it. You think I need the details? You think I want you to describe how the two of you started staring into one another's eyes over your margaritas? Let me guess, her knee brushed against yours? Your hand landed on her thigh and you don't even know how it got there? You started confiding about how your bitch of a wife was going to deprive you of the chance to be a daddy?"

Something flashed across Garret's eyes and Poppy knew she was bang-on. *That arsehole.*

She forged on. "And next thing, I show up—completely clueless and ruin the moment for the two of you. But from then on, you're exchanging secret little glances of longing, and before you know it . . . you're fucking one another. That's how it went, right?"

"Poppy, don't do this. Karls and I, we both still love you. It tears us up that we're hurting you, it was the last thing we wanted, but it was like we didn't have a choice in the matter."

"Oh yeah, she sure looked all torn up inside."

"You know what she's like, she puts up a front, she's all business, but it's only because she's trying to hold it together."

"Business? So what, this is just a neat little business transaction to her? We switch roles, she becomes the wife, I ▶

become the best friend, the third wheel,
and we go on like nothing ever happened?
And you think you can sit there and tell
me you both still love me? You two make
me sick."

Garret reached once more for her
hand but Poppy lurched backward, almost
falling off the seat. "I never want to see
either of your faces again."

She stood and fled. Karleen didn't try to
stop her when she passed her on the front
porch.

In the car, Poppy drove aimlessly.
She didn't know where to go. Usually
if you had a fight with your husband,
the person you turned to was your best
friend. But obviously Poppy didn't have
that option anymore. Not that she and
Garret had really fought much throughout
their marriage. Was that another sign
she'd missed? Did their lack of arguments
equate to a lack of passion?

She couldn't bring herself to head over
to her parents' place. They would try their
best to comfort her, but ultimately they
wouldn't know the right things to say.
The same went for her brother, Nolan.
He'd be lost for words, and probably
want to punch Garret in the face, which
wouldn't necessarily be a bad thing. It was
a shame she'd never become close with
Nolan's wife, Megan, but Poppy had really
only ever had the one female friend—
Karleen, who had been her friend since
primary school when she'd walked up

to her in the playground and asked for a
turn of her My Little Pony toy.

"You can play with my Cabbage Patch
doll if you want?"

Boom. Just like that. Friends for life.
Well, that's what Poppy had thought
anyway. She thought that's how it worked.
You start with your family, and then
you make your friends as a child and
they stick with you, and that right there
is your safety net. Then you fall in love
and you get married and your best friend
is your maid of honor.

Her maid of honor. Her maid of honor
had slept with her husband.

Eventually she pulled over on the side
of the road and simply sat in the car.
Hands gripping the steering wheel. Her
body shuddering with sobs as she let
herself completely succumb to the self-
pity, not caring who might walk or drive
past and see her broken form.

Her mind swung from one gut-
wrenching moment to the next.

The moment she'd touched her fingers
to the freshly made bed.

The moment Garret had whispered
those words: *Poppy, please.*

The moment Karleen had dropped her
bombshell: Garret does want kids.

She still couldn't really believe it.
Not wanting to have children had been
something they had agreed upon so early
in their relationship. Yes, of course she
had been the instigator, but Garret had ▶

never once expressed even the slightest hesitation on the matter.

"Kids are expensive," he'd agreed, "and they take over your lives."

Okay, so his reasons for being on board didn't exactly stem from the most deep-seated of desires, but regardless, he'd said he was all for it. He's said that whatever made her happy made him happy. And not having children made Poppy happy.

She couldn't really pinpoint the moment when she'd come to that decision for herself. There was no single defining incident. No one driving reason. It was a combination of things. It was the immense relief she felt when she held someone else's baby and then she got to hand it back. It was the pride she felt in knowing her choice was the environmentally responsible one. It was the freedom she knew she had to do what she wanted, when she wanted. Knowing she could travel, knowing she could grow her career, knowing she could spend her money on an expensive outfit without compromising her hypothetical child's future education.

And lastly, it was the acute absence of any maternal desire or instinct within. When it came down to it, she simply didn't want to be a mother. And she knew she never would.

So in truth, what would have happened if Garret had brought up his change of heart instead of straying? He wasn't wrong when he'd said that not having children was a deal breaker for Poppy. But surely he should have given her the chance to at least talk it through. There might not have been any easy solution, but couldn't they have found a way to work things out?

Or did she mean she might have been able to talk him round? Change his mind back? And would that have been fair? Either way it didn't matter, because Garret hadn't given her the chance. Instead he'd found his own simple solution. Trade his wife in for a different model, a better model. Was Karleen better than Poppy? Simply because she was ready and willing to give Garret the thing his heart suddenly desired?

A thought occurred to her then. Was Karleen being so cold and hard throughout their confrontation because she believed she was actually doing the right thing? Rescuing Garret from an oppressive wife who was refusing to bless him with a family. It certainly would have made it easier for Karleen to reconcile her part in all of this if she thought that Poppy had somehow tricked Garret into agreeing to forgo children. Karleen had always been the prissy do-gooder. Never one to break the rules and becoming the "other woman" in her best friend's marriage was one hell of a rule-breaking move. But if she imagined her role as the noble savior of a man trapped in a loveless marriage, then she'd probably decided it was all for the greater good. Bitch.

Poppy tortured herself as she tried to replay any and every interaction she'd ▶

witnessed between Garret and Karleen
over the past few months and saw the
two of them through her new, hyperaware
lens. She saw the time Garret picked a
leaf out of Karleen's curls when they'd
picnicked at the park. She saw the time
Karleen had dropped around with tomato
soup for Poppy when she was sick with a
bad cold. Poppy had been laid out on the
couch in her old terry-toweling dressing
gown with a tissue stuck in her nose.
Karleen had been wearing a short skirt
and her favorite silvery top. She'd
disappeared into the kitchen with
Garret, and Poppy had thought nothing
of it at the time. Now she wondered,
had he pushed her up against the fridge
and kissed her then and there, while
Poppy coughed through an episode
of *The Blacklist* in the other room?

The image of the two of them kissing
made her double over in pain. Who knew
heartbreak could hurt so physically?

Four months! How could this have
been going on behind Poppy's back for
four whole months? How could the two
people she loved most in the world have
betrayed her in this way?

In one afternoon, she'd lost her
husband and her best friend. She pressed
her forehead to the steering wheel and let
the tears overcome her.

Poppy and Garret's separation was pretty
easy. No kids, no pets, no mortgage.
Separate bank accounts, one car each.

And their rental lease had been due for renewal. There was a shared savings account they'd each been depositing money into to buy a house one day, and they simply split it down the middle. Admittedly, Poppy earned a little more than Garret, so she'd probably put more money into the account than he had, but she didn't care. She didn't want to have any arguments. She didn't want to delay things any more than she had to. She just wanted to get Garret and Karleen out of her life as quickly as possible.

Garret got the sofa; Poppy never liked that pattern anyway.

Poppy got the coffee table—it was an antique from her grandmother.

Garret got the bed. Poppy got the bedroom furniture.

Garret got the coffee machine and Poppy got the kettle.

Garret got the toaster and Poppy took the blender.

Garret took the LCD TV and Poppy took the plasma.

And of course, Garret not only kept his best man from the wedding—his mate from high school—but he also cleaned up with the maid of honor too. How nice for him to collect the set.

It was an amicable divorce settlement with a nauseating rhythm.

And ultimately, it was the catalyst for the group. ▸

PINNED POST

Poppy Weston—Hi all and a big welcome
to any new members. A reminder that
this group is still in its infancy and we're
ironing out the main guidelines and
trying to keep it quite small and intimate.
If you know of someone who you think
might like to join, please make sure
they fit the parameters BEFORE you
invite them as we want to keep this
group a secret from the general public.
Thanks! ∽